HEINOUS

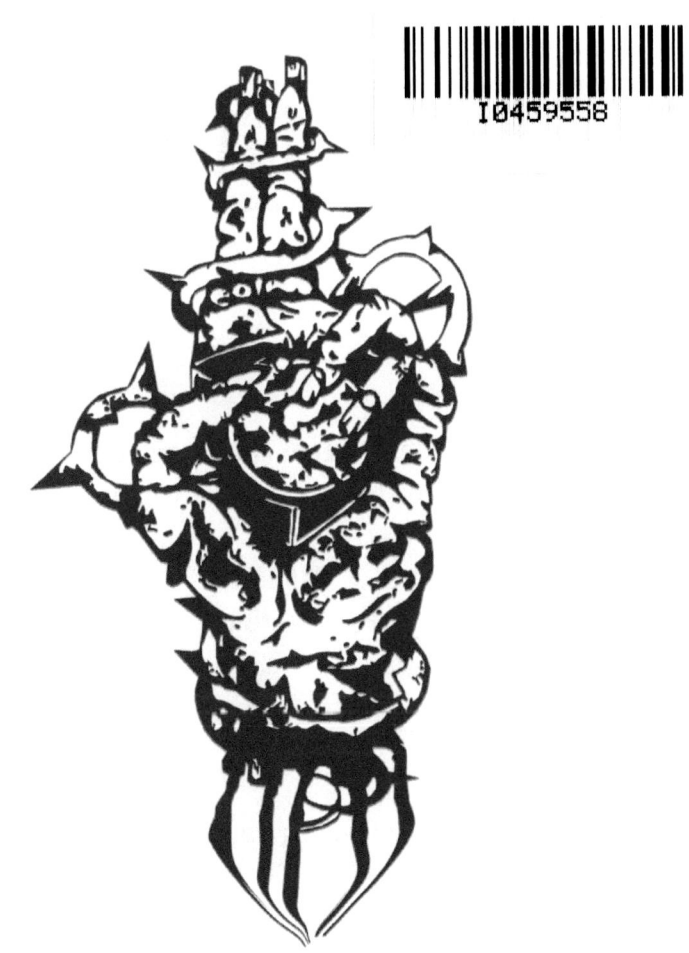

By Jonathan Moon

-- Hoo Doo Heathens --

Hoo-Doo
HEATHENS

A "Hoo Doo Heathens" Book
Published by arrangement with the author.

"HEINOUS"
By Jonathan Moon

Praise for Jonathan Moon's *Heinous*

"Imagine looking out the window and seeing your infant child standing in the middle of a busy street. That sunken chest punch in the gut feeling is all I can compare HEINOUS with. Jonathan Moon shows no mercy."
-- William Pauley III-author of *DOOM MAGNETIC!* and *The Brothers Crunk*

"Uniquely disturbing, disturbingly unique"
-- Jessica Brown-*horrornews.net* and *darkmarkets.com*

"*Heinous* will suck you in with its easy, lyrical style so that it can electroshock you with straight-up gorgeous fear. Lines like, *My memories are ghosts. Ghosts wrapped in barbed wire* will haunt you to sleep. This book kicks ass. Jonathan Moon is one scary dude."
-- Kevin Shamel, author of *Rotten Little Animals* and *Island of the Super People*

"*[HEINOUS is]* A breakneck hell-ride through the heart and mind of a rising talent. Once you're in, there's no stopping."
--David Dunwoody, author of *EMPIRE'S END* and *UNBOUND & OTHER TALES*

"Get to know a man named Gavin Wagner and his dark friend inside, *HEINOUS. Heinous* will possess you to keep turning the pages into his world, and it is a dark one. What starts out as a vivid nightmare twists its way into a brutal reality of depravity and violence. This novel jolts you into and out of reality in whiplashes of macabre dreamscapes and morbid intent. Jonathan Moon is a name in Horror to be reckoned with. His words bleed with dim adjectives that blanket the reader in a gloomy sense of dread. Moon skillfully guides you down a pitch black path... with something sinister waiting around every corner and for you, the reader... there is no light."
-- Jason Hughes-author of *Without Notice* and screen-writer of *Dead Girls Don't Cry*

More Praise for Jonathan Moon's *Heinous*

"From the haunting, mesmerizing opening to the stunning, pitch perfect conclusion, Mr. Moon weaves a tale of raw brutality and sheer terror that will stay with you long after you finish reading. In a word - Brilliant. "
-- Bryan Hall, author of *Containment Room Seven*

"Like a claustrophobic nightmare, Jonathan Moon carves out a dark dreamscape filled with ghastly images and dark terror in Heinous."
-- Bowie V. Ibarra-author of the *'Down the Road' zombie series*

It's like Jonathan Moon ripped out my inner child and beat it to death with a shovel. *Heinous* is an easy contender for horror novel of the year."
-- Timothy W. Long, author of the *'Among the Living' books*

For Shannley- The Light in My Darkness

A Note from the Editor

There is a reason you're reading my words at the beginning of Jonathan Moon's opus of terror. It's not just because I know this book backwards and forwards (Heinous = suonieH, see?). It's not just because Mr. Moon was flattered that I once called him the nicest psycho I know (which is still true).

You're reading my words at the beginning of Heinous because Jonathan Moon is a tough act to follow under any circumstances, let alone when he's dealing with a vicious, brutal, unstoppable ... Ah, but that would be telling.

Suffice it to say that I'm sneaking my bit in here because I'm the editor and I can. So there. The original incarnation of Heinous was the first of Moon's works that I ever read. As chance or luck— or perhaps a writing imp that enjoys a good dose of gore—would have it, as I was reading his tale, he was reading a story of mine. I'd submitted a weird little tale involving souls, cannibalism, and a duck named Waddles to a Bizarro anthology that Moon was compiling. In each other's work, we each recognized a kindred— albeit extremely disturbed—spirit. And since then, I've had the pleasure of working with Moon on a number of projects, as well as the honor of calling him a friend.

Sweet, right? Nice and heartwarming and fuzzy?

Hold onto that feeling. It'll come in handy.

As you travel through the tortuous mind of Moon, you'll bear witness to strange and terrible things. He'll speak what you thought was unspeakable, imagine what you thought was inconceivable. And once your poor psyche has been bludgeoned until it resembles roadkill (and we're talking *old* roadkill, not a nice fresh possum strike) ... well, then you'll know he's good and warmed up and ready for the real pain to begin.

So ... soft little kittens. Puppies with big, sad eyes. Pixie dust and cupcakes and nauseatingly cute Internet memes. Whatever gives you the warm fuzzies, you find that thing and hold on tight. Think of it as a blankie for your soul.

You'll need it soon enough.

Trust me. Mine is the last friendly voice you'll hear for quite some time. All that remains is for me to wish you well. Enjoy Moon's macabre masterpiece. Good luck. Be strong. And go with God. 'Cause Heinous sure doesn't.

-Stephanie Kinkaid

4/2/2011

Table of Contents

Dream: Limbo

I have this dream …

My eyes are closed, but a weak light shines through my eyelids, sending blurry blue worms wiggling through the darkness. I open my eyes slowly, mindful of the dim light surrounding me and the soft clouds floating around me. My eyes adjust for the most part; a few worms still twist and burrow into nothingness, and I realize the clouds are really a thick yet wispy fog. My senses settle, and I look above me. No sky, only fog. To my left and right, only fog. I have about a six-foot ring of visibility around me before the fog presses tight enough on itself that I see nothing. I watch my hand reach up and grab at a wisp of fog floating close to my face.

I catch a look at what I'm wearing, and it looks homemade. Simple pants and shirt made from what feels like semisoft cloth. I would describe them as colorless rather than white. To call them white would be giving something they are just way too plain to have. Clothes sewn together for the Post-Apocalyptic Boogie—when the fashion police, like everyone else, are dust. The shirt is too long and cut too wide in the neck, so it flops back and forth. The pants are rolled up like they only come in one size and I'm just too damn short.

I notice my bare feet and the ground below me. The terrain is grayish sand with hundreds of circular white pebbles speckling it. I tap a few of the pebbles with my toes, and they crush to smears across the gray sand. I look closely at the new stains, and I see tiny faces etched with agony staring back at me from the sand. I blink; the small stains remain, but the pained faces are nothing more than random patterns of white on gray. When I dig my ankles in and let my piggies wiggle, the sand feels more abrasive. Oddly, it is not an unpleasant sensation, like pumice ground to a dust without losing its harshness. I burrow my toes in the sand and look around me.

I try to get my bearings, and for some reason—the gray, most likely—I wonder if I'm on a beach in Oregon. I went with my parents when I was young. It was a time of smiles and innocence. There is no

11

innocence here. I don't feel any air move on my face, but the fog drifts and twists all around me as if stirred by my confusion. Two voices buzz in the distance, and they give me something on which to focus. I take a few steps, and the fog steps with me the way it stays at the end of your headlights when you drive into it on dark nights. The fog distorts sound and seems to push it toward the harsh gray sand underfoot, so I bend at the knees and lean forward to hear better. I catch more tones and pitch than words, but I can identify the voices as the nervous chatter of teenage boys. I shuffle in the direction of the voices, leaning slightly forward, my ear tilted down and leading my cautious charge.

The fog moves like the smoke from a thousand incense sticks, and it crowds closer around me like a scentless wall until I'm forced to wave my hand to stir it. The voices rise and fall, and their tones intensify. I catch phrases like ghost words springing from the fog, "Pit to Hell" and "bullshit." The fog stirs as if from the strife in the boys' tones and reveals a tree in the near distance. The closer I get to the strange tree, the more appear around me: thick evergreens that reach into the fog and disappear a few feet above my head. That doesn't stop me from leaning back, mouth open in flycatcher mode, to see for myself that the tops are hidden. The fog wraps tight around the thick trunks above my head, and searching for the tops is useless.

When I look back down, I'm standing in a forest. I'm surrounded by tall pines and thick, gnarled cedars, small jagged rock formations and bright green ferns. Fog drifts and twists around everything, though it has a softer feel to it. I look around, and I can see to the top of the giant trees now, although there is no color in the sky around the ancient treetops. I reach out to touch the nearest magnificent pine, and it stirs to colorless fog around my fingertips. An illusion, but somehow it looks so real that I'm sure I could feel the bark if I could just keep it from falling to wisps between my fingers. Everything around me looks solid and real, but as my eyes adjust, I see that the entire forest is fog. The mist has somehow taken the millions of shapes and earthen rainbow of colors of an entire forest. As I stare at it all, I see the fog still moving, twisting on itself back and forth, over and under. The detail in the fog forest is amazing, and it sets my eyes and mind at odds. I feel like I'm in a dream inside a dream, where it is twice as hard to wake up.

I'm in such strange awe of the fog and its magic trick that I've nearly forgotten about the voices and their "Pit to Hell" talk. Then two teenage boys—made of fog but colored like teenage boys—come bounding at me. I stumble backwards with shock and trip ass over teakettle. I fall through the false forest floor to the gray sand and white pebbles beneath. The fog loses its color and drifts, stirred by my falling ass. As I hit the ground, I roll backwards even more, and my flailing right foot catches the first boy in his hip. My foot moves right through his side, pulling fog back with it. The second boy is so close behind that my foot tears through his left shin. Instead of either boy slowing, the fog stirred from my ass joins with the boy in the lead from his knee to his third rib. The fog I kicked from his hip drifts quickly down and replaces the second boy's kicked ankle. The fog I kicked from that ankle floats into place as the rocks, sticks, and ferns that make up the forest floor. I stand and watch them run farther down a path I hadn't noticed before.

I'm surrounded by thick forest on all sides. The beauty is breathtaking, but between my mind and my eyes, the illusion only remains solid for a few seconds no matter what I'm looking at. Anytime I stop and focus, my eyes adjust, and I see the fog swirling on itself. It drifts lazily, but the colors flow quickly. The fog appears the moist brown of tree bark, then swirls effortlessly into the bright yellow-green of a young fern, and from there it twists hypnotically into the reds and yellows and browns of the forest floor. Nothing ever loses its shape; it just fills in blank spots where wisps of fog drift. I am standing in a rich and vibrant painting come to life on the plain, bleak fog. The more I look at all the colors twisting and rolling into each other, the more my stomach turns. Everything is creeping into everything else, though nothing ever looks like anything else. The giant pine in front of me still looks like a tree even though it is constantly drifting into the trees next to it and the ground below it. Even as a large wisp becomes a pile of rocks on the hillside behind it, the tree maintains its shape and presence. There is only a split second of colorlessness when one wisps moves and another takes its place. The forest waves and turns like it's crawling around me, and the feeling clenches my guts like seasickness. It all looks twitchy and wrong—too much twirling and rocking over itself.

The fog boys stop not far away from me, and I follow to catch as much of this weirdness as I can. Even though I'm feeling a little twisted in the tummy from the nasty trip of staring deep into the forest, I can't help but watch the ground when I walk. I can see the pinecones, broken branches, rocks, dirt, and red clay of the forest floor, but when I stare deep at the twisted and rolling colors I see the circular pebbles below, begging my bare feet to stomp them into the gray sand. And stomp them I do. The fog-ground scatters for a second with every step, and I see a trail of white smears that appear to be agonized faces on the real sand floor but, again, only at first. A blink and they are gone.

Staring at my feet instead of my surroundings seems to help calm my turning stomach, and I catch up to the fog-boys quickly. I stop next to the bigger of the two boys, the one I kicked clear the hell back into his little buddy. He looks like the All-American Lad with his blond hair, blue eyes, and a smile that might get him out of almost as much trouble as it gets him into. He reminds me of me. Since he is made of fog and doesn't seem to give half a shit anyway, I crowd right on in. The second, smaller boy is blocking the path up ahead with his palms up like he is begging off a beating. He is scrawny and birdlike, wet eyes behind thin-rimmed glasses.

I'm guessing that while I was staring at my feet like a one year old, the smaller boy ran around the bigger boy, who was moving much faster and with greater ease through the forest, and stopped him in the middle of the worn path. The small boy stands catching his breath in front of us. I stand and watch him wheeze while his face drifts into the trees behind him and back. I watch the ankle I kicked twist first into a small tree stump next to him and then into a scattering of branches. It's starting to make me feel shitty again, and I wonder out loud how long it takes a boy made of fog to catch his breath. Not even a full minute later, he speaks, his voice shaky and on the verge of tears. I

14

almost want to hug him, even if that means he will float into the forest around him and back without even knowing I had taken the time to comfort him.

"Leave it here," he pleads. "Can't you feel it? It makes my stomach queasy."

The first boy, obviously tired of the conversation, answers in a rigid tone, "Look, I'll give ya it's kind of a strange day. That hole was creepy, but we've never been back into that wicked thorn patch before, so we don't know that it hasn't always been there. I like this little stone. Sure it's weird, but satanic or something? Come on, man." He adds in a snarky tone, "This is almost as stupid as the time you told me hookers don't have feelings."

Something in the smaller boy's already wet eyes deepens and rages. "Arrrghhh! I never said hookers don't have feelings! I was trying to have a conversation with you about how the scars of our youth plague us well into our adult lives, and you come away with … hookers have no feelings!"

The smaller boy's voice reaches a high-pitched crescendo that surely would shatter glass, were any glass handy. The bigger, blonder boy just stands there smiling his winning smile at his little buddy, who stands in the middle of the path with his hands on his hips, gasping and wheezing after having set off like a teakettle. The little guy shoots his friend an exasperated look, turns to the heavens above with the same glance, and then trains his shaky gaze back on his friend.

"Fine, I'll put it back if you promise you'll calm down and not die out here. Deal?"

A frenzied nod that becomes a foggy blur signals total agreement.

"And use your damn inhaler. Your mom gives it to your frail ass for some reason."

Relief flushes the smaller face then slips right off his cheek into a rotten log nearby, and he mumbles, "Your mom gives it to my frail ass."

They start back in the direction from which they came, walking next to each other down the path. I follow behind, kicking fog as I go.

It's still easier to kick the fog below me and catch glimpses of the harsh gray sand and white pebbles than to stare at the trees or even the boys for more than a few seconds at a time. As we move, everything around me swirls and dances in place. It's *nothing* trying to be *beautiful,* and it makes my stomach roll and twist. We walk in total silence. They stick to the path, and I walk around piles of rotten logs and thick standing pines, slapping the fog as I move. To pass the time, I kick out their ankles in turn. They never slow as their ankles reform from the ever-twisting fog. I notice that when the boys aren't talking, there is no other sound from the fog forest. No chatter of squirrel or chipmunk. No creaking of the ancient trees as they sway. No birdsong. They slow their pace, cut off the path, and drop down the steep embankment to a small creek. The water makes no sound as it flows; clear wet fog through deep, ever-shifting fog. Across the creek is a mess of thorn bushes that crowd up to a sheer rock wall. The boys bound to it.

My throat goes dry, and I get the opposite sensation of sweat forming on my forehead. I feel a cold bead slip down my nose, and I tilt forward to watch it. The drop of sweat cuts through the fog like a wet bullet. It lands on a white pebble, and the pebble dissolves into nothing. A tiny wisp of fog drifts up from the small wet spot and twists into the forest floor.

I look back to the boys and see that they've pulled back some thorn branches with a stick and are ducking and waddling carefully through the bramble. I follow right behind, turning the thorns that tore at them to colorless fog as I pass. We all stop in a small clearing flush against the sheer mountainside.

The smaller boy tells the bigger one, "There it is. Now throw it back in there and let's get the hell outta here."

His words turn muffled and distant when I notice the big kid is holding something that isn't made of fog. It's a smooth deep-black stone of some kind, the shape of a large glass eye. It is circular and bulges in the center. Thin, delicate fins adorn three sides of the stone. He tosses it in the air, and just before he catches it, his hand drifts to nothing for a second—only to be reformed as the stone lands in his palm. The stone remains black, but I can now see colors swirling across the swollen center. I want to steal from his fog hands. I want to hold it. I want to stare at it. I want it to be mine. I step toward him, stirring the forest floor as I move, but he clenches his fist and turns to the other boy.

"I'm keeping it. I'm sorry we walked all the way back to this hole in the ground. It's mine. It means something, and I get the feeling it's meant for me. So don't start your crying and shit. Just deal, man, okay?"

The challenge in his voice is unmistakable. The smaller boy's eyes fill with tears again, and I have to look away. When I do, I see the hole they were talking about. It's as real as I am, as real as the stone. I take two steps closer and stare into its depths. The hole is a good three feet by three feet: big enough for a kid to crawl into. It sinks back about a foot and then drops off for who knows how far. It's dark in there, and it looks like it is sucking in the fog. It almost seems to be slowly breathing, pulling whatever lush colors the fog had out and deep into the darkness. I can see the gray sand right up to the rim, and I see it trickling into the hole from a few different spots. As I stare, I feel the sensation of sound from the hole, but before the actual sound comes, the smaller boy shrieks, and I jump to face him.

"Liar! You lied to me!"

The bigger kid opens his mouth to say something but instead uses it to catch the smaller boy's fist. The small kid unleashes an onslaught of flailing rights and lefts at his friend. Several of the blows land, blurring the bigger kid's face like TV in a snowstorm and sending fog masquerading as blood flying. A fist smashes into the bigger kid's nose, and both boys are instantly dirty bloody messes. The bigger kid makes no effort to fight back, only sidestepping and leaning back, but he finally shoots his right arm out straight. His palm is flat, and it hits the smaller kid dead center in the middle of his chest like a running back's stiff arm. The littler kid and several wisps of fog go flying backwards. The fog boy hits the dirt and bounds right back to his feet. He tears through the thorn bush, and I plow through behind him suffering far less damage than he sustains. I see bright red under the rips in his shirt. He is mumbling and crying as he crawls up the creek bed. He reaches the path and runs down it with both arms flailing. He becomes a blur running through the forest, being made of fog himself. Watching not just him but everything around him drift, twist, and roll makes my stomach clench and turn again, but I can't look away. It's like a carnival ride without the lights. I feel strapped in and forced to watch, no matter how it makes my guts churn. The boy is out of my sight, but the ripples he made while charging through like a madman continue to distort the fog around me. I want to turn my head, but I get the strangest feeling that whatever is happening behind me is far worse than the waving reality in front of me.

Just as the ripples settle, the smaller boy comes back up the path. He is talking to himself, rehearsing his apology. I get the feeling the little guy doesn't have many friends—at least not enough to cut his big blond punching bag loose. Watching the smaller boy trot up the path talking, reasoning, and pleading with himself gives the bad feeling about looking behind me time to pass. The smaller boy reaches the thorns at the same time I do. He crawls through much more slowly and carefully than last time. The landscape offers me no resistance, so I am already standing in the clearing while he is still mumbling words and navigating the treacherous thorns. I look around for the blond kid to see how he is handling the bloody nose, but he and his stone are gone. I walk around the fog- and sand-swallowing hole and stare into its depths. Nothing. As the little guy finally makes it through the thorn bush, I wave my way through in the other direction. I squint my eyes and try to see the second fog boy. I scan the forest, despite how it makes my stomach turn, figuring if I can't see him, at least I might see the stone for which he took the beating, as it is real. If I see it again, I'll take it from him. He is made of fog, and they've offered no fight against me displacing them yet. People made of fog are notorious sissies. I'll take it, and the fog boys can play out whatever they need to play out without the stone. My stone.

I'm still thinking about kicking some fog ass and getting my stone when I hear a scream from behind me that sets the hair on the back of my neck on end. The fog wall behind the bush is a twisting blur that moves so fast it almost can't regain any color before a second scream and a more terrible unseen thrashing blurs it again. Whatever has gotten hold of the fog boy is whipping so furiously it is pulling the entire fog forest forward. It's like a vacuum cleaner that screams and growls as it swallows illusions whole. The screams become constant, and a deep growl roars when the fog whips. As the growl grows in volume, it pulls the fog forest toward it. Soon the growl echoes around me, and the forest is finally starting to lose its shape as it is pulled into the screams. A chorus of hungry growls thunders behind the blurry bush, and the pull becomes constant and powerful. I stagger forward a step from the force, and the smaller boy comes diving halfway out of the bush, reaching and screaming. Only now he isn't made of fog; he is as real as I am. His tears are real, the blood smeared all over his face is real, and the terrified look in his eyes is even realer than my own body at the moment. His wide, panicked eyes meet mine, and I know he sees me. He opens his mouth to say something, and blood and teeth spit out instead of words. The unseen terror behind him pulls him back through the whipping fog. The pull increases, and the forest is reduced to muddy-looking blurs as it rushes all around me. One final scream slices the air, and the entire illusion is gone, sucked forward. The force of the final pull tugs me face first into the ground. I push myself up and spit out a mouthful of the dismal-tasting sand. I look around and notice the forest is gone. The thick colorless fog drifts lazily around me.

I stand, crack my neck, and notice I'm at the lip of the hole. My bare feet slide toward it, forcing gray sand to fall into the pit. The air is calm again. The fog is floating as thick and plain as it was before the weird trip in the forest. The hole in front of me is still pulling wisps of fog down into itself at oddly timed intervals. I step back when I notice sand and pebbles falling from all around it. I picture the hole swallowing the fog forest, then the fog, then sand and pebbles, until I have nowhere to go except into its dark maw. I get the feeling that this hole is no good. This hole is bad. In fact, judging by how strong and clear the boy's screams were moments before, this hole is a downright shitty place to be.

I back away, scanning the ground around the hole for the black stone while trying to keep an eye on the sand-swallowing hole itself. I wonder if the first kid made it safely home to his fog house and fog family or if he was caught by the same terror hidden behind the whipping bush. If he had, he would have dropped the stone. I still want it.

I figure I'm far enough away from the hole that it's safe to turn around. When I do, I spin face first into steel bars with absolutely no give. My body follows my face and walks hard into the unforgiving metal. My face slides down the cold steel bars before I fall backwards into the sand. I feel like a one-man pileup crumpled on the scratchy ground.

"Well, that's one way you can't get in."

The voice from above me sounds exactly like mine.

I sit myself up slowly, trying to see the top of the bars, which turn out to form a massive gate that disappears into the fog overhead. It's a battered and used gate that must have been built eons ago. Thick mottled bars line the gate, which is governed by a built-in lock. The lock looks like it takes a simple old-fashioned skeleton key. Oddly enough, standing next to the lock is me. The other me looks younger and happier than I ever remember being. Where I let my blond hair shag to my neckline, he is bald. He face is also hairless where I have a well-trimmed goatee. He is wearing an outfit like mine, but his fits him and is a light sky blue that stands out against the bland fog. He is also barefoot in the sand. All around him, the sand is covered in tiny white smears. I picture him stomping on the white pebbles out of boredom until I came spinning out of nowhere and into his gate.

He looks at me with my blue eyes, and I feel the need to help him.

"Are you locked out?"

He smiles very sincerely and tells me calmly, "I let people in."

He is looking at me like he either wants to hug me or tell me a sad secret. I know because his face is mine and I've made that face. I've made it at sad times to sad people. The look passes quickly, and he looks like he is happy to see me after waiting a long while. I want to ask him if he has been here stomping people into the sand, but because of his initial look, I ask, "Is there something you want to tell me?"

"Is there something you want to ask?"

"Yeah, lots. How much time you got?" I joke.

"Oh, we got plenty of time." He doesn't sound like he is joking.

It doesn't change his attitude or smile at all. Looking at him is like looking in a mirror. His happy smile is my happy smile, and I can't help but smile it right back at him.

I look beyond the gate and ask him, "Do I know anybody in there?"

"I'm afraid not," he answers very simply and politely.

"Oh," is all I can say, and I sound like a dumbass when I do.

I try to think to myself. I feel like I have to know somebody behind the fog, but my mind is a blank sheet. My mind is racing so fast it blurs blank. Thoughts bounce and roll into each other like the surrounding fog. I can't slow a thought down enough to think it, and as they flip, they are as fuzzy as a memory of a dream. I can't think of a single person I've ever known in any way. I can't think of a single name, face, bra size, phone number, birthday, or anything else about anyone I could ever have known. I have to have known people. I know people. Why can't I think of anyone? People are everywhere on Earth, so much so it's kind of irritating when you can't recall shit. As blank as my mind is, every name and every thought is right there, on the tip of my tongue. The faces are almost in focus. I feel so sure I'll think of someone that I start talking before I have any idea what to say.

"What about ..."

"I'm afraid not."

He tilts his head just slightly and nods. Since he is me, I know what he is telling me. I could sit and think forever (Oh, we got plenty of time) without his answer ever changing. I'll never be able to think of anything about anybody. Whatever face I make, he must recognize, because he tells me, "You'd be the first."

This fills me with a great sense of pride. He is me, but his aura is proud, strong, and protecting like an older brother who would pick me up and dust me off if I fell. I'm the older brother I never had, and he smiles at me. I puff up my chest, and he looks at my loose-cut shirt, frowning slightly.

"Even *here* you can't help getting someone else's blood on you?"

His smile fades for the tiniest glimpse, a small facial tick. It reminds me of telling your grandma you are going to jail, again. That look of "you is a stupid bastard, but I love you anyway."

I grab my shirt and pull it so I can examine it for myself. I see a few spatters of blood that look like they came from different directions making an off-kilter X across my chest. This is the first time I've noticed it, and I can't remember where or when it got on me or whose it is. The harder I think about the answers to my own questions, the faster my thoughts spin. Everything is still just out of reach mentally, right on the tip of my tongue even as a mystery. I still can't think a sentence all the way through, but that in no way slows my urge to speak.

"The Thing," I tell the him-me with utter conviction.

He nods our understanding nod and lifts his hand. "Of course, the Thing. It gets almost all of them."

His smile doesn't waver, but I feel he is being serious. Maybe I'm just falling for my own bullshit. I can't be sure, but it all seems less important by the second. I struggle for memories, but if I just stand and stare at the fog with the him-me, my stomach settles and my mind slows to a comfortable useless crawl.

The fog beyond the gate glows as if a great light has been illuminated at my realization. I'm enjoying standing here, thinking nothing, just smiling at the other me. This other self appears to be so content. I see happiness in his-my eyes. Have I ever been that happy? I try to think of that one song that one band did clear back when I was in high school, but it's no good. The thought is gone before I can even finish thinking it. We just stand there staring at each other while I try to half-ass process thought. He reaches his foot forward and taps two white pebbles with his toes. I fully expect to see pained faces in the small smears, but when he pulls his foot back, the smears offer no faces no matter how abstract. Simply white smears.

I ask the him-me, "Is this how you spend time while guarding the gate? Smashing defenseless pebbles to smears?"

He laughs, and the sound makes me laugh. He reminds me of a kid who stole his older brother's favorite hat out to play and got caught. We smile and laugh again.

"It passes the time," he smiles even wider, "and you took a while to get here."

"Yeah, I got held up ..." I start but don't finish. What the hell have I been doing? I feel like I've been in this fog for a long time now, yet I can't think of anything before the gate and the him-me. As I stand here, even the memory of walking into the gate seems fuzzy. I feel frightfully disoriented and totally carefree at the same time. My mind is still wild and unyielding, so I seek no more answers from my other self or my own confused mind.

"The *thing*," he finishes for me with a chuckle and a grin. I think he sees me snap back to our conversation with confusion tattooed across my face. I pretend to remember what the hell we were talking about. I snap my fingers and say, "Yes, that's it!"

He laughs at what I attempt to make funny, so I laugh along. Our laughter sounds very similar, but only his sounds sincere. We share a smile in the fog as I grip tight to the thick steel bars. Their cold solid realness is an anchor I can latch to in an increasingly disorienting world.

"The thing," I repeat respectfully, "it's not in there, is it?"

"Of course not, that's why we have the gate."

He almost sounds like he wanted to call me "silly." He is having fun and enjoying my questions. Am I being funny? Is my situation funny? Is he me, or do we all just look the same? His bright blue eyes mirror my own; a twinkle of mischief lies in the reflection.

"What's it like in there?" I ask in a far more hushed tone. It feels like a big question, and I really don't want to get this other me in trouble. The light far beyond the gate glows more intensely for a moment or two as if hearing my question despite my whisper.

He turns away from me and reaches high on the bars. He leans in so his face rests between two of them. He says nothing and keeps staring. While he stares, I try to think of where I was before I started talking to him. How did I find him? Did he find me? I'm gonna have to stop asking myself questions, because they just keep leading to more questions.

He turns back to me, and his eyes are glazed over with a slight green and purple sheen. He looks like he has spent a lifetime looking into the fog. His eyes look blind and knowing, but he blinks a few times, and they shine our beautiful blue. Looking in his eyes, I see quick flashes of the mysteries beyond the gate, back where the light glows. The images melt into each other rapidly and are distorted (squished and bright, almost like tunnel vision with floodlights), rendering the whole experience more confusing than helpful. He blinks again, and the visions stop. Back is the confident grin. He looks slowly, deliberately, to his left then his right before leaning closer.

"It's not near as crowded as you would think," he answers finally—whether with pride or jealousy, I can't distinguish.

This seems overly deep, but I nod like I can dig it. He returns my nod and smiles even wider. Too wide for the handsome face we share.

I swallow my nervousness and ask, "So can I get in?"

"If you give me your key," he says, the corners of his mouth high on his cheekbones, forcing his face to elongate slightly.

I panic at the thought of losing something as necessary as *my key*. I frantically pat myself down in search of it. For some reason, I start at my nipples—I guess in case a key had been taped there all along. From there, I pat down my chest, stomach, and each leg in turn. I slap the front of my thighs … nothing. I slap halfway to my ass and feel something solid against my hand. I reach into a pocket I didn't know I had and pull out a smooth key.

I marvel at its simple beauty; it has of the look of an old skeleton key but is made of a bright green marble with deep, bold purple swirls. I run my finger up its smooth shaft to the end, which has three small circles set atop each other in an awkward pyramid. The surface is as cold as it is smooth, so I rub it to warm it. It doesn't work. The cold seems to pulse from within.

The other me gets a good look at what I'm playing with, and his eyes go as wide as a boy seeing his first booby. I hold it up to show him, and his eyes continue to swell as exaggeratedly wide as his stretched smile. His face is too happy, too wide, too much.

"Excellent! That's the ticket! Congratulations!"

He words run into each other with a giddy whine, and his hand shakes with excitement as he reaches for my key. His excitement is contagious, and I beam with pride. I wonder how wide my smile and eyes are. He stares intently at the key, rolling it over with his fingers, holding it up, squinting at it. He runs his finger along the shaft and over the pyramid of circles as I did. I feel like I made this key and now my project is being graded. I feel like I'm back in high school, except I don't have any pot on me. Just to be sure, I do one more quick pat search in the same nipple-to-ass pattern without taking my eyes off him.

He turns his distorted gleeful face at me and throws in a cheerful wink of one large eye.

I passed! MY key! I can enter the gate in the fog! Safe from the thing!

"Now, this is a beautiful key! This lock is old, and it takes me a minute to work the keys in. Bear with me."

He digs his bare heels into the sand and turns away from me to the lock. I put my hands on my hips so I can push my chest as far out as it can go. He jiggles the key a few times, and it clicks into place. He glances over his shoulder, eyes bugging with joy. He turns the key, and I hear what sounds like hundreds of smaller locks within the large lock. Deep clacks and high-pitched clicks echo off the fog and back to me. He looks over his shoulder again, more slowly, his eyes and smile returned to normal size and clouded with darkness. His eyes betray worry, and it makes me worry in turn. He rolls his eyes then his head forward to face the gate. He leans against the bars and moans an exaggerated sigh of disappointment.

A wave of regret and doom washes over me like a kick in the nuts. I don't mean to offend the him-me, but I feel his discontent pulsing off him. I worry that I have blood on my face or in my hair. If I do, I already know I can't explain it. I'm blushing and worrying.

He turns the key back, and I hear all the locks inside slamming shut again. Hundreds of clacks and clicks hammer home my sudden failure. He pulls the key out of the lock and holds it between his palms. He leans on his palms and utters a quick prayer with words I don't understand. I feel uncomfortable. My skin is too hot and too tight.

The him-me turns slowly and faces me. His body language is standoffish and his voice angry and stern. "You cannot come in … with … him."

By the last two words, he can't hide his disdain. His good-looking face is an uncomfortable grimace, and his voice drips with something heavier than hate. My shoulders slump, and my mouth drops open. I don't understand. Confusion. Again.

He sighs and reaches up to close my mouth for me. I stand up straight and look him in his eyes, my eyes. Except they've abandoned our bright blue to become cold solid cobalt orbs. Anger burns furious in his frozen eyes, and he nods to my right.

I feel a sudden weight on my shoulder and turn to see a dirty clawed hand resting there. The fingernails are long and dangerous looking. Claws a madman would earn by sharpening them against concrete. Each nail is uneven and deathly sharp, capable of severing arteries with a flick of the wrist. The dried blood caked to the bottom of each nail underscores this impression. As I stare at the skin of the hand, which seems old and sundried, I feel the weight of an arm across my back. I realize that my right arm, in turn, is draped over the owner of the dangerous hand and heavy arm. We are standing facing the him-me like two old pals posing for a photograph.

I'm so amazed at the monster I'm half-hugging that I ignore the cobalt-eyed gatekeeper. The monster stands as tall as I do and has long greasy hair hanging in clumps down his back. The dark hair looks

26

as if it is beginning to dreadlock itself from all the blood, grease, and dirt in it. For as unkempt as it is, he has taken the time to hollow out chunks of bones and slide random handfuls of hair through them so they hang like beads. When I squint, I can see small black faces screaming in silent agony etched on several of the bone shards. I can only see his left ear, and it looks as sunbaked and leathery as his hand. It also looks like someone has chewed the top of it off. Two thick hoop earrings made of the same purple and green marble of my key pull down on the lobe so it hangs obscenely at me. A black beard, knotted and decorated with bone beads like his hair, shags halfway down his chest.

He wears an outfit similar to mine and that of the him-me now staring at us with furious eyes and gritted teeth. Only his is gray or even a faded black. Either way, it is light enough that I can see the unmistakable bloody handprints all over him. Different sizes and different shades for different victims. It is brutal fog fashion. I half smile when I see his pants are rolled up like mine. The smile slips away when I see his toenails are as long, sharp, and bloodied as his fingernails.

He turns and faces me, and I notice his other ear is just as chewed and sports two more dangling marble earrings. Several deep furrows score the leathery hide of his forehead. Smack in the middle is an inverted cross that looks as though it might have been freshly carved with his talons only moments before.

Had I been standing here hugging him while he dug those nails into his flesh?

A rivulet of blood trickles down his nose, through his mustache, and to his dry lips, where he licks it away with a forked serpent's tongue. He smiles wickedly at me, and I see his teeth. They aren't filed to points like I expected. Instead, they look like bone chipped into a predator's teeth: jagged and sharp as his claws. His teeth would destroy meat and tear away at the soul within it.

A second small river of blood draws my attention back to his forehead. I notice his eyebrows, each an incomplete jigsaw puzzle due to the numerous scars around his eyes. I look into his blue eyes, and under the malevolence, I realize he is me as well. He winks. I feel gut punched, but wink back.

"Do you believe this bullshit?"

His voice is raspy like mine if I had been screaming for hours. As dry as his skin. I hear it with my ears *and* echoing inside my head. Oddly enough, the voice my ears hear sounds less familiar. Since we are within kissing distance, I can feel his breath—not just warm, but hot. Hotter than anyone's breath should have reason to be. It reeks of burnt meat and decay. My stomach turns, and it is the most familiar thing in my universe.

I shake my head as if hoping to rattle some sense into things. I look back to the gatekeeper-me. He is scowling at the monster-me, his cobalt orbs darkening even more. The monster-me ignores the baleful glare.

"I'll handle this," he growls at me and faces old Blue Eyes.

"Calm down. The kid wants in. Let him in and I'll beat it. I'll be gone, daddy, gone." His tone is raspy but deep and calm. It echoes in my head and buzzes in my ears. I'm calm. The gatekeeper-me must be calmer, because he blinks a few times and his eyes look like ours again. He speaks calmly but firmly.

"I cannot. You know I cannot."

I look back and forth between them as they have a conversation with their eyes. I get the feeling it is an old conversation. The gatekeeper-me's face is unflinching steel. The monster-me snarls and spits at the gatekeeper-me's feet. The yellow saliva hisses and smokes when it hits the ground. I watch the puff of smoke rise, and I see more twisted, tortured faces before it blends with the ever-rolling fog.

"After all he has done for you?" The monster-me doesn't even try to conceal his disgust.

"More bones?" comes the gatekeeper's unimpressed reply. His face looks less and less like mine as their voices grow louder and angrier.

"And ASH!" the monster-me yells so loud it echoes all through the fog.

I hear muffled sounds respond all around me. Soft slithering noises and distant laughter tease my ears, but the fog distorts their origins. The gatekeeper looks nothing like me anymore, save for his blue eyes. They are surrounded by an old face that I think I should recognize but can't. The face is pale and worn, with deep lines and a white beard. I feel their discord on the fog and step backwards. The gatekeeper's eyes flash back to the solid cobalt orbs and he yells, "Enough!"

The monster-me's eyes glow like coals of Hell. He growls loudly in response, and I hear the ghosts of sounds around me again. The gatekeeper turns his back on us and faces the distant light beyond the fog. He places one hand on the large lock and bows his head. The monster-me turns away with a snarl. The gatekeeper ignores me while mumbling something over and over under his breath. I don't know what to do other than follow the monster-me into the fog.

We walk along silently, together but alone. I have a million questions for him but am trying to figure out how to word them in order to avoid the claws swinging at his sides. As usual, once I'm getting close, I open my mouth. The monster-me silences me with a clawed finger to his dry lips. The faint yet unmistakable sound of laughter finds its way to my ears but dissipates and distorts in the fog. The monster-me inches toward the laughter and nods for me to follow. The laughter gets clearer with every step until I can tell it is actually two very different voices. One is a high-pitched female giggle and the other a booming male "ha ha ha ha." Both peal nonstop, leaving no time for breath. We are finally close enough to see dark blurs in the fog ahead of us, and he stops.

"I'll let you check this out yourself. I've seen everything this place has to offer." He bows and ushers me toward the laughing shadows. He smiles his bone teeth at me, and a chill dances the length of my spine.

I walk cautiously toward the shapes, and the monster-me tells me, "I'll be waiting right here."

The words bounce around inside my head as if my ears missed them but my brain caught them. It feels normal. Almost familiar.

I trust him, even covered in blood, even with the inverted cross flayed into his forehead, because he is the only thing that feels familiar. I take a few small steps and turn back to make sure he hasn't disappeared. He hasn't moved a muscle, and he winks one scarred eye at me. As I approach the laughers, my heart pounds in my chest and ears. The fog around them moves as if forced by their sounds. They go from darkly amusing to overtly creepy as my small shuffled steps take me closer. From this distance, I can tell there is something very wrong about the laughter; it is too intense and goes on too long. The hairs on my arms stand on end. If I had spider-sense, it would be all a-tingle. The sick feeling in my gut makes me seek more assurance from the mind-speaking, inverted-cross-carving me. He is still standing there, expectant and brutal, nodding to the source of the laughter. He fixes me with an impatient glare, and my body turns around on its on accord. My head remains twisted facing him, and he shows those deathly sharp teeth in a smile. He speaks into my head.

"They can't hurt you. Now hurry up."

The voice is loud and clear in my head, as if he were using my own brain to talk to me. It's a bit like a conscience, except a million times meaner than some little cricket in a top hat. The voice sounds ancient and not to be questioned. It manages to be both calming and commanding. His tone reminds me of someone petting a cat the wrong way until it is all hunched and half angry and then petting the kitty aggressively the right way until it resumes lying there and taking any love you give it. Using a heavy hand to calm the beast whether it wants to be calmed or not. I feel his heavy hand in my head. Not wanting to anger someone with such savage claws, I obey and walk forward into the fog.

I take a few steps and wave the lazy fog in front of me. I'm standing in a clearing, and the laughter is so loud I think my ears will bleed. Looking down with my ears covered, I get the feeling that whatever is laughing is right in front of me. I also get the feeling that whatever it is, it is terrible. I take a step backwards, planning on telling him I saw nothing, and his gravelly voice echoes in my head.

"Look."

My hands fall away from my ears, and the laughter drills into them, suffocating silence and reason. I feel the muscles in my neck tighten, and my head tilts up to behold the horror I sense. I can't close my eyes; invisible pins prop them open, so they dry and tear intermittently. Instinct fights to close them but the more I struggle, the more they burn and weep. My body is obeying other orders than mine, and it crushes my spirit under spiked wheels of defeat.

I feel hopeless.

When I give up control, my eyes blink. I blink them again and again and let thick tears roll down my cheeks. My vision clears, and I see that the things making the noise really can't hurt me.

Before me hang twin abominations, a nude man and woman wrapped to a thick pole with barbed and razor wire. The pole disappears a few feet above their heads up into the fog. I walk a slow, transfixed circle to get a better look at the man hanging a good three feet off the ground. He looks as if he should be dead. The strands of wire dig into his flesh, covering most of his nude form with a sticky layer of his own blood that drips quickly off his toes to the sand below him. For as badly as he is bleeding, he still has color to him. I always thought losing blood led to pallor. He thrashes madly against his cruel bonds, but he only moves a quarter to half an inch at the most. He shakes and twitches and lurches against the wires, all while laughing uproariously. I can see his chest heave and the wires dig into deep grooves in his flesh. A strand of barbed wire wrapped across his face holds his head up at an awkward angle. A rusty strand of razor wire covers his eyes. It most likely kept them closed at one time. There is so much gore dripping from them now that I can't tell if the man still has eyeballs. I doubt it. He looks to be screaming, but as the sound leaves his dry cracked lips, it turns to maniacal laughter. I continue my way around the gory spectacle, in awe of the sheer brutal madness of it all, to gain a better look at the female laugher.

She is held in place in much the same fashion, except her head is tilted up in the other direction. I stand in front of her and see that the strand of razor wire only covers one of her eyes. The unobstructed eye rolls wildly in its sunken socket, forever scanning the thick drifting fog. Her tears are streams running down her bloody face, clearing little trickles across her reddened cheeks. The wild eye lands on me and stops rolling at once. It opens wide enough for me to see the green iris and the red cracks across its surface. A few of her long eyelashes hang low, clumped thick with blood, over the eye. She stares at me and laughs, high and cheerful, though it is clearly meant to be a scream.

She fights against her vicious bonds, causing the wires to rip at her mangled flesh. She thrashes, the wires tear, and a few fans of blood splatter me from above. She twists and throws her body at the wires (still laughing, always laughing), and the blood continues to spray. One strand of barbed wire has worn clear through her jugular. The open vein gushes and flings blood aplenty. Her laugh is an irony that claws at my soul and her eye a hand reaching for salvation from the pits of Hell.

The eye focus on me with pained intensity, and her laugh slowly dies. The man on the opposite side of the pole still struggles, and the wires across the woman dig into her terrible gashes as he does. She is breathing deep, every breath an exercise in astonishing pain. With the longest, deepest of her exhalations, small clouds of red mist puff out and land on her chafed lips and pale cheeks. She works her lips, silent and determined like a wolf-child struggling for its first English word. Her eye is shining over with wetness that begs and pleads, but I can't tell if her pleas are meant for me or for her vocal cords. I can hear condensation in her lungs. She is having one hell of a time.

The man wrapped opposite her finally notices that she has stopped laughing, and his laugh dies a slow, nervous death as well. Once neither body is fighting the bonds, she slumps forward against the wires. With high creaking noises, the wires constrict themselves until they dig fresh grooves into the captives. A section of razor wire that crisscrosses the woman's temple slips under a piece of her scalp with a wet whisper. The man laughs once but cuts it short. In the silence that follows, I hear their blood running down the pole between them like a morbid, hellish creek. Without their thrashing, I see a monstrous hook protruding through her chest. I imagine the man has one as well. They've been hung on hooks and then double-wrapped with razor and barbed wire for good measure.

Her lips still struggle to make phantom words, and she looks like she is blowing me kisses with each breath. She focuses on me, though she winces when the wire across her throat shifts deeper. A sound, weak and hopeless, rises in her shredded throat. Once it leaves her lips, it's a feeble, whiny chuckle. Her eye fills with tears and anguish while her face contorts to a scream again. Her laughter rings all around me, high and joyful, and the man joins in with renewed fervor. Her eye rolls with pain and frustration, and she resumes thrashing. I take a step backwards as fans of blood fall again.

I walk around to the side where the man is bound and confirm for my own twisted curiosity that he has a matching hook. He does. A horrible thought occurs to me, and I look at the pole above the man's head, trailing my gaze up the foot and a half of exposed pole before it vanishes in fog. I see trails of brown blood—dried, cracked and flaking. I know without needing to see it that the pole rises far up into the fog with hooks every twelve feet or so. Just these two hang for now, but I know more people had hung (and would hang again) on however many hooks are lost in the fog above. I can almost hear a chorus of hellish laughter echoing back to the tortured souls trying to scream for forgiveness, for mercy or release. Souls trying to scream for the comfort of it, be it the physical release of giving sound to agony or the small comfort in yelling for loved ones and just hearing their names.

Blood from the man's tattered and torn femoral artery splashes across my shirt and face. The warm stickiness seals my eyes momentarily shut like crimson candle wax. In the darkness under my eyes, I see ghostly faces distorted in anguish. The sight tugs me back into my twisted reality with a mental jolt. I cup my hands and drag them from the corners of my eyes to my tear ducts and flick the handfuls of blood at the sand. I wipe my face and then wipe my bloody hands on my pant legs. I stare at the whole gory spectacle one last time and let it wash over me. I should feel something more than curiosity and mild annoyance, but I don't. The laughter goes on and on. I frown at the hung people, unsure of myself and entirely unsympathetic to them, and turn back the way I came.

I wonder to myself why their skin held the flushed tones of life instead of the black-green color of rotting flesh. I wonder how long they've been there and how long they will continue to hang there bleeding into the sand. I wonder about the height of the poles. I imagine how the pole would sound when covered with laughing people wrapped tight to it with wires that rend their flesh. Then one thought dismisses all others: what hung these people on those hooks and then took the time to double-wrap them?

My mind trips over itself like my feet as I stumble through the fog back to the monster-me. He takes one look at the blank expression on my blood-streaked face and falls backwards with his own raspy laughter. Holding his sides, he rolls back and forth, screaming with amusement the entire time. I hear it with my ears, and it echoes inside my head so loud it stomps away any chance of processing another thought. His laughter is harsh and cold, the guffaws of a bully. The two different laughs from the hung people drift from behind me, and the monster-me's chortles join from in front. All the eerie laugher swirls and dances within and around me. My knees go weak, and I double over. I blink my eyes at the sand, but they refuse to focus. In between my blinks, I can see the fog swirling madly around me in time with the twisting laughter. The different laughs each take a physical form in my mind's eye as they dance around me, leaning close and then backing away from me so they all roll over each other.

When the hung people lunge forward at me with screams on their faces but joy on their lips, they are still wrapped tight in their own personal coils of wire. I blink and turn in what I think is a small circle, casting blurry glances at each of the horrors surrounding me within the confines of their tortured laughs. The hanged man still has wire wrapped around both his eyes, and he snaps forward with blind fury. The woman's eye is now a dark maroon color where the blood vessels have ruptured. The monster-me has a priest-eating grin on, and he points at me while they circle me. Blood trickles down from the cross on the monster-me's face and from the numerous gashes and wounds on the man and woman. I hear them in my head and with my ears.

Or maybe I'm moving. Maybe I'm stumbling and swaying. My stomach clenches. Tears form in the corners of my eyes. The air feels thicker, and the laughs have whipped into a hurricane. My eyes shut tight to avoid the fun house gone straight to Hell, but the laughter still screams inside my head. I feel the madness in the air as it squeezes and bends my body. It is a dull pickax mining at my sanity.

My knees buckle, and I slump to the ground, dropping beneath the circling madness. I hear it reach a crescendo above me and then stop instantly. The spinning sensation ceases with the force of a bus hitting a brick wall at 90 miles an hour. My stomach rolls again, deeper than before, and I retch. Tears run down my cheeks and drip off my face, pink after mixing with the blood. All that comes out of my throat is harsh gray sand. It flows from my mouth in steady, forceful streams. The violent eruption sprays random flecks into my eyebrows and goatee, where they stick. The sand scratches the inside of my throat and my lips. I try to stop, but I can't suppress the gagging. I continue spewing more sand until my sides burn and the sand is speckled with tiny drops of my blood. I spit out a few more mouthfuls and collapse into the mess I just vomited. I bury my face in it. It cuts the tender skin of my eyelids and plugs my nose.

I can't handle this. Too many terrible things are hidden in the fog. I can stay buried in the sand forever. But the monster-me stands above me, with a leg on either side of my prone body, and he grabs me under my armpits with his clawed hands. He tugs me to my feet like I'm a three year old. He stands me back up, roughly wipes some of the gray sand off my face, and says, "'Ere we go."

I wipe the rest of the sand off my face, and the air stings the hundreds of tiny newborn scrapes bleeding dully across my face. I sway in place on my weak knees as a small whimper escapes my dry lips. He looks at me with my blue eyes.

"Pussy."

He says it through a smile of buzz saw bone teeth in a tone molded with disgust. There is a challenge in his eyes. He means it as a verbal poke in the chest, but I just stand and stare at him like he is trying to explain why hookers don't have feelings. The challenge melts away, and he winks, striding past as if nothing had happened.

He walks and I follow. The sudden silence is eerie and disorienting. I can vividly remember the horror of the hanging people, but I have no idea where in the ever-swirling fog they are. Just as I'm about ready to unleash my barrage of questions, I hear a sound somewhere ahead of us. My legs freeze awkwardly when the peals of rambunctious children's laughter meet my ears. My stomach sinks and rolls twice as hard before. He spins around so fast he is a bloody greasy blur.

"I dare you!" he shouts even though it thunders inside my skull as well.

I stare at my feet in response. A shiver runs the length of my spine, and I see the man and woman wrapped to the pole. I hear their laughter as they thrash against their bonds, succeeding only in shredding their nude bodies to ribbons. Somehow, I hear the sound of their blood trickling down the pole. The laughter of children is closer now, and the dreadlock takes a step closer to me. I watch my feet take a slow step backwards, and I shake my head even more slowly. Just to be sure he understands me, I flip him the bird with both hands in the universal "no thanks" gesture.

He laughs to himself, and it vibrates my spine and brain.

"Fuck you too, pal," he tells me in my head while smiling his predator's smile.

A loud siren-like wail drowns out the sound of the laughter, and the monster-me raises a bloodstained finger to his lips. He smiles as the wailer first becomes a blur in the fog and then stumbles fully into sight. A tall, tubby white guy stands before us. His short blond hair is messed up, and his bloodshot pale blue eyes are alive with panic, though they don't see us. He has a deep, jagged wound across his throat that in no way hinders his high-pitched wail. He is wearing an outfit like mine, though his looks small for him and just about my size. I notice the crotch of his pants is one giant bloodstain and decide against offering a trade. Without noticing us, he rubs his eyes, whimpering. Then he unleashes a shrill wail that hurts my ears and makes me cringe away from him. He hits notes I never though possible, and I feel a vibration behind me. The monster-me feels it too. He smiles and pushes me a few feet to the shrieking man's left.

The man wails next to us, and I feel the vibration on my skin like the heartbeat of the wind. I see a huge shape in the fog where there was nothing a moment before. In the next blink of my eye, a massive horrible beast stands before us. The monster-me raises his finger to his lips again. Light gleams off his talons even in the dimness of the fog. The wailing man has his head in his hands and is screaming hard enough that blood gushes from his throat in small shooting streams. He doesn't notice the newcomer.

The horror is easily fifteen feet tall but somehow appeared with a silence of which I thought only ninjas capable. It stands on legs like cedar trunks that end in big two-toed feet that resemble hooves. It wears what looks to be the biggest pair of leather chaps I have ever seen. The green-gray leather is covered in scuffs and wear and sports an obscene bulge in the crotch. A colossal and solid-looking stomach hangs over the beltline. His mammoth right arm flexes and relaxes down to an enormous fist silently twisting a giant barbed hook made from some strange purple metal. His left hand reaches over and scratches his ample belly. His hand has three fingers (birdie, pointer, and thumbkin), each ending in a wicked thick nail. Where the other two (ring and lil' pinky) would be on a human, there is a small blunt horn that reminds me of a rhino's smaller horn.

The abomination has a face only an ugly mother could love. The creature looks like some kind of giant demon troll. His massive underbite accommodates two large horn-like teeth on either side of his mouth. Just above where his upper lip should be are four small slits I assume to be his nostrils. Above the nostril slits are two eyes nearly the same size as the teeth, and they are both sewn shut tight. Two thick twisting horns rise out from the small forehead above the unpleasant ocular stitching. Two floppy ears, which vaguely resemble those of an old goat, hang to his hunched shoulders. They twitch toward the sound of the scream, and the monster shuffles silently forward until he is right in front of the howling man.

The monster grunts, a sound that makes my breath catch and burn my lungs. The wailing man stops screaming and looks at the monster with his mouth agape. The tubby guy staggers back a step and inhales deeply. His wound spurts fresh torrents of blood at the force. The monster-me steps back a few steps, and I follow as though he is the leader. The monster roars, and hundreds of different laughs echo from all over in the fog in response. Laughter rings from behind me, from above me, from any direction I face. It sounds close, but I can hear it rising in the distance as well. The laughter of men, women, and children scream along with the behemoth. The screaming man bends his knees and shakes his hands in front of his face in some kind of terrified tantrum.

The beast focuses on the scream, grunts in triumph, and swings his massive left fist toward the sound. It connects horn to forehead with a crack like dueling rams. The man's eyes cross, and he rocks back on his heels until he tips flat on his back. He lands sprawled and screaming like he plans on making a sand angel. The instant he hits ground, the monster swings his right arm in a high arch, aiming the hook at the supine man. The hook hits the man in his chest with a loud crack as it shatters his sternum. The sound of bone splintering is followed by a spurt of blood that shoots high enough to splash across the monster's face as it follows through its swing. Feeling the warm sticky blood, the monster screams again, more triumphant than before. Again, laughter rises from all around to answer the roar of the beast. The man's scream gurgles in his chest and turns to giggles when it hits his lips. He curls up like a bug sprayed with poison and claws weakly at the massive horned hand grinding the hook into him. His feet kick in twitches at the swirling fog.

The monster holds tight to the hook and pokes the man in his forehead with its other hand. It takes three such pokes to make the man uncurl and fall back into the sand. Huge tears stream down the man's face, but his laughter sounds like that of an excited teenage girl at the mall. His deep breathing is punctuated with bursts of high girlish giggles that send spurts of blood to the sand around him in fans. He stares at the hook piercing his chest and arches his back and digs his heels into the sand. As he does, his throat gapes open, causing him to choke on his laughter and blood. He rolls to one side and spits out mouthfuls of blood and squeals of joy through clenched teeth. Then he returns to his back and repeats the process.

Giggle, stare, giggle, arch, choke, and spit.

On the third repetition, I move my foot just out of range of a splatter of blood propelled by the force of his laughter. He finally notices us, but the words he tries to scream turn into furious chuckles when they pass through his lips with mouthfuls of claret. His pale blue eyes lock on us and do all the screaming his voice cannot. I stare back unspeaking, lost somewhere between shock and sick amazement. The monster-me smiles and licks the razors masquerading as his teeth. The man gags on his blood and spits it out with a weak giggle. He then locks eyes with the bloodstained fiend beside me. The man's eyes grow wide with terror; the monster-me's are mere slits. The monster-me ends the staring contest with a wink.

As if on cue, the great horned behemoth gives a third deafening roar that brings another chorus of the damned laughter. I stare at the madness in front of me: the blinded colossus, the monster-me with his talons and teeth, and the man with the hook and the giggle. Yet somehow, as the laughter rises, my mind wanders.

I close my eyes, and I see the man and woman hung and wrapped tight to the pole, blood trickling, as incessant as the ringing of their laughter. The fog parts, and I see more people above them, two by two up the length of the pole. Men and women thrash at rusty barbed wire and shiny razor wire, flinging a red rain down on me. Long strands of wire connect at varying points on other newly visible poles nearby. Hanging from the wires by massive gore-dripping hooks are more people. They swing and flail, and the blood rains. The longer I stare, the more poles connected with morbid wires I see. Everyone laughs as though this were an amusement park ride. I open my eyes, and all the noises stop, save for that of the pierced man still giggling like a girl in front of me, and the horrible vision fades.

The beast's nose slits sniff at the air. It seems satisfied and grunts, deep and throaty. The giant three-fingered hand pulls away from the hook it embedded into its prey, revealing a thick leather cord bound to the weapon. He takes a massive step, his cedar-sized legs missing the man by a few scant inches. At first, I think the monster is going to walk away and leave the man to roll around with the hook spearing through him and gagging blood, but then I notice the four other leather straps trailing into the fog behind the monster. After his next giant but eerily silent step, the behemoth becomes a blur in the fog. One more step and he is a dark distant blur. The leather cords pull four people into our little clearing. Three men and one woman, each sporting the same fashionable hook as the man in front of us, are dragged before us. They roll and crash into each other as the cord tugs then goes slack before tugging again. They give nervous chuckles and chortles in place of moans. The hook in the tubby guy pulls tight, and he rolls like a log into the others. They slam together, laugh like old school chums, and push each other away with dirty, bloody hands. The cords tug again, and the five twist as their hooks shift, sending arms and legs flopping helplessly into each other.

I can see a small black dot on the woman's forehead and a massive sand-crusted crater on the back of her head. Fresh blood trickles over the dry, frayed edges of the wound. They push and scream with laughter, and I see one of the men has a matching wound. I don't see the fatal wounds on the other two, but I know they are there. Their hooks tug them forward, leaving a slick trail of gore on the sand and a fading quintet of laughs.

Once I can't even see the blurred shapes of the monster and his wretched tail, I turn to the monster-me. He stares after the beast and pays me no mind.

"What the hell was that?" I whisper.

He just smiles his bone-toothed grin at me and turns back the way we were heading. After a few steps, he looks over his shoulder to make sure I am following him. I stare at the sand at my feet. Faces have formed in the trail of gore and sand left behind by the monster and his crew. They all stare madly at me with silent screams. I look back to the monster-me, who is regarding me with one eyebrow raised. I shake my head and jog to catch up to him. When he speaks next, it is only in my head.

"He is a hunter."

"He hunts chubby people?" I whisper with a grin.

"He hunts the wandering damned. His eyes are sewn shut. What the fuck does he care what they look like? He only hears the terror in their screams, and he only knows one way to make it stop. They call to him like a siren's song."

He regards me briefly, and I see in his-my eyes that he is not in a joking mood. Knowing this makes the hair on the back of my neck stand up and dance.

"So I'm not damned?" I ask in a serious, almost reverent tone.

"Are you wandering?" he snaps back.

I don't know how to respond, and my head throbs suddenly and painfully enough to distract me. My knees are getting weaker, and my feet stumble over each other as I follow him. I feel myself losing control of my limbs as they grow heavy and obstinate, disregarding my mental commands. I stagger a few more wobbly steps before I fall to one knee in the sand. My hand follows my knee, and my face follows my hand. The harsh, mocking laughter of the monster-me echoes inside my head.

"Get up or I'll leave ya."

My body twitches and jerks, and I stand up in a crunching reversal of exactly how I fell. The monster-me stands facing me with a deadly Cheshire cat grin. He takes an exaggerated step to one side, revealing a torch adorned with eight skulls, tied to the torch and to each other by their long, knotted hair. Death looks out in every direction from the torch. I focus on the skull facing me. The fire from above reflects off the smooth forehead and somehow makes the empty eye sockets seem deeper and darker. Small tortured faces dance across the skull in the reflection of flame, silently screaming at me.

I find myself looking into the eye sockets, and I hear a quiet, oddly timed drumbeat rising inside my head the same way the monster-me's voice does. The rhythm is like nothing I've ever heard or imagined, both primal and complex. I feel a pull forward, and my stomach cramps a warning to turn back. I can turn now and leave this monster-me here. If I can find my way back to the gatekeeper-me alone, he might twist that beautiful key into the lock of a thousand locks and let me hide behind the thick steel bars from all this horror. The gatekeeper kept my key. I feel flushed and dizzy.

The drums are getting louder.

The pounding beats smash my thoughts of retreat under their thrall. I can't break eye contact with the skull. I stumble forward a step, and the drums intensify in speed and volume. My knees bend, and I stumble past the torch, my movement controlled by the drums. The monster-me gives a loud whoop and dances past me. He jumps and twists and kicks the sand. Shaking his dreadlocked hair so the bone beads clack together, he lifts his hands slowly in the air and claps to the beat that is tugging me forward stumble by stumble. I realize he can hear the drums, though I still only hear them in my head. My ears hear nothing but the leather-handed clap of the monster-me. The high ringing sound of silence is an eerie contrast to the growing momentum of the drumming inside my skull. The sharp buzz of silence cuts out when the monster-me claps, like a radio edit of a gangster rap song. The monster-me dances a wobbly circle around me that weaves when I stumble. He whoops again and cartwheels around the torch pole, then cuts back around me in a figure eight. He laughs, and it buzzes like distortion between drumbeats.

Using every bit of willpower I can, I stop stumbling forward and stand up straight. I close my eyes but still hear the drums inside my head and the random clapping of the dreadlock. My body wants to move forward, but my mind is in full-on panic mode.

"C'mon," he growls. The pulse of the drum promises no hope, but I open my eyes and shamble forward.

The abrasive gray sand is getting sharper underfoot, and bigger chunks poke out and cut at my bare soles. The more I focus on the drums, the less I feel my now-bleeding feet and the faster I move forward. The less I fight, the less my stomach turns. I let go of panic, hope, fear and give myself to the drums. Immediately, my stumble becomes a confident stride. The drums slow into a groove—still oddly timed and alien—and everything slows down with it. The monster-me does a languorous cartwheel in front of me, and I notice the fog is lifting. When he raises his hands, they move in slow motion, but the sound of the clap keeps place with the relentless drumming.

I turn my head to follow his wild dance and notice a solid black wall to my left. It is so dark that it seems to pull the fog into itself. I follow the wall up with my eyes and discover it has a ceiling only a few feet taller than I am. I follow the ceiling to the wall on my right and realize with numbed worry that I've followed the drums into a deep black rock cave. Torches, like the one where the drums wormed their way into my head, line the wall every fifty feet or so. I've only just noticed the cave around me, but when I look back, the entrance is miles away and cloaked in forbidding darkness.

Carved into the stone walls and ceiling are faces in torment. Hopeless screams of torture and pain etched in the cold dark stone. Carved alongside some of the images are hands reaching out for mercy they will never receive. Others have arms in defensive poses across grimacing stone faces. As the wall rolls into the ceiling, there is a carving of a man upside down, reaching for me. His frozen stone eyes seem to hold a warning. A carving on the wall can't hear the drums calling me forward. The carving ends at the man's belly button, and a woman screams for eternity with her hands pressed to her cheeks where his knees would be. So the carving will never have to stumble forward on what I can now tell are bones. Mostly smaller slivers and shards, but as I near the first torch, I kick half of a human skull out of my way. It bounces away and rolls on its strange axis into the wall, which seems ever closer. We pass the torch, me limping slightly and leaving a slick trail of my blood, and the monster-me dancing circles around me like a drunken sailor around a fat girl. I notice the skulls hanging from the torch, but I manage to avoid looking into the dark, hollow eye holes. The light from the torches' flames makes the carvings across the walls and ceiling come alive. Pained stone faces turn to me. Hands thrash and reach for me.

Intense feelings of impending doom and crippling despair soak into me. My thoughts scream and then fade under the drums into nothingness. The nothingness is thick and physical, and its presence staves away complete madness at the beat of the drums. My emotions are as frozen as the stone faces surrounding me. I should have felt something at witnessing the horrors in the fog, but each only managed to fill me with strange wonder. Even the blind behemoth shocked me with his size and brutality, but fear never raised its head in its presence.

Now, as I slip on human bones and progress deeper down a slowly contracting black hall, haunted in stone, fear hums in my head alongside the steady drums and the leathery clapping of the monster-me's hands to form a disturbing trio. The bone-littered floor is angling down. A slow glance to the ceiling above tells me it is slanting lower to match the gradual drop in the floor.

The space between the walls narrows with each revolution of the dancing monster-me. We pass another torch as we begin our descent. The shards of bone sticking up from the ground have my feet in shreds, and my toes throb as I kick femurs and spines with partial ribcages still attached out of my way. My toes throb uncomfortably, and the deep grooves in my soles beg for mercy, but my body refuses to stop. The drums care not for my pain or discomfort. The dreadlock comes around my right side as he rears back and spits at the wall. A mouthful of bright red blood splashes across the stone face of a girl who seems to cry and sway in the light from the torch. The stark red drips from the girl's eyes and lips like tears and drool. The monster-me says something, but the drums drown out his voice. I see his lips move, but the jagged bone teeth behind them make lip reading impossible. With great effort, I shake my head and point at my ear so he knows I only hear the beckoning of the drums. His lips move again as the drums grow ever louder. I only hear a faint crackling break in the steady awkward groove. He claps, and it is silent but in time. He leans his head back and I think he whoops again, but the only thing I hear is the drums.

The drums are so loud they echo not only off the walls of my head but off the dark carven walls around me as well. I can feel the madness rising now. It starts with a roll in my stomach. It churns the sickness in my stomach to calmness. It flows down my still-shuffling legs to my torn and bleeding feet. The filthy gashes in my feet tingle with pins and needles as they go numb. I allow the drums to pull me, and my limp lessens while my speed down the narrowing slope increases. The monster-me adjusts the speed of his taunting dance to maintain the same bug-the-fuck-out-of-me circle even closer as the walls close in. I turn an ancient skull to dust when I step on it. The tingle rises to my ankles.

I turn and look behind me without slowing my pace. I can only see to the last torch; beyond that is a wall of darkness that swirls and oozes like the fog had before. The carved faces that were in front of me as I passed have all turned to watch me leave. Some of the visages appear to wail at me as the light and shadows dance in cadence to the drums across the stone.

The dreadlock passes in front of me and makes eye contact.

Thought is impossible. No words or pictures or clever symbolism can withstand the furious pounding. Since he is moving so slowly, I have time to stare into his-my eyes. They are alive with wicked glee. I catch a glimpse of my own reflection in his eyes, and I see the smile on my face. It is an awkward, crooked grin but a grin nonetheless. His smile is wide and maniacal with razor-sharp bone teeth poking over dry lips. He winks when he notices my own grin. He raises his hands inches from my ear and claps. I feel the air move from his hands striking each other, but no sound stands a chance against the drums. He spins away from me, continuing his strange jig.

The decline in the floor increases at every torch, and the walls get closer as we drop. I look at the floor behind me and notice the trail of bright red blood my feet are leaving. My blood is the brightest thing I see: a stark and violent red across the dismal gray and white path of bones. As I watch, the bones absorb my blood. Within seconds, my gore trail has faded into the bone and ash. A thirst rises from the bones, and a hunger reaches from the darkness.

I turn back around to feel the tickly tingly sensation work its way up my sides. My chest tightens and then goes numb. The pins and needles work from my armpits to my shoulders and then down my arms. As the feeling reaches my wrists, I realize I've been clenching and unclenching my fists without knowing it. The force controlling me allows one more clench before the pins and needles tingle through my fingers.

The monster-me dances past me again, and I notice that the inverted cross on his forehead is bleeding again, more profusely than before. Blood streams from the wound and down his hairy face. Most of the sticky red runs into his dreadlocked beard, dying bone beads crimson and plastering his shirt to his chest. Blood trickles over his lips, which take on a sudden and incongruous look of good health, and into his mouth. He smiles, and blood oozes from the corners of his mouth.

He leans his head back as if to howl and shakes it furiously. Drops of blood fly through the air in slow motion and land on my face. The pins and needles have reached a stalemate with the pounding drums at my tingling shoulders, and I feel the unpleasant kiss of sticky droplets on my skin. The blood is not as warm as it should be. He leans back and shakes then leans forward and shakes, blood flying from his beard and hair as he does so. Seeing him hunched over and shaking, blood spattering in all directions, makes me think of a rabid dog attacking its first meal in weeks. I watch his dance until he disappears at my shoulder.

I turn back around, and the hallway we are following ends suddenly at a large archway lit by torches on either side. My legs carry me closer, and I see the light from many torches flickering in what appears to be a great hall. Another step, and I'm standing in the archway. The great hall is dark save for the torches, and the light they cast gives the impression of immense size.

The drums are louder than they have ever been. Heavy and sedative. The echo of the strange rhythm bounces off the inside of my skull and the hallway behind me, and it sounds like an army of the damned pounding away in the great room before me.

I feel a warm trickle run between my eyes and down my nose. The drums pound, and the flames flicker. I wipe the trickle and look at it in slow motion. When I see the unmistakable bright red of my blood, I instinctively reach for my face. I feel a large weeping gash on my forehead and use all five numbed fingers to assess the damage. Somehow, I have acquired an inverted cross to match that of the monster-me. The oils from my skin make the fresh lesions shriek. It burns so fiercely that the pain stabs through the drums for an instant. The drums pound back furiously and build toward a thunderous and awkward crescendo. It shocks my numb body, and I'm jerked into the hall.

I feel a whoosh of foul-smelling wind as I am slammed forward. My feet touch down into the hall, and the drums go silent before they can reach the climax toward which I felt them building. The tickling sensation I assume to be madness works its way up the back of my neck unopposed by the drums. The silence rings in my ears and inside my head. The great hall is brobdingnagian in size, stretching much farther and taller than I can see. Still, one step carries me most of the way across the immense space. The archway through which I came looks to be over three hundred feet away. Matching archways dot the far wall, each lit with the same torches, complete with long-haired skulls. I am an ant in a museum, hiding in the shadows of the flickering flames from the torches set every thirty feet on the dark stone walls. The torches should be closer together. There is a space between each one where the light from neither torch reaches, leaving a cold dark spot of menacing shadows. Thirty feet above the torches are more, and thirty feet above them are even more. Up and up until I can't see any farther.

Bones and full skeletal remains litter the floor, but my numb feet feel cold stone below. The monster-me moves at full speed as if someone turned off his slow motion mode with the push of a button. He cartwheels into my line of sight, but rather than continuing his circling pattern, he shoots out straight in front of me. He rolls back to his feet, facing me with a wink, and lets his momentum carry him backwards. He leans his arms back, and his body follows in a perfect back handspring. He twists in midair and lands momentarily with his back facing me. He raises his arms like a blood-covered gymnast and somersaults forwards. As he rolls, he launches himself back into the air, where he twists again so he is facing me. He lands on one knee with his arms up, palms even with his shoulders.

"Ta-daaa!" The firelight adds a new depth to his eyes, and I see rolling darkness in them.

His gymnastic routine leaves him kneeling before a thirty-five-foot archway. Strange words and symbols are carved into the great black bricks that make up the ancient archway. Beyond it is darkness that repels the flickering light of the torches. On either side of the archway are two ten-foot drums. Each is set on a pedestal of stone so they look like they are resting in the monster-me's open palms. Behind each drum is a twenty-foot hunter behemoth like the one we saw hook the chubby guy with the girlish giggle. They don't move or twitch, and I realize right away that something is different about them. Both are covered with different patches of colors: green, gray, red, purple, and black.

They are dead—chopped and rotten.

The tingle reaches my jaw line and buzzes just beneath my ears as I realize the atrocious truth. My eyes adjust, and I see strands of barbed wire holding the corpses of dozens of people in place to form the shapes of the horrific creatures. They are massive morbid sculptures in a corpse-meat medium. The arm closest to me looks to be four or five human bodies, all in various stages of rot, all tied and bent as needed to form the minutest details of the beast's arm and hand. The hands are wonders of macabre skill: human arms and legs bound tightly into the shape of three long-clawed fingers and one blunt horn. Each hand holds a large stick with a bolder affixed to it lying motionlessly across the drums' heads. The bodies that make up the terrible sculptures are all in varying states of decay, yet I can see details on the monsters right down to the razor wire sewn across the heap of bodies to form the creatures' eyes. The archway-then-drummer pattern repeats around the colossal hall, each morbid drummer lit by torches above and below.

The tickle nibbles at my earlobes and inches up the back of my skull. The pins and needles keep me from giving in to my body's urge to get sick at such a sight. The monster-me smiles his buzz saw grin and takes slow, exaggerated steps backwards. As each foot falls, the drums sound a single brutal beat. I look to the drums next to me, but even as they pound again in my head, the monsters remain lifeless, gripping unmoving drumsticks. The drums don't stop the tingling now, and it numbs my face. The darkness of the archway swallows the monster-me's leg and the back half of his body. The drums pound again. He winks and leans slowly back. I lunge forward, driven by something between merciless rage and mindless terror as his face disappears into the blackness. The way his wide, dangerous grin is there one second and gone the next reminds me again of the Cheshire cat. I picture something fat and purple waiting for me in the darkness, though I doubt it is as harmless as a floating grin.

I reach and grab his beard with one hand, holding fast to bone beads slick with blood. My other hand finds a grip on his blood-soaked shirt. His momentum carries him backwards and me forward. The drums pound again. I watch helplessly as my hands disappear into darkness with his beard and chest. I feel like I'm reaching into an ice pond. I can no longer tell if I'm still gripping anything; all I sense is undead cold.

I feel the tingle dance on my scalp, and my mind spirals.

My last thought as my biceps sink into the shadows is of the Cheshire cat: plump, purple, and laughing down at me from the steel gate to which it is bound with barbed wire. The drums pound again, and I try to scream. Out of my mouth comes the honest laughter of a man in the full embrace of madness. Tortured screams echo in my head, and my laughter rings in my ears. I feel a coldness so frozen and stubborn that it burns the gaping cross on my forehead as I fall into the darkness.

Then I wake and start my day.

My Sick Story: Becoming Hate

My name is Gavin Wagner, and that was my dream. But before I get there, let me fill you in a little bit. I was born to the late Shannon and Dennis Wagner in 1978. I was their only son, and they gave me a great youth in a little town on the Washington/Idaho border, which even now I won't tarnish by speaking its name. Both of my parents were professors at the college in the next town over. Dad taught some long-fancy-word math, and Mom taught some long dead history of some ancient peoples. I never really cared enough to know much more about it. Then again, I might have had not they both died before I reached college age. Mom passed on in February 1996, and Dad followed her mere days later. Sad story; I'll get to it to in a minute.

First the dream. It began a few years after my parents' deaths (Y2K, I think), and it has been reoccurring ever since. Long enough that the memories jumbled and replayed in fog during the dream seem blurred when I remember them when wide awake. My memories are ghosts. Ghosts wrapped in barbed wire. I made them ghosts; I might as well have wrapped them in barbed wire myself. And even if I did, do you think I'd know better? I can't. I can't feel my past all the way. No remorse. No sorrow. I miss things. Their absence when they're gone. I feel longing and loss but nothing more. The dream makes me remember. It opens my eyes to the ghosts, and I always stare. I'd chant a mantra every morning as I shook them away and got out of bed: "Even Madness Ends."

I'd only half believe it.

The first part of the dream is easy. It's a very specific day. I lived that day. I'm the bigger kid. The smaller kid is my best friend, Joshua Austin. I always called him Joshie, even though he hated it. The day in the dream is a day that replays in my head a lot during my waking hours as well. The darkest day in my extended funeral of a life: the day I met Heinous.

It was a Saturday. Joshie called early, as I knew he would. He wanted to go out to the forest. I was raised near the woods and never passed up a chance to walk in the trees. He was the same. His parents

50

were professors at the same college where my mom and dad worked. They had been friends for years before Joshie and I ever came along, and they had the photos of muttonchops and bellbottoms to prove it. Joshie and I were born a few months apart and knew each other our entire lives. We crawled together and took our first steps side by side. He shared his toys, which were always the coolest around. I shared my sarcasm and unwanted nicknames. On some strange level, as different as we were, our senses of humor would crisscross, and no one made me laugh like that. Or has since, for that matter. Most of the time, other people wouldn't understand what we were laughing at, and never once did we care. He hung around me like a shadow that would come alive with a snarky comment and send me into fits of hysterics. People would look at him, surprised they'd forgotten he was there, and stare plain-faced at his awkward grin. I could talk to anyone, especially the ladies. Joshie only talked to his parents, his overworked doctor, and me.

The forest in which we would hang out was about ten miles out of town. The land was donated by some rich old nature lover and maintained by the college, which meant college kids would walk the paths drinking brewskis and chainsawing logs in their way. It wasn't a huge patch of forest land, maybe three miles long and five or six deep up the mountain, but the town loved it. People would hike the paths that wound up and around the mountain during every season. People would bring their dogs out to run through the trees and splash in the small creek. The local schools would have field trips to the forest to show the children the wonders of animals and plants in our woodland environment. People rode mountain bikes on the paths or, just as often, made their own paths. People were respectful and cleaned up after themselves, making it a great place for a family to spend a lazy summer day watching the sun stab through the trees. All the kids from school went out there. Joshie and I would go year round even if we had to dig through five feet of snow. I like to think we had a special connection with the forest.

When we were still in junior high, we would ride out there in packs of ten or more wild, crazy boys to burn our prepubescent energy playing *armywarhidedeathkill*. Joshie would deem himself my team's engineer every time rather than participate in an actual play battle. He would dig holes between trees and build rock walls around them for our team to hide behind. Joshie would always be wearing the only camo he owned: a safety orange camo vest, easily two sizes too big, and an old army bandana. If he was ever confronted during our war games, he would fall to the ground and cover his ears before the bitter smell of burnt cap could fill the air. He would stay huddled there on the ground until I came back to tell him the war was over.

As nervous and scared as he seemed of other people, he would surprise me with his fearless attitude to other things. The road into the forest ran across the top of a small ridge that looked down into the lower part of the forest. The road wrapped halfway around the mountain before it dead-ended into its side. You would park on the rim of forest and take any one of several ways down into it. On the far end of the forest, hidden by tall pines and fat, round cedars, was an old abandoned house. People swore you could find it at night by following the festering feeling of evil through the trees. Joshie and I stumbled across it exploring one day, and Joshie had to see the inside of the creepy old bastard.

It was a nice spacious two-story home that was probably beautiful when it had inhabitants. However, for as long as I'd known about it, no one had ever lived there. It just got creepier and more rundown year after year. No one our age knew the real story behind it and that only increased the legend. Adults never mentioned it other than to tell us to stay away, so of course it was a popular place to explore and smoke pot when we should have been in school. Joshie and I spent a week exploring and mapping it out. The old home had two "secret passageways." One went behind two small rooms in the basement to a small stable attached to the farthest end of the house, and a second, cooler, one followed a twisting stone staircase from the stable room up to the kitchen, where it was hidden by a protruding wall. At some point in the house's history, a fire raged through it, scarring the logs of the living room and blackening the wooden staircase up to the loft. The large hand-built stone fireplace was covered with a layer of grimy ash and dust but showed no fire damage. We found boxes of old magazines, strange sexual magazines featuring rape and torture, that sent Joshie on rants about morals and values disintegrating in America. They kinda turned me on even then. Joshie would copy down all the strange nonsense words scrawled all over the house in hopes of translating them while I flipped through page after wrinkled, blackened page of twisted violent sex. It wasn't like looking at other nudie mags (hey, we were teenage boys, and we'd seen loads of porn); it was more personal and deep. Blood, metal, and cum. I don't think Joshie ever did figure out what "Tagen Noob Cel Fhatgen" meant, but I learned all about violent sexual depravity. The fact that it rolled my boulder … well, I kept that to myself.

Our little forest was the first place I ever smoked a joint. Joshie stood watching with a smirk I could see under the hand used to stifle ridiculously fake coughs the entire time. Our little town was a hippy town, and not only was pot not a big deal, it was almost a right of passage into enlightened adulthood. Joshie would never smoke anything, especially something that could make him dumb. For a while he tried to call me Stony every time I called him Joshie, but I was far more determined as far as annoying nicknames went, and it never stuck. Not even when I was calling him Joshie from inside a thick yellow cloud of reefer smoke.

Our little forest is where I kissed a girl with tongue the first time. Her name was Sarah Jackson, and she went on to become Homecoming Queen, beauty pageant winner, and crack whore, in that order. While she and I were up the mountain swapping spit like we needed more mucus to live, Joshie was listening to Nirvana on his headphones and building a dam in the creek. Sarah kissed me deep and ran her fingers through my hair. She dug the edges of her nails into the flesh behind my ears and then moaned softly into them. I pictured her hands with every finger broken, twitching and clawing at me while she groaned seductively in my ear. I controlled my sudden and violent urge to break her pretty fucking fingers, but I misread her slobbery signals. I grabbed her left tit and gave it a gentle squeeze. Her reaction was immediate and severe, and it resulted in a hand-shaped bruise I wore for a week and a half across my face. She stormed down the mountain in a state of righteous anger while I stumbled behind, rubbing my already swollen cheek and uttering frantic apologies.

As we reached the forest floor, we came into Joshie's view. He was working his way upstream to build a second dam "to ease the pressure" on the first. He noticed Sarah's tussled hair, and he told me later that she looked like she wanted to register me as an underage pervert with the first law enforcement officer she could find. He looked from the disheveled and disgusted Sarah to me rubbing my red cheek and looking as embarrassed as he'd ever seen me. He added everything up in less than a second.

"You touched her booby!"

Now, it wasn't typical Joshie style to yell anything, much less something about the female anatomy. He didn't understand the female of our species, and he never seemed very interested in them anyway. He treated all females with a quiet cautious respect, save for my mom, who was the brunt of countless harmless and lame "your mom" jokes over the years. However, on this day, Joshie had his Walkman on max, blasting Nirvana straight to his brain, so he had no idea how loud he had just shouted. Sarah turned on the heel of her LA Gears and slapped me hard across the as-yet-unscathed side of my face while I stared at Joshie, shocked beyond words.

A few college kids were playing hacky sack in a small clearing just up the path, and by then they were laughing out loud. Sarah turned away from me, gave Joshie a glare that screamed, "Die, you little freak" and ran down the path as she let her tears flow. The female college student slugged one of her two male companions in the arm and told him to "Shut it, bucko."

She stepped in front of Sarah, who crumpled into her arms after the everlasting trauma of my boob squeeze. The college girl hugged the hysterical Sarah, pushed the hair out of her tear-streaked face, and asked if she needed a ride. Sarah nodded, and the college girl told the guy she slugged that she was taking his car and they could ride home with "those perverts." She told us all how ashamed we should be, and—her arm protectively around Sarah—the two girls walked up and out of the forest. The two college guys stood in stunned silence looking from the girls to the ground to us and then back. Joshie and I did the same to them. As the girls reached the foot of the old wooden staircase, I could hear the Nirvana cassette destroying Joshie's hearing even though he was seven steps away. The college girl turned back and shot us all one last hateful glare before they marched up the stairs.

Joshie's cassette ended, and at the click, the two college guys looked over at us. We heard two car doors slam and then what sounded like one hot rod of a car peel away from the gravel at the side of the road. At this, Joshie burst into chirps of laughter.

"Did she call us perverts?" he asked, still rather loudly.

I stood there with a hand over each stinging cheek. I smiled at him and nodded.

More of his chirpy laughter filled the still forest air. The sound of his high giggles made the two college guys crack up. Joshie and I enjoyed a good hearty laugh and then, while we were still trying to catch our breath, walked past the two guys to the stairs. The two college guys fell in behind us and followed us up the stairs with Joshie still giggling in short quiet bursts. I remembered her telling them they would have to ride with us, and I knew Kurt Cobain was screaming in Joshie's ears the whole time and he hadn't heard anything. I'd let him tell them; it'd be funnier that way.

When we reached the top of the staircase, I turned to them and said, "Sorry about that, guys. I thought our makeout session was going a completely different direction."

"I feel ya there!" the guy who got socked in the shoulder told me.

We all laughed again. They started looking around for our ride at the same time that Joshie began grabbing branches from the side of the road and tossing them aside. After a few seconds, he revealed our bikes in the hiding spot where we covered them with downed branches for camouflage and protection. Our little town was safe as far as little towns go, but we got a lot of outsiders and college kids who would steal anything that wasn't nailed down. So we hid our bikes when we went hiking. It was a goodly bike ride there, and a walk was out of the question if someone took them. Besides, our bikes were nice, and we had both spent two summers in a row earning money for them. We mowed and raked countless yards, had our hands stained black from paper routes, and had been dragged all over our little forest town by dogs of all shapes, sizes and temperaments. We grew up watching college kids throw away couches and brand-new VCRs at the end of every semester. Our parents taught us respect and appreciation for the things we worked for, and we treated our bikes accordingly. We covered them when we went to the forest, and we locked them to bike racks when we were in town. I used a lock and key I kept on a key ring with my house key, and Joshie used an old numerical combination lock. Sometimes he would take as long to lock up his bike as it would take me to go into the store and grab what I needed. Just as he'd snap his lock shut, I come bounding out and unlock mine with a quick turn of the key. He hated it, but he would chirp a chuckle and work on opening his combination lock as fast as he could.

As Joshie dug through the branches, the college guys began to understand something was up. I looked around, pretending to look for the car I had already heard hot rod off down the road. Joshie, sensing everyone standing around staring at him instead of just taking off in their own rides. He had a question in his eyes, and I did my best to answer with a nod toward the college guys. Joshie turned to them.

"Sorry again, guys, for how tonight worked out, but we don't need a ride or anything, so … take it easy."

They both stood there staring at him.

"Cindy took my car. She told us to hitch a ride with you two perverts."

Joshie blinked, and I saw the realization sparkle behind his glasses. He wrapped his hand around the still-covered handlebars of his bike and gave one final tug. The remaining branches fell to the ground, revealing his bike. The guys rolled their eyes at their luck, and Joshie told them through a grin that barely held back his laughter:

"We are perverts on *bikes*!"

The four of us shared one more laugh at our predicament. They introduced themselves as Troy and Mike, who happened to be the one who lost his car and got slugged. I offered them my bike and rode back into town on Joshie's handlebars. Joshie would never have let a stranger ride his bike, even though they were never once out of our sight the entire way to campus. When we got to their dorm, I hopped off Joshie's handlebars and walked gingerly to my bike. Mike had also drawn the short straw and had ridden on my handlebars. We pulled up and he shimmied off, walking like a short John Wayne badly in need of a beer. He had both hands on his ass cheeks as he waddled toward the door and the small crowd gathered around it.

"My ass hurts!" Mike said, more than a little loudly.

"At least you're used to it!" Troy answered right back.

The shouting and the raucous laughter that followed drew more curious dorm dwellers out into the cool evening. The crowd doubled in size as the college kids told the story of their night, and how it ended up as an adventure with two kids, with Mike embellishing details, flinging curse words about, and clutching his ass cheeks all the while. The rush of new faces panicked Joshie, and he got silently back on his bike and slunk away from the group. I watched someone give Troy and Mike beers, but instead of drinking his, Mike held it to his ass, and everyone laughed. I inched away quietly and caught up with Joshie at the end of the block. He shook his head and chirped, "You touched her booby."

Another time, we were hanging out in the forest at a big old rope swing that swung out over the shallow creek. I was selling pot to a few football jocks, and Joshie was sitting on a half-decayed log watching chipmunks gather food and doing his best to ignore me and my illegal pastime. It worked out well, because the football players ignored him and his anti-drug stance. I think they might have forgotten about him completely until his chirps of laughter echoed off the pines and cedars when the biggest of them (a big dumb bastard nicknamed Bull) lost first his grip and then his pants in mid-swing. The big boy shouted something unintelligible, but the solid, unforgiving ground met him with a sickening thud and interrupted his cry. Bull landed with his pants around his calves. When he thumped into the mountainside, both of his shoes flew off in opposite directions, and a loud wheezing sound came from his crumpled form. Bull's football player buddies and I roared boisterous ganja-fueled laughter down at the pantsless Bull, who only groaned weakly back at us as he rolled onto his side. Joshie hopped up off his log, chirping his signature laugh to himself, and went after the far flung shoes. Bull groaned again and sounded a lot like his namesake beast—a wounded and embarrassed one at that. The fall had forced the air from his lungs harder than any rival ever had on the football field. We who had been swinging with him felt no mercy, and our laughter rained down on him as he tried to pull up his downed pants without standing up. He tugged and rolled, but the pant legs twisted and rolled into tight knots when they slid off his kicking tree trunk legs. We laughed even harder at his failure. The big bastard just rolled back and forth, tugging at his twisted pants and groaning uphill at us.

He was halfway down the hill from us, but we could see his pain and embarrassment from our position by the trunk of the tree where the rope swing still swung past us erratically. Being teenage boys and all, we laughed even harder. Joshie walked back up the mountain with one of Bull's big-ass shoes in each hand. On his way, he shot me a glance that told me in no uncertain terms that I was a dick. He knelt next to Bull and handed him back his shoes without a word. Bull rolled toward Joshie, and Joshie helped him to his knees. Bull hitched up his pants and stared at us. His eyes were a swirling pool of emotions: embarrassment, confusion, and pain.

Bull's eyes filled with tears against his will, and I gradually redirected mine to the ground. Joshie stared at me until I could feel his gaze burning into my cheek and had to look. I could see the pity he had for this big jock who normally would have enjoyed pulling Joshie's tightie-whities over his head and stuffing him in a garbage can. As I looked into his eyes, I understood that he had felt that stinging embarrassment before and I had been the one to make people stop laughing at him. The realization hit me like a gut punch, and my head lowered again with shame, but not before I noticed that the other two football players were staring at the ground as well. I wanted to ask if it was Joshie's look or the fear of Bull kicking their asses that hung their heads, but I never did.

Joshie looked like a frail flightless bird as he helped Bull regain his bearings. The big clod stepped into one shoe and then the other without bothering to tie them, while Joshie kept his big ass from swaying. After both shoes were on, he looked uphill at us with eyes every bit ashamed as ours. The big boy mumbled a "thanks" that sounded like "tanks" to Joshie, and the little guy smiled from ear to ear in response.

From that day forward, no one on the football team ever picked on Joshie. The three who had been there did their best to become Joshie's friend, even going so far as to invite him to sit and dine on fine high school cafeteria cuisine at their lunchroom table that damn near radiated coolness. I never even got invited to sit there; I was only their friend when they wanted something to get high on. Just the same, Joshie was an odd fit, and he only sat there twice. Still, nods and waves were directed at him, at school and around town, for the first time in his life. I don't think he ever had a full conversation with any of them aside from Bull, but they all treated him in a friendlier fashion. Bull only called Joshie "Joshua," as per the smaller boy's request.

I think it was Bull who told us about the hole, that fat son of a bitch. Someone had found a hole behind a thick thorn bush against a sheer rock cliff at the end of our forest. According to high school chatter, it was so deep that those who saw it called it the "Pit to Hell." We had to check it out.

Joshie had a very logical mind, and the idea of Heaven and Hell simply boggled him. Since he had never spoken with someone dead, he had no idea what happened after death, and he refused to make any assumptions not based on solid facts. He felt the Christian Heaven he heard about as a child seemed ancient and silly, with all the people hanging out in white robes and chatting their time away in the clouds. He thought Hell was an ancient place dreamed up to scare bad children into being good. He explained to me once the scientific reasons for the ten biblical plagues. I was stoned, but I remember something about blood-red mold and poisoned meat. In that same rant, he disproved lakes of fire, Noah's flood, and hookers with feelings.

Hearing the name kids at school had given the hole, I assumed it was a big deep-ass hole. Joshie heard all the same words, but they meant something else to him. If kids were calling it a "Pit to Hell" then, damn it, Joshie expected to see more flames than a Motley Crue video and devils dancing while torturing the damned souls sure to reside within. He called things exactly how he saw them, and it confused him that other people didn't. He viewed a tiny empty white lie with the same disapproval with which he viewed the act of cheating on one's spouse. Joshie was harshly honest at all times, and he expected the same of everyone in his small universe. He would never had called anything "Pit to Hell" unless he saw the Devil's smiling face and felt the heat of hellfire on his skin. I think on this dark day he was out to either feel those flames or disprove the rumors stirred by a high school full of gossip and hormones. We heard about the hole on a Thursday, so by ten o'clock on the next Saturday, Joshie had worked himself into a chirpy little frenzy.

I was still dreaming about cheerleaders and girl fights when someone knocked on my door. I faced the door, then clamped my eyes shut, hoping to relive some of the fantasy from which I'd been disturbed. Behind my eyelids, I saw girls fighting with knives instead of pillows, blood and gore spackling the walls of my dream where, moments before, billowy white feathers had floated. The next knock flushed the strange, violent visions away and pried my eyes back open. I rolled over and gave my alarm clock a dirty look. It read three minutes after ten, and I knew it was my loving mother knocking with an excited Joshie on the phone. I knew he had been up for at least three hours and had just been waiting until ten to call me. I knew that he would wait for as many knocks as it took my mom to wake me up. I also knew my mom loved Joshie like she loved me—maybe more so, because he never dug for cash in her purse—and she would knock as long as it took for me to open it. The two of them could sit outside my door all day long, knocking and waiting, my mother judging my progress by the noises behind the door, and reporting accordingly.

I sighed loudly and grumbled, "Come on in."

My beautiful mother poked her head inside my room. Her big happy smile was so honest and warm it could melt igloos. The rays of morning sun that pierced the darkness of my room gleamed off the lenses of her black-rimmed teacher glasses. She was temporarily blinded, but she smiled even bigger and stepped into my room and out of the path of sunshine. She gave me a wink, as was the custom in my family. I instinctively winked back. Her smile never waned, and she covered the phone with one hand.

"It's Joshua," she told me quietly.

"I know," I told her as I buried my head under my pillows.

"He seems really excited about something," she whispered.

"I said I know," I answered, a little too rudely for her taste. She scolded me with her eyes and handed me the phone.

"Be nice, Gavin," she told me in a mock-threatening whisper, "or I'll take the keys to your Aries, and you'll have to drive the bug!"

My eyes stretched wide, and I gasped playfully, knowing full well that Joshie had told her she would have to use this threat. We shared a smile, and she tossed me the phone. My mom winked again, and I mouthed a "thanks" as she glided out of my room. I rolled my eyes and spoke with an exaggeratedly sleepy voice.

"Hello … hello?" I did my best to sound as if the phone had been draped across my still-slumbering face. Joshie saw right through my bullshit, and he had no time for it.

"Gavin, I need you to take me to the forest," he squawked excitedly into the phone.

"I'm sleeping here, Joshie. Ride your bike," I growled at him from under my blankets.

"That is BS, and you know that I know it. So get your lazy butt outta bed and pick me up." His thin, shaky voice was trying its hardest to be firm.

"I can't," I scoffed, feeling like a genius. "My mom took the keys to the Aries, and I ain't driving the fucking bug, man."

There was a short pause on the other end of the phone line. I heard a hand cover the mouthpiece and peals of muffled chirpy laughter. After a second, the hand rumbled across the speaker and Joshie spoke in a serious tone.

"Gavin, this is important. Give your mom the phone. I'll take care of this."

I scoffed at him as I stood and stretched toward the ceiling, letting my muscles strain the stiffness of sound sleep away. I laughed under my breath and told him, "Shut up, Joshie. I'm up and moving, thanks to you. Give me a minute to get up and out the door, then I'll pick you up."

"Okay," he said hearing every word I spoke, "I'm walking over right now."

We hung up, and I staggered from my bedroom to the bathroom and back again, getting ready. By the time I finished, Joshie was sitting on the bottom step of our front staircase eating a piece of wheat toast my mom had made him. He smiled up at me, and I playfully tussled his hair as I sprang past. He stood slowly and followed me through our dining room into the kitchen. Four pieces of wheat toast and half a grapefruit sitting in a ceramic bowl were waiting for me.

"I talked your mom into giving you back your keys," he told me slyly, "and it was my pleasure."

"You're a dick," I told him as I gobbled a piece of toast in one bite.

"She had to go to work … but she left you ten dollars … for gas. She told me … she was going to give you … a Volkswagen … for graduation. Then she would only have … to leave you five dollars … at a whack," he explained between bites of buttery toast.

Long before there was any serious talk of a gas shortage, hippies like my parents knew it was coming. I drove an old Dodge Aries from '88 or '89. It was a box on wheels, and it sounded like shit, but it drove like a dream. It drank gas like it was taking it through a straw, and it made the local hippies crazy to see it smoking and rumbling through the tree-shaded streets. Subarus and Volkswagens were the local favorites, being the economic and family-friendly rides that they are. My Aries stuck out like a sore thumb, but I didn't give a shit, and I took it up into the hills and down twisting dirt mountain roads. I treated the Aries like a truck and, in turn, it treated me like a king.

The only flaw I saw in the Aries was the cassette player that had chewed up so many cassettes that we called it the Destroyer. Joshie would never put the original cassette of any album into the Destroyer's mouth. Instead he recorded them to cheap-ass blank cassettes, on which he wrote the name of the album followed by "Destroyer Mix." He saw them as sacrificial cassettes to keep the Destroyer happy. He only recorded full albums, never any mix tapes. A mix tape, he explained to me once, went against the intended sound. He bought the cassettes from the photo counter at the grocery store in town, four for five dollars. Joshie would buy ten at a time and spend entire nights recording Destroyer Mixes for the week. I think we went through at least twenty copies of Nirvana's Nevermind album, as it was Joshie's all-time favorite.

Kurt Cobain had put his own brains on the wall behind him about six months prior, and Joshie had been crushed. The first two months were the worst, but Joshie was finally beginning to pull himself back from the darkness of depression. He had loved and respected Cobain for the way he translated the pain he felt into song. Joshie had told me on more than one occasion that Kurt Cobain was the last honest man in music—aside, of course, from Tom Petty. I wasn't about to wear flannel and long johns under my shorts, but I could never argue with Joshie when it came to his idol. I listened to it so much that I liked it whether I wanted to or not. I believed Joshie when he said Cobain changed the face of music and gave Seattle more than the rain to talk about. I always preferred my music heavier. It was just one more thing to separate me from the rest of my little hippy hometown. My favorites were thrash masters Testament, Obituary, Exodus, Sepultura, and, of course, Slayer. Joshie loved a lot of different music, and he called mine "headache tunes." Nirvana was Joshie's favorite, but he loved Tom Petty and Elvis Costello almost as much. He also liked the hippy songs by Phish and the Grateful Dead that we grew up listening to. Jerry Garcia, the iconic stoner frontman for the Dead, died just a few months after that terrible day in the forest.

That morning, after I finished my toast and grapefruit, we hopped into the Aries and headed to the forest. Joshie got comfortable and pulled a tape from his pocket. It read "Pork Soda/Destroyer Mix 4," which meant that three others had gone before, and the Destroyer had done its thing to all of them. Pork Soda was the newest Primus album, and it was wild and weird as hell. It sounded like nothing we'd ever heard before, except maybe more Primus. I smiled at my little buddy, pleased with his musical choice.

Joshie had a recent and strange interest in Neil Diamond. At first I was amused by it, but after hearing The Greatest 1966-1992, the second tape of a two-cassette set, on an all-night drive to Seattle, I was less enthused. I remember silently praying that the Destroyer would chomp that shit, but it never did. Neil Diamond played until it flipped over and played the other side. Then it flipped again and played all the way through. It was the only tape we had that the Destroyer wouldn't eat. Joshie believed this to be a sign, and he started listening to it more and more, trying to find a life-changing message just for him. He did the same with Nirvana, and he found loads of lyrics that he assumed were sent straight from Kurt Cobain to Joshie himself. I told him that if you listened to anything long enough, your brain would form messages from it.

The road to the forest slunk over and around the rolling hills of our region until it started climbing up the mountainside. At that point, the road twisted and tucked around big wide blind corners lined with evergreen trees. As we rounded one of the final corners, the strange sounds coming from the speakers slurred, then sped up, then squealed. Pork Soda/Destroyer Mix 4 had been consumed by my hateful cassette player. I reached up and poked the eject button without taking my eyes from the corner I was navigating. I pulled the cassette out, but the tape remained stuck in the player so that a crumpled length hung limply between the mouth of the Destroyer and my hand. The next corner was even more treacherous, and as I leaned into the turn, I handed Joshie the cassette with the tape still dangling. He squinted behind his glasses and stuck two small fingertips into the Destroyer's open mouth. He slowly and carefully pulled the folded tape from the Destroyer without breaking it all the way.

"That's good," I told him, "it didn't break, so you can play it again."

"No I can't. See how it's folded all weird?" Joshie let the cassette fall to his lap and showed me the worst part of the mangled brown tape between his fingers.

I glanced quickly at the tape and then back ahead of us to the next turn. Once I was sure I was safe, I nodded for him to continue.

"This chewed part will get caught in any cassette player now. The Destroyer just took a little nibble, but it marked this for death if it ever gets played again." Joshie spoke softly, as if he were carefully studying the dreadful monster that was my car's cassette player.

He stared at it with contempt and reached into the pockets of his green fatigue jacket, letting the crumpled tape fall back on the cassette in his lap. Out of the corner of my eye, I watched him dig in his pocket. He found what he was hunting and, with a triumphant chirp, showed me the cassette he was putting in next. I winced when I read "Neil Diamond" and scoffed as I turned back to the road. As the first few bars of Brother Love's Traveling Salvation Show came through the speakers, Joshie started clapping along and singing in the deepest voice he could manage, which wasn't very deep at all. I couldn't help but laugh out loud and smile at my odd little friend. We pulled around the last corner and eased to the side of the dirt road. By the time the chorus ended for the second time, I was turning off the car and stuffing the keys in my pocket. I stepped out of the Aries and slammed the door, as I normally did. Joshie waited inside until I was out. Then he locked my door from the inside before he slid out his side. He locked his door from the inside and closed it without slamming it, as he normally did.

We walked across the dirt road to our favorite entrance into our forest: a little winding path about a quarter mile up the road from the staircase. Joshie dug in the bushes next to the path and pulled up the walking stick that left he left there every time we left. I took my normal long downhill strides around the tree trunks and half-buried boulders in my way. Joshie's steps were half the length of mine, but he moved every bit as fast in his excitement. We had thundered down the winding path so many times that we knew every rock that could trip us up and every branch that could slap our faces. We avoided them all and moved quickly and fearlessly into the forest. We came to thunderous stops where the ground leveled back out, and we each took a few deep breaths of moist forest air.

It was normally about five to ten degrees cooler down in the forest than outside of it, but I remember it being even colder that long-ago Saturday. It seemed thick with shadows and darkness too. I looked around at the forest I had known and loved since my babyhood, and it had a new sinister feeling. Shadows from the massive cedars overpowered the rays from the springtime sun as it slunk in between the wide moss-covered trunks. It had an oppressively dismal feeling to it, overly shaded when it should be warm with the noon sun. I watched the shadows dance, and a chill crept up my spine, raising the neck hair in its wake. I looked at Joshie, and he was looking around at the same shadows with a hesitant look on his slender face.

"Well, Captain, where did he say it was?" I asked to break the silence that was feeling thicker and thicker every minute.

He scanned the forest in front of us one more time then darted a gaze back up the path we'd just taken, as though he were having second thoughts about the entire thing. He still looked nervous, but he swallowed it as he cleared his throat.

"He said it was behind the thorn bushes against the back of the mountainside."

"The thorn bushes across the creek?" I asked.

"Yes, Gavin, the only thorn bushes against the mountain," he answered in a snide tone I knew would restore some of the confidence the prematurely darkened forest had sapped.

I held up both hands and motioned for him to calm down. He chuckled at me, and we started out next to the creek instead of taking the well-worn path. We figured it to be a more direct route, since the hole was behind the thorn bushes that were directly across from the creek. I knew the thorn bushes he was talking about, but I could have sworn they grew right up to the face of the mountain. The mountain was climbable from every angle except that one. It was a sheer rock wall covered with brown and yellowed moss. Sharp thorns grew wide and thick, right up to the cold stone. There was no room for a big mysterious hole behind the thorn bushes. I was sure of it. I mentally cursed the fuckers for telling Joshie about the hole, because even though I knew there was no room for a hole behind the thorns, I would have to crawl all the way through the sharp bastards to touch moss-covered stone before he would give up.

I made a mental note to sock Bull in his oversized gut next time I saw him. Maybe I would punch him one time for every scratch I got from the thorns. I could see myself unloading on him with shots to his fat stomach and his square-jawed face. I saw blood running down my arms from my fists, tangling my blond arm hair as it dripped. I could see him cover his wide surprised eyes with his hands, trying in vain to stave off my attack. While he shielded his face and head, I hit him in random spots like his ears and neck as hard as I could. Specks of blood covered my face as I hit him more and more. He would roll away from my fist, and I'd kick him in the ribs to force him back over. In my mind, I was screaming, "How funny is it now?" My screams punctuated my kicks, which echoed with the crack of bones being smashed. The vision was so real I was caught up in the sheer violence of it all, and I paid no attention to the creek by which we were walking.

"Gavin," Joshie shouted. "You're walking in the creek, dummy."

He looked from my soaked shoes to my face.

"What the heck is so funny? That's a big dumb grin if I've ever seen one." His tone was uncomfortable and nervous.

I stared at my shoes, trying to remember walking in the creek, but my mind was blank. I couldn't tell him what was so funny, because I couldn't remember. I just remembered the feeling of dominance. Even in my memory, I felt savage glee building within me with every sickening thud of fist on flesh and every wet crack of bone as a face gave way to my fury. I couldn't remember whom I had the sudden urge to beat or why. Something told me that whoever it was, he deserved it.

I shook my head and shrugged, unsure what else I could tell him. My confusion had been so real and so strong that I couldn't even come up with a lie as to what had made me smile. Joshie knew how quick-witted I was, and he, being the smart son of a teacher that he was, caught my brain fart. He looked around nervously and shook his head to himself. Then he nodded upstream as if to ask if I was going to stand in the creek all day long or go look for this big over-hyped hole. I could tell that, between the unnaturally dim coolness in what should have been a nice sunny forest and my mental stutter step, Joshie was fighting a panic. To ease the tension, I flipped him off and stepped out of the creek. I was wearing my black Chuck Taylors, and they didn't protect my feet in the least. I took a long two-step head start up the creek bed, and Joshie followed with a chuckle. He used his walking stick to pull himself up the creek bed and right next to me in a few quick steps of his own. We both laughed out loud when every step I took was accompanied by the sloshing of my soaked shoes, which sounded like something incredibly dirty to our seventeen-year-old minds. We were still laughing when we reached the thorn bushes.

We didn't come around to this far side of the mountain very often. The edge of the forest dead-ended at the mountain wall. The path cut hard up the mountainside away from the creek. As it wound upward, it turned into the rockiest, steepest part of the mountain. If you could brave the initial roughness of the trail, you could follow it up and over where it forked. One side of the fork offered a breathtaking view from the top of the sheer rock wall and down to the thorns below. The other led toward the middle of the forest and joined with a number of the more popular trails deep in the forest.

We reached the bushes, and they looked, as they always did, as though they grew solid to the rock wall. Joshie squatted down and scooted back and forth, trying to get a glimpse of anything beyond the prickly branches. I knelt next to him and scanned the bushes as he was doing.

"It looks like there *is* a clearing back in there," he said without looking at me.

"I don't see sh-" Then I saw something sparkle in strange dark colors, and it stole my voice.

The bush looked thick, too thick to climb through for sure, but I had seen something shine in the faded sunlight. I had seen a flash from a dark-spectrum rainbow. Shiny black, blues, purples, and greens flared up from inside the bush and then dropped back down into nothingness in the blink of an eye. My eyes widened, and I searched the bushes for a sign of the lights again. I even slid down the creek bed to get a closer look. Joshie giggled and followed me down. He leaned his walking stick against a little pine and hunched over with his hands on his knees. We spent the next few minutes staring down the imposing thorn bush.

"I see it!" he finally shouted.

I thought at first that he had seen the same light I had, so I asked him, "What is it?"

"*It* is a way to get through without getting cut to shreds." He smiled at me and danced across the creek.

The thorn bush was three or four feet beyond the creek, so he had room to squat down and stab his walking stick into the thicket. He pulled the stick back toward him, breaking a few branches and moving far more, to reveal a small clearing just beyond. Joshie wedged the bottom of his walking stick between two rocks on the ground, and it held the thorny branches back like the flap on a circus tent. I smiled at Joshie's genius, and he gave me a big cheesy thumbs-up.

"Son of a bitch," I said more to myself than to him.

I was staring into the space he had opened up when the colors flashed again. This time, the flash was slower, and it shone in my eyes as it rose from the ground. A battle-scarred landscape flashed in my mind, and I saw a field of bodies. Filthy blood-streaked corpses stacked and strewn for miles replaced the thorn bush and mountain that were there a moment ago. Piles of the dead burned with pale greasy flames and flooded the sky above with rolling black smoke. Still-smoking corpses tied to tall poles twinkled like cinders in a wind

I couldn't feel on my face. The dark light shone through it all, and then the battlefield disappeared. I was blinded by the terrible colors for a second, but as it faded, I sprang forward to chase the light.

I dove into the bush right next to where Joshie was squatting. The first few feet were easy, thanks to Joshie's stick holding the thorns back, but beyond that, the path was more of an illusion as angry thorns tore at my face and back. My momentum knocked most of the branches out of my way as I plodded through them. Joshie was only a few steps behind me, and I heard him wail as the thorns sought his blood as well. My adrenaline was flowing and my heartbeat pulsing in my ears as I half crawled, half rolled out of the bushes and into a small clearing that, minutes before, I had believed to be complete bullshit. Since I was a little kid, I'd sworn the bushes grew right up to the face of the cliff. The bushes grew thick, and the big razor-sharp thorns kept even the most die-hard rock climbers at bay.

Yet I stood there with the thorns to my back and a big deep hole between me and the rock wall. The hole was three feet by three feet wide, a gaping maw in the solid earth in which roots from the nearby thorn bushes stuck out, giving the impression of the sarlacc's teeth in Star Wars. A shiver worked its way up my back, and I looked from the hole to the wall behind it. Dozens of bloody handprints covered the powder white and dismal gray of the wall. I was staring at them when Joshie thundered out of the bushes behind me and bumped me forward. I felt like I was falling off a cliff, and I took an exaggerated breath as I caught my balance. His bump also forced me to take an extra step, right to the lip of the strange hole. Joshie grabbed my shoulder to help balance me, and we exchanged shocked expressions.

"Holy shit!" I told him.

"Indeed," he answered, eyeing the hole.

I looked up the wall and saw no bloody handprints. I'd seen the view from the top looking down, but the view from below was every bit as breathtaking. The rays of sunlight that filtered through the trees danced across the pale surface, illuminating every small crevice and imperfection. I blinked and the handprints were back. Dozens of bloody handprints of all sizes crawled in every direction in the pale sunlight. They were different shades of reds and browns, some fresh and dripping, some dry and flaking, like autumn in Hell. Some were clear and deliberate; others were messy splotches and upward swipes like someone had been pulled up the wall. I took a few short, panicky breaths and blinked my dry eyes again. When I opened them, the wall was clean.

"What's that by your foot, Gavin?" Joshie asked, looking at my foot mere inches from the hole.

I looked down, saw how close my foot was to the hole and pulled it back like I was doing the hokey pokey. I saw what Joshie was talking about. A small, oddly shaped stone shimmered back up at me in the dimness of the forest. I knelt to pick up the strange stone, and Joshie took a quick step forward.

"Don't!" he shouted at me with an awkward urgency in his voice.

I stopped in mid-squat and turned to him. Joshie had gone as white as a sheet, and he shivered like he was naked in a snowstorm. I finished my squat but maintained eye contact with my little buddy. He shook his head, looked from the stone to the hole to me, and shook his head again. While I squatted there, waiting for him to form words to go with his panic, I thought I heard a noise from deep inside the hole. I leaned closer to the hole, still looking at Joshie but straining to hear the noise that rose from the darkness. Joshie spoke, and I turned away from the hole, figuring I was hearing things.

"Okay, Gavin, it really is here, and we really saw it. I don't like it at all, and I'm ready to leave." His voice was as shaky as his hands.

Joshie was getting spooked, and it was rubbing off on me. I had the fierce, sudden urge to run. I wanted to bolt back through the thorns, down the creek bed, and back to the shitty Neil Diamond waiting for me in the car. Instead, I reached down and picked up the stone before Joshie could stop me. It felt warm in the palm of my hand and seemed to pulse in response to my grasp.

"Gavin! What the heck? Can't you feel that something is wrong? I feel it in my gut."

He held his hand to his stomach to punctuate his words. He was so pale I thought he was going to pass out. He pointed a trembling finger at the hole.

"There is something wrong about *that*. It wasn't here before." He said the word "that" like people say "Nazi." He turned his shaking finger from the hole to the stone I held tight in my hand. The stone pulsed against my palm, and I looked at Joshie. His face was a dead face, covered with torn and tattered gray skin pulled too tight over dry bones. Behind his glasses, his eyeballs were sunken in and rolling wildly in their sockets. He opened his mouth to talk, and I could see daylight through gaping slits in his ancient-looking skin.

"And there is something very wrong about *that*!" spat the pointing corpse with Joshie's high-pitched voice.

I squeezed the stone tight, and warmth pulsed into my hand. I blinked and Joshie stood before me, pale but not decaying.

"Okay, okay," I told him absently.

I opened my hand and looked at the stone. It was circular with three thin fins around it. It was relatively flat for the most part, but it was swollen and bulbous in the center. I held it between my finger and thumb to get a better look at it, and the dark rainbow shone in my eyes again. Everything around me was dead. The trees surrounding me looked rotted and burned, and the ground was littered with craters and pools of a boiling thick red fluid. The handprints were back, and there were twice as many. I could see layers of them in a few places. I didn't see Joshie standing in front of me, but his hand came out of nowhere, reaching for the stone. *My* stone. I pulled it close to my chest and took a step back, crashing into the thorns as I did. I winced as they tore my shirt and drew fresh blood on my back and shoulders. I took half a step forward, but my t-shirt was held firm by blood-tipped thorns. I shook myself loose and snapped at Joshie.

"What the hell, Joshie? I saw this shining when we were still standing by the creek. It's mine."

He looked at me with a whine rising in his throat. He started to say something, but then shook his head to himself. I stared at him with a dare in my eyes, and he stared at the ground.

"I don't think you should. I think you should throw it back in there," he said in a quick whiny voice, jerking his thumb at the hole. "And then we should get the heck outta here and go to church or something."

I giggled at the thought of going to church, and Joshie smiled at the sound. With his smile, the tiniest hint of color crept back to his pale cheeks. I motioned for him to lead, and he laughed his singsong laugh and nodded for me to go first. I always went first; it made Joshie feel safer. I clutched the stone tight and dove into the bushes. I swung my fist with the stone in it wildly in front of me, breaking branches instead of trying to move them. Behind me, Joshie ducked the thorny branches as they fell behind me. We had managed to stomp out a faint path going in, so leaving was quite a bit easier. I could feel blood trickling down my back and my shirt sticking to me. On my last step, a branch slapped down and tore a bloody gash on my left forearm. I rubbed the wound with the back of the fist that still clutched the stone. It felt like it was humming a slow, deliberate tune as my blood covered the back side of my hand. Joshie saw me snag, and he grabbed the branch low and snapped it. He made a grimace like he was fighting a snake, and then he smiled triumphantly when he broke it free. He threw it to the ground and stomped on it. The more he smiled, the more color returned to his cheeks.

"Thanks," I told him, still rubbing my wound.

He looked at me rasping the scratch and shook his head low and to himself. He looked across the creek bed and down the forest path.

"Let's just get out of here," he said without looking at me.

I crossed the creek and ran up the other side of the creek bed in a few long strides. Once at the top, I waited for Joshie. He hopped across the creek like a bird and stood ready to run up the creek bed when he realized he had left his walking stick stabbed into the bushes behind him. We both looked back at the stick at the same time. It still looked like the open flap to an old circus tent, but the path beyond was much darker than before.

"Dang it," he whined.

"C'mon, we'll find you a new one."

I offered him my wounded left arm. He grabbed my wrist, and I tugged him up the creek bed with ease. Without any more words, we headed back down the path toward the waiting Aries, Joshie walking double time to keep up with my long strides. My heart raced. I could feel my pulse against the pulse of the stone in my palm. I gave the stone a squeeze, and everything around took on a reddish tint. I blinked, and the red tint faded, but strange things hung from the trees above me. I looked up to see what they were, and blood dripped onto my face. It landed on my forehead and rolled down the right side of my face. I reached up and wiped it, then looked at my hand. Brilliant crimson blood shone on my fingertips and cast a dark rainbow, like the stone's, but weaker. I blinked and still felt the blood, warm and sticky, on my face. Two human feet dangled high above me from the old, wide pine next to me. As I stared, blood dripped from the toes and rained down on me. Joshie's voice broke the vision.

"What the heck are you smiling at?"

I felt tiny thorny fingers dig into the gash on my arm, and my head cleared instantly. I howled in pain and stepped away from a wild-eyed Joshie. He eyed me suspiciously as I felt my face. It was soaked with sweat, but there was no blood.

"Gavin, what the heck is going on?"

Again, I had no words for him. I shook my head dumbly and shrugged. I could vaguely remember blood—bright and warm and sticky. I couldn't tell Joshie what was happening. He would have shit his pants and run the ten miles home. Rather than think of something smart to say or some word of comfort to set him at ease, I told him to "fuck off and hurry up." He did his best to stay one step behind me as irritation lengthened my stride.

"It's *that* rock, isn't it?"

The words seemed to rip my head in half. A dull but jagged pain tore across my forehead, forcing my eyes closed. I remember taking deep breaths. I remember how the taste of soil in those breaths turned to the taste of ash. I opened my eyes, and I was standing in a wasteland. Most of the marvelous trees around me were broken and reduced to still-glowing embers on the forest floor. Others were burnt stumps. Any left standing had been stripped of their branches and had naked human forms tied to them with barbed wire. A thick, dark chemical sludge flowed where the creek should have been rolling lazily along. Craters dotted the blackened forest floor, some burping foul plumes of smoke and others hissing and boiling thick red ooze that spat and dripped over the edge. The sky above me was a bright scarlet with menacing black clouds blooming from a dozen fires on the horizon. The smoke burned my throat and my eyes. Tears formed, and I closed my eyes to let them soak in my sorrow. I could sense Joshie behind me, going silently insane waiting for an answer. I opened my eyes and saw my beautiful forest as it had always been: lush and full of life.

"It's a fucking rock, Joshie. Nothing more." I didn't look at him, because I knew I wouldn't be able to explain my tears.

"Dang it, Gavin." Joshie huffed, and I heard his steps stop in the middle of the path. "Gavin …"

I stopped and sighed. Before I turned to face my little friend, I rubbed the back of my hand into my forehead like I was massaging out a headache. My head throbbed, and I felt the stone throb back. Joshie shook his head at me while exhaling argumentatively out his nose. I could see his paranoia turning to panic.

"No," Joshie said with a firmness I had never heard before that day, "it's not … and you know it."

"What?" I asked in a rude and incredulous tone.

"If it's nothing special, let me hold it," he reasoned softly.

"Ha! I fucking knew it!" Birds took to the sky from various hiding spots around us at the booming sound of my voice.

"No!" he shouted back, confused more than angry. He looked like I'd slapped him, hurt rimming his eyes with tears.

"I'm not trying to argue, Gavin, but I feel something bad about that. And I think you feel it too." He paused and waited to gauge my response. I said nothing, and he continued. "It makes me feel sick, Gavin, like a seriously bad feeling. I don't want it. I don't want either of us to have it. I want it to be far away from us."

I acknowledged his feelings with a raised eyebrow, but no words left my mouth. As his whine grew higher in pitch with each word, my head started to feel like it was being sawed in half. My skull vibrated, and my face throbbed angrily. I reached up and rubbed the back of my left hand against my forehead, swaying on my feet from the sudden and intense pain. Joshie leaned forward just in the nick of time, using his entire body weight to stop me from falling. My momentum made us stumble a few steps, but he guided us to the trunk of an old cedar. I leaned forward and rested my head on his shoulder while he hyperventilated. The stone in my hand pulsed along with my headache. I could feel heat seeping from it, and sweat dripped from my clenched fist.

Joshie sighed and reached his bony fingers toward my hand. "Just give me the cursed thing."

In one smooth movement, I shoved him into the tree and used the force of the push to shove myself away and down the path. "Lay off it, Joshie," I yelled over my shoulder as I thundered away. I heard him take a deep breath and follow me. I jumped over fallen logs and zig-zagged across the path, refusing to wait for him. Joshie ran at full speed, sticking to the path. He didn't always pick up his feet all the way, and he kicked branches and pinecones as he hurried along. I looked back at him over my shoulder, and he used my momentary distraction to circle around me. He came to a sudden stop, and a cloud of dirt puffed up around his feet. He threw his hands up and waved his palms at me while he struggled to catch his breath. He shook and wheezed with each sharp burst of breath, but he maintained his stance smack in the middle of the path, blocking my passage. Joshie was not used to any sort of physical exercise beyond hiking, and his poor lungs looked, by the grimace on his face, to be burning within his frail form. His rolled wildly in their sockets as he tried to slow his breath. I could see hysteria rising in my little buddy.

When he finally spoke, his voice shook, and tears teetered on the red rims of his eyes. "Just leave it here. Can't you feel it? It's making me queasy."

I was feeling something all right, but it was fear. My head still throbbed, and the stone in my fist matched it pulse for pulse. I knew deep down that something was wrong. After all, I didn't normally see bloody handprints on walls or bodies dripping blood down on me, but the visions left me feeling dangerous and powerful. I couldn't tell Joshie anything I'd seen. He would lose his mind.

When I spoke again, it was much more sharply than I meant to. "Look, I'll give ya it's kind of a strange day. That hole was creepy, but we've never been back into that wicked thorn patch before, so we don't know that it hasn't always been there. I like this little stone. It's weird, but satanic or something? Come on, man."

Joshie and I had both been raised with the concept of a higher power, but we never called it God. When bad things happened, it was never because of Lucifer or any other names that rascal devil had. We were raised with science and reason in place of religion. I, being the cynical bastard I was, always made fun of church people in their stiff clothes with their stiff walks and their stiff smiles. I made fun of their lofty beliefs and reversible morals. Joshie was far more tactful than I, and he would seldom curse and would never take the Lord's name in vain—if only out of respect for those who did believe in that Lord. I knew better than to think Joshie thought the rock satanic. It wasn't logical, and Joshie only looked at things logically. The more illogical I acted, the more the situation felt like it was spinning out of his control. As his panic rose, the fear and dread he felt plastered themselves to his pale, sweaty face. Before he had time to chastise me for my foolish belief that he thought the rock satanic, I snapped out something from months ago that was entirely off the subject.

"This is almost as stupid as the time you told me hookers don't have feelings."

I could see his eyes roll and his mind snap against the strangeness of the day: the darkness of the forest, the hole beyond the thorns, and the rock his increasingly odd best friend refused to give up. He grimaced and threw anger at the situation instead of logic. Joshie squeezed his fists tight at his side and squealed so loud the birds fled into the safety of the sky once more. My head throbbed painfully as I watched them scatter.

"I never said hookers don't have feelings! I was trying to have a conversation with you about how the scars of our youth can plague us well into adulthood, and you come away with … hookers have no feelings!"

He yelled so loud and hard that it took his breath away again. From the pained look on his face, I knew his lungs had caught flame again. My statement wasn't only rude and out of place, it was the straw that broke the camel's back. I knew I was pushing him, and I knew he would react this way, but I did it anyway. I could see his fear rising to a crescendo. I could almost taste it on the air, and the stone in my palm emitted warmer heat as I looked past his glasses to the frightened eyes behind them. He was thinking about running and not stopping. I was pushing our friendship harder than I ever had before, and I knew he wouldn't talk to me again if he did leave. I don't think he could see the visions of death and destruction, but I think he could somehow feel them.

When the tear slipped down his cheek, my heart sank. I caused that tear to fall, and my headache faded as a terrible and honest guilt rose within me. Joshie was an oddball and a dork. But he was also my best friend, so he was *my* oddball dork. Before that day, I had never made Joshie cry, not even by accident. Joshie had never tried to make anyone cry, and there I was trying not just to make him cry, but to completely break down his fragile little world. My headache vanished as if chased away by my shame. I didn't want him to leave. and the thought of being alone in our happy place, now somehow tainted and strange, gave me a feeling of dread to hum along with my guilt. I wanted to leave with Joshie, and if that meant leaving the stone, then that's what I would do.

"Fine. I'll put it back if you'll promise you'll calm down and not die out here. Deal?"

He didn't answer with words, but he smiled weakly. His fear didn't leave him entirely, but it sank deep enough not to burn in his eyes anymore. He dried his eyes with the long sleeves of his army fatigue jacket, and the stiff cuffs left red but bloodless scrapes above his eyebrows. Behind his glasses, his eyes still gleamed with tears but when he looked at me, I think he saw my apology. His smile solidified a little.

"And use your damn inhaler. Your mom gives it to your frail ass for some reason."

He chirped at the unexpected verbal jab, but he answered back so fast one might have thought he'd practiced it. "Your mom gives it to my frail ass."

I laughed out loud, and the strange stillness of the forest seemed to lift. Sunlight stabbed through between the trunks of the massive evergreens, and birds chirped in response. I reached over and wrapped my arm around Joshie, and we went back toward the thorns. We kicked rocks and pinecones but didn't say anything. The dust we kicked up as we walked danced through the rays of sunlight and left dirty clouds behind us. The walk back seemed to take forever, and the closer we drew to the bush, the heavier my legs became. Joshie's eyes still wore a troubled look. He looked at me long enough to make me a little uncomfortable before he smiled at me and dropped down the creek bed and across the creek.

His stick was still there, pinning the branches back. He stood next to the opening, and the faint pounding of drums rose from within the darkness of the thorn bushes. My legs felt like concrete, and I swayed in place out of some primal, subconscious fear. Something inside me told me to throw the stone, run like hell back to the Aries, and listen to Neil Diamond and fucking like it. I opened my mouth to tell Joshie that I didn't even want to go back in the thorns, that I'd just throw it from where we stood. But before I found my voice, I saw the thorns on the branches grow. At first they grew slowly, and they twisted as they did. I could hear the ancient branches popping as they took on the extra weight. Sharp barbs defined themselves on the tips of the thorns. I felt the blood draining from my face as I looked above the bushes to the rock wall, now covered in hundreds of bloody handprints. My words came out a gargled choke, and Joshie rolled his eyes at me before ducking back into the thorn bush. No sooner had he vanished from my sight than the thorns themselves started bleeding as they twisted and grew. Thick, dark blood pooled at the base of every thorn and trickled down the branches like spring creeks.

The stone twitched in my palm and began vibrating more intensely. My legs came unglued from the ground, and I dove after Joshie, carefully avoiding the sharp, ravenous thorns. The stone in my hand felt alive—not just vibrating, but slithering and jumping against my palm. The heat it radiated sent a deep tingle from my hand up my shoulder, across my back, down my legs, and up my neck. I dragged my feet gradually, and time seemed to slow down. I couldn't see Joshie, but I could hear him just ahead of me. I reached up and moved branches out of my way, careful to avoid the growing, bleeding thorns, only to reveal more branches and even bigger thorns. It seemed like an hour before I stumbled out of the bushes and into the small clearing next to Joshie.

I stood there for a second and stared at him. His eyes were sunk back in their sockets, and his skin looked gray and dead. He tilted his head at me, causing his glasses to slide to the tip of his decayed nose and send a small storm of gray flesh flakes off his face. He looked dead and half rotted, but when he spoke, it was with the same firm tone he had used earlier.

"There it is. Now throw it back in there, and let's get the hell outta here."

He shivered visibly as he finished, and his face returned to normal. His eyes darted from me to the hole and back again while he jumped in his skin like a meth head at a slot machine at three in the morning. I could see the fear in Joshie, and I could smell it. A heady musk of sweat, blood, and shattered nerves filled my nostrils. I slowed my breathing to take in the smell of his fear. It was sweet and hot like sugar, sex, and burnt wires. I looked back to his fear-clouded eyes, and they were the picture of panic personified: darting back and forth, focusing on nothing while seeing everything. I wondered if they caught sight of the bloody handprints on the rock wall. Maybe his panicked orbs saw the burnt and devastated landscape with the boiling craters. Perhaps the blood-red clouds blooming in the blackened sky above drew his attention and kept him on edge. Thinking these thoughts, I stood in my vision again. A feeling of power coursed through my veins, warming them like a drug. My eyelids fluttered closed, and I tossed the stone up into the air. I opened my eyes to watch it flip while airborne. A rainbow of dark neons shone from it as it spun in midair. The lights shone in my eyes, and I felt powerful within the destruction. The instant the stone landed back in my hand, the vision was gone and I was standing next to an ever-more-impatient Joshie looking at the hole in the ground. Even as the vision faded, I felt the leftover sensations of power, strength, and domination. I felt like the king of the damned standing in that eerie little clearing. The rock hummed warmly in my palm, and I knew without a doubt it had everything to do with these feelings. I couldn't throw it away. I wouldn't. It belonged to me, and even then, I belonged to it.

"I'm keeping it. I'm sorry we walked all the way back to this hole in the ground. It's mine. It means something, and I get the feeling it is meant for me. So don't start your crying and shit. Just deal, man, okay?"

I locked eyes with him, and my desire for the strange stone refused to allow me to break the stare or back down from my statement. I was watching when his anger pushed big wet tears out of his already red and watery eyes. The guilt I felt before was there somewhere, but as I stood there, the forest burned around me, and the roar of the blaze muffled any feelings I had. Joshie stood in place while the vision flashed around him. He took a few sharp breaths and screamed at me.

"Liar! You lied to me!"

I was going to explain to him the feeling the rock gave me. I was going to tell him about the gory visions I was seeing, and how it had to be a sign. I was even going to tell him he could hold it, if he wouldn't be a little prick and throw it. I thought I could explain it to him. After all, he was my best friend. But I never got the chance to say anything. When I opened my mouth, he promptly shut it with a tiny fist. They were small knuckles, but bony and sharp. My lips split, sandwiched between knuckle and tooth. I tasted blood and couldn't hide a grin. Joshie had snapped and wouldn't have listened to anything I said anyway. I had pushed him too far and told a big lie at the wrong fucking time. I deserved my punishment, and I held my hands at my sides faced the fury attacking me. His small, sharp fists smashed into my nose, breaking it and sending blood gushing down my face to my chest. Knuckles driven by rage bounced off my eyebrows and chin. A wild haymaker hit me high on the cheek, right under my eye, splitting the skin and swelling the eye shut immediately.

The stone twitched in my hand, and my other arm shot straight out in front of me. My open palm caught Joshie square in his chest, and I felt his breath on my face as it was forced from his lungs. Blood ran into my good eye from another cut near my eyebrow, obscuring my view of Joshie. I did hear him hit the ground with a thud and a whimper and then jump right back up. I reached up to wipe blood out of my eye with the back of my right hand so I could at least have an idea of what my little anger-fueled friend would throw at my face next. Nothing hit me, and I heard him crashing back through the bushes as I blinked the last of the warm blood out of my eye. I could see the branches falling roughly back into place as I held the back of my hand to the gash above my eyebrow and applied pressure, hoping to ease the flow of crimson into my eye.

Instead, blood spurted into the crack of flesh between my thumb and finger. The stone quit vibrating and was quickly covered in my blood, managing to be both slippery and sticky. I clenched my fist in a near panic over the sudden stillness of my newfound treasure. As I squeezed it, I felt it change, first crumbling against my kung fu grip, then folding two fins down. It squished like a sponge and collapsed on itself. I opened my hand and rolled the stone to my fingers to get a better look at it.

Even beneath a sheen of my blood, dark, strange colors swirled under the black surface. The colors shone and danced along with the steady pulse of my thudding heart. I watched a ripple of movement under the surface of the stone. One fin would lift and wiggle a time or two before it dropped back down to let the next fin rise and flicker. The hard center rolled like a slowly growing marble as the fins did their slow-motion stretch. With every rotation of the fins, the center grew, and the movement of the fins was more defined and controlled. I pushed the hard center with my thumb, and it collapsed flat. It rose slowly when I pulled my thumb away. The stone felt warm, uneven, as though it were wrapped in toad skin. I pushed again, and something inside the stone pushed back.

I yanked my thumb back and watched with stunned amazement as all three fins rolled underneath the stone's bulk and lifted the center up. The fins moved the stone in a circular pattern, and it reminded me of some kind of space spider dancing drunkenly in my palm. I held my hand open and palm flat so it had room to move. I watched breathlessly as it continued the same staggering walk toward the tips of my fingers. When it reached them, one fin went over the edge, so I rolled my hand over to give it continued traction. The stone held tight and rolled through with my motion. It didn't slow or miss a beat as it wobbled up my forearm, tickling slightly as it moved. I turned my good eye back the way Joshie had left, half hoping he was seeing what I was. Just before the stone reached my elbow, it walked off the edge of my arm, but I felt it grip with the fins until it reappeared and skittered in the circular motion up my bicep. It twirled its way to my shoulder, where it spun in place like a tiny faithful pet bird. A chuckle escaped my lips, and at the sound, the stone moved toward the back of my neck. It moved faster than I could ever have imagined, and when I slapped at it, I missed and hit myself hard across my now-vacant shoulder. I reared away from its aggressive new dance as panic churned in my guts, but it followed my movement and skittered across my face. As it passed my nose, I smelled blood and sickly sweet decay. It passed over my eye, and I saw it moving like bugs in a sack before it scrambled into my hair. It spun over my head, twisting knots in my hair as it moved.

When it reached the back of my neck, where the spinal column meets the base of the skull, it stopped traveling and spun in place. The fins grew sharper with each hurried rotation, and I felt them tear into the tender flesh of my neck. My head slumped forward, and my eyes closed as the fins cut deeper and deeper with each spin. My breath was quick and shallow, and I couldn't scream for Joshie even as I realized how wrong I had been. I felt nerves sever in my neck, and my arm reached back to slap the stone away out of some long-buried primal instinct that I had been ignoring. As my hand came toward it, the stone slipped completely under the skin of my neck. When I slapped my neck, I felt it move inside of me. I felt one of the fins cut forward, tearing through muscle and tissue to allow room for its bulk. I felt it wrap itself around my brainstem with unholy speed and fervor. The pain was inconceivable, and it made my weak knees buckle. I feel in a heap less than a foot away from the hole that started the whole mess.

All at once, my body went rigid and then stood up stiffly. I felt like I was slammed to the back of my body by something else inside me. If my body were a bus—my face being the front and the back of my head being where the cool kids sat—then I was thrown into the fire exit while a madman took the wheel. I immediately became aware that I was sharing my body with something else. Something evil beyond my previous understanding of the word. Every muscle in my body went rigid and hard, including my dick. Trust me, at that age I was used to an uncomfortable boner, but it and every other muscle was more swollen and harder than I would have thought possible.

I felt pinned against the farthest reaches of myself, held in place by my own skeleton. I was no longer in control. I was aware of my body, but the sensations I was feeling were numbed, and nothing responded to my panic. My clenched and unclenched at my sides, obeying orders I hadn't issued. My swollen eye opened, but everything looked distant and blurry. Looking out of my eyes was more like looking out a dirty window than really *seeing* things myself. I was staring out of my window eyes when my mind started to race. I found myself reliving long-forgotten memories and thoughts I'd had since birth. I realized with a sickeningly helpless feeling that the something else inside me was reading my mind and soaking it all in. It was studying me and raping my mind at the same time, and I could feel its malevolent glee as it worked.

The intruder knew everything about me as it dug deeper, uncovering subconscious thoughts buried so far down I'd never even realized I thought them. The thing inside me knew me better than I knew myself, and all I could feel from it was power and hatred. My mind was wheeling in shock and pain when I heard a noise that sounded miles away. My head turned, powered by this foreign force inside me, and faced the direction from which the sound had come. Through the windows of my eyes, I saw the branches shaking and moving as they gave way to something behind them.

I felt my throat muscles move, and they worked out the word "Joshie."

It wasn't the scream for which I'd hoped, but a barely audible growl—and hardly in my voice. My body stepped back into the thorns behind me. I barely felt the thorns tear at me as my body eased back. Another step back and thorny branches fell in front of my window eyes. I heard Joshie stumble out of the bushes and into the clearing. I felt my fists clenching and unclenching, but I couldn't stop them.

"Gavin, I'm so sorry." I saw his shape moving beyond the branches; he didn't realize I wasn't still standing there. "I don't know why I got so angry."

At that point, I think he realized he was standing alone in the clearing. The silence following his words hummed distantly in my ears. I wanted to wave my clenching fists in the air and tell him to run. I wanted to give him the keys to my Aries, tell him to keep it and rock the Neil Diamond often. I had lied to him, toyed with him, and even shoved him harder than I even knew possible, but he still came back. I knew he was in more trouble than I, and I wanted to help him. My loyal little buddy had returned for me, but I couldn't stop what I knew was coming next.

"Gavin … Gavin?"

His voice rose and fell like he was looking around himself, looking for me. Brutal thorns that twisted and grew were all I could see.

"Gavin?"

I could hear the fear in his voice and even smell it in the air. As the musk of his fear entered my nose, my muscles all tightened and flexed. I saw my bloody right hand reach up and move the thorn branches out of my view. I saw Joshie standing with his back to me, facing the hole in the ground that had been the cause of everything.

A strange hunger growled from within me. It did not belong to me, but to the invader. I could only feel a small piece of my stomach, and the tiny fraction I could feel felt sick. I could feel a tiny piece of my heart, and it was racing, blurring the windows that my eyes had become with each pulse. The small part of my lungs I could still feel burned and gasped for air. At the same time, I could feel them—as well as the rest of me—working just fine and dandy for the strange thing inside of me. I could barely even feel my body; I certainly could not control it.

My legs took one slow, quiet step forward and closer to Joshie. I could still see thorn bushes out of the side of my window vision. In front of me, Joshie bent at the waist and peered into the hole. My legs took another silent stride out of the thorns and stopped right behind my kneeling friend.

"Gavin," he said, on the verge of tears as he stared into the darkness of the hole, "please don't be in there."

I felt my throat move, and words tumbled out in a voice that was harsh and thirsty and did not come from me.

"He's not."

As Joshie turned to face the voice, I watched my hands shoot out in front of me. My left hand grabbed his shoulder and neck. My right fist, already caked in blood, slammed into his cheek as he was turning. My left hand held Joshie still while my right rained blows down on him with more strength than I knew I had. Joshie tried to curl up, but my fist repeatedly knocked him in and out of consciousness. My right hand grabbed him by his face and hair and slammed him face first into the lip of the hole. Joshie shrieked short screams in between slams. I watched helplessly as his glasses snapped in half and his nose shattered on the hard ground surrounding a hole. He bucked in pain and terror as his vision blurred and blood gushed down his face. My hands clawed deep into his shoulders and got a better grip. I realized as my body leaned down that I was smiling like a maniac and an evil laugh poured from my mouth.

Joshie turned his battered face to me and locked eyes with me. I still felt like I was looking out a window, but I could see the confusion and pain in his eyes.

"Gav …" was all he had time to say before my hands slammed his mouth into the lip of the hole. I saw teeth skitter across the forest floor in several directions. My body stood over him, a foot I could hardly feel planted on either side of his prone, whimpering form. My hands pulled him in a backward arch as my body crouched down above him. My hands folded him in the wrong direction until his ear was next to my mouth. A strange voice spoke to him.

"*Gav* is going to kill you now, Joshie."

I cringed within my flesh prison at the name of my best friend spoken by the violent evil in control of my body.

"We are going to beat you to death with these two hands."

To punctuate its point, the fiend used my hands to slam Joshie's face into the ground again before pulling him back for more taunting.

"We'll beat you past death. We'll bury you deeper than Hell, and we'll enjoy it."

My hands pulled Joshie's limp form off the ground so that his feet dangled helplessly. With a growl, we threw him over the hole at the rock wall behind it. Joshie was too scared to scream, but I heard him take a few wheezy breaths as he sailed toward his sudden rocky stop. He cracked against the rock wall so hard that blood splattered the white stone, and the wet thudding sound of his skull bouncing off the rock echoed around us. As he flew back at me, my hands reached up and caught him in midair before slamming him, back first this time, onto the ground next to me.

Joshie's upper half landed in the thorn bushes, leaving his legs and lower back to take the brunt of his fall. He plunged headfirst into the thorns, blinded by the loss of his glasses and the blood flowing freely from all over his face. A thick branch slapped across his beaten face hard enough to knock him back into the small clearing. He rolled over and held his arms up to protect his head. My body leapt into the air and came down hard on Joshie's knees. I heard several of his bones shatter from the force of the jump, but when he opened his mouth to scream, both my hands shot out and smacked him hard in his face. His head snapped back a few inches and slammed into a rock that was almost completely buried in dirt.

I watched with shock numbing my lips as his eyes crossed to look as his nose and then rolled back in their sockets for what I knew would be the last time. A primal howl of triumph rose from my throat and echoed all around us. Joshie was gone.

I stepped back from my windows, and my tiny piece of heart broke. Joshie had gone the way of his idol, Mr. Cobain. My hands had killed my best friend, had beaten him savagely to death.

I felt tears that wouldn't quite fall and then I felt my leg rise slowly and stomp back down furiously. I stared out of the eyes I was borrowing from the real killer as my foot stomped down on Joshie's frail, unmoving chest. I felt it give way to my foot and heard a sound like a watermelon bursting. My lungs wouldn't take the breath I needed to cry. But my leg stomped down again, this time on Joshie's left shoulder. His head popped up in a postmortem nod as his collarbone snapped. The voice that had taunted and killed Joshie spoke to me, not out loud but with undeniable clarity in my head: "every bone." I knew at once that we would stomp his battered little corpse until every bone was broken. And we did.

The invader took its time walking my body around its prey and picking targets for its powerful stomps. I tried to run, but my legs would only stomp. I tried to fall down, but the force inside me held more control over my body than I did. I couldn't turn away or cover my ears. With every stomp, I heard bones shatter and split. Joshie was jarred and jerked into a different position every time my foot fell. He waved when we smashed his elbow, as if the nod weren't enough of a goodbye.

The eyes from which I stared never blinked but never went dry or shed any tears; they just stared at the carnage at my feet. My face felt numb, but I could still feel the grin that spread, wide and vicious, across it. The monster inside me stood and stared at Joshie's broken corpse for a long time. It inhaled deep breaths of cool forest air with my lungs and forced me to stare along with it at the body of my best friend in the world crushed before us. My mind was racing; thoughts of despair and sadness clambered over each other and mixed with anger and fear.

The fact that I had killed someone as special as Joshie was starting to sink in, but there was nothing I could do. I could hear his grunts, could hear him saying 'Gavvv …' in his frail, scared voice over and over and over again in my head. The loud, wet cracking of bones boomed between his tortured cries. Each grunt and snap quickened the beat of the small piece of heart I could feel. I tried to force the sights and sounds of Joshie's terrible demise out of my mind, but they only rang louder. The grunts and cries were beginning to sound like a sick song whispered in dark alleys and cold, lonely rooms in insane asylums.

When a part of me started enjoying the song and welcoming the feelings of power and domination I hadn't felt when stomping the holy living dog shit out of Joshie, I realized that my mind was linked with something else. These weren't my thoughts; they were being forced on me. I remembered the feeling of something raping my mind, digging deep into my subconscious and my memories. It knew everything about me. Then I realized our minds were sharing the same space. I felt raped before, but once I realized this, I felt the exact opposite. The sounds of pain and death around me, pushing in on me, were dirty and painful … but deep down, it was exciting. It felt like a crack head hooker rubbing her sex on me while I was chained to a wall covered with little spikes.

I felt it inside my head and got a better sense of my invader. It was so cold, it felt like tiny shards of ice moving slowly through my bloodstream. It was ancient and evil. I felt a million sensations at once: physical, emotional, and mental. My entire body shuddered as the sensations shot through me, as the evil wrapped around my brainstem, rubbed its coiled hatred on my soul, and gave me a small glance at its true self.

It felt like pain, fear, agony, desolation, despair, hate, and unbridled fury. It was ageless and knowing, wicked and mean, violent and sexual. And because of it, I felt the stain of the bloody hands and broken souls of its former hosts through the ages. I heard the never-ending wails and screams of those who received death at the urging of the evil. Each victim unlucky enough to cross this unrestrained evil became a small part of it—and thus a small part of me.

I saw through the eyes of strangers as they killed their brothers and lovers. I watched a kindly old woman being beaten mercilessly with an umbrella before being shoved down a flight of stairs that disappeared into darkness. I saw a rock used to cave in the most beautiful face I have ever seen until it was just a pulp of gore, flesh, blood, and bone, covered with wisps of blond hair. I witnessed children drowning and parents set aflame while watching the television. Within a matter of seconds, I watched hundreds of terrible deaths. I felt the sick thrill pulse through my body as my invader cherished every painful, bloodstained memory. My muscles were all flexed again, my prick was swollen against the crotch of my jeans as the monster forced its conquests of gore on me.

With every new vision, I heard Joshie say "Gavvv …" and then the grunts and wet snapping sounds would echo again in my head. I watched two pale thin hands grab a man around his waist and tip him over the edge of a tall bridge. The man opened his mouth, and "Gavvv …" was the sound I heard. The sound of Joshie's bones splintering overpowered all other sounds as the man landed headfirst in the shallow rocky water forty or fifty feet under the bridge. I heard "Gavvv …" as I saw a baseball bat swing wildly and hit more than one person. As the snapping sounds started, I saw the wooden bat broken in half and left in a gas station attendant's head—or, more precisely, left in the quivering mound that remained on his shoulders. I stared out of someone else's eyes as the handle of the weapon was tossed aside and the killer walked up a blood-streaked store aisle strewn with candy bars. The eyes through which I watched darted back and forth before finally settling on a woman clutching a seeping wound on her side as she sidestepped toward the door. She saw the person whose eyes I was borrowing and screamed. A fist hit her hard in the mouth, sending two teeth skittering across the bloody floor in two different directions. The fist then wrapped itself up in her tussled hair and slammed her face into the hard tile floor, much like mine had done to Joshie only moments before. I kept staring while the woman was dragged to a back room. I tried to turn away during the violent first-person perspective of her brutal rape on the cold restroom floor, but I couldn't. For a while, her soft broken sobs and desperate cries rolled with Joshie's whimpers and grunts as the next vision started: a vision of a very unnecessary surgery for which I'm positive no one would volunteer.

The horrors kept flashing, jarring me back and forth through time, stopping at moments of incredible pain and suffering.

I followed a pair of sandaled feet up the rocky hillside of a faraway land. The young boy fleeing from us scrambled ahead, scraping his knees and hands and leaving fresh smears of bright crimson on the rocks between us. My muscles were coiled steel as the boy slipped and fell within our reach. I saw a hand clasp tight to his bleeding ankle. The boy turned to us with tears streaming down his face. He said only one word.

"Mercy."

The same raspy voice that taunted Joshie told the boy, "Mercy is an affliction."

The hand tugged hard on the ankle, and the boy lost his bloody grip on the slippery rocks. We turned to watch him tumble and break down the jagged hillside. His simple robes were torn and bloodstained by the time he came to a sudden stop, wedged awkwardly between two massive boulders. A woman came climbing up toward us, screaming unintelligible words.

"Stop," a voice pleaded weakly in my head.

I pleaded along with it. "Stop."

A voice growled at the plea in the memory and scoffed at me.

I watched the hand that sent the boy downhill curl into a fist and greet the woman with a broken nose. She stumbled back against a boulder and took three hard backhanded slaps. One hand grabbed her by the hair and rammed her face against the rock while the other tore at her robes. The assailant raped her while looking at the broken body below.

I screamed, but it only sounded in my head. The memory dissipated quickly, as though it were made of fog, and in seconds, I was staring at Joshie's twisted corpse again. To say my mind was reeling would be an understatement. To say it twisted and collapsed in on itself would be slightly more accurate. I stared wide eyed at Joshie's body, trying to absorb everything that had happened, but I could feel the evil slithering under my skin. I felt a connection to it. It sensed my question before I had words to match the initial feeling of wonder. The gravelly voice spoke inside my head.

"I have no name. No genus or species. I've been called many things throughout time. Demon, Devil, Monster, He who Follows the Shadow, Harbinger of the Damned, the Hate Within, the Slouching Beast, the Fourth Eye of T'Nartha, and many more that would make no sense to a waste of a human such as you. I was born in the fire at the beginning of time. The fire burnt to life and creation. As time and reality began to live, it began to die, and a part of it burned instantly into the abyss. No names were ever truly bestowed on the creatures and horrors of the abyss. Some crawled blind and insane through the darkness and space while others, like myself, balanced on the brink of the abyss and slithered into reality. We walk in nightmares and darkness. We are the uneasy feeling in the air and the stirring in the calm. We are every unnatural fear, every starving child, and they very idea of war. We walk between Life and Death, before the Beginning and after the End. I have made brother kill brother, parent kill child, lover kill lover. What is sacred to you is laughable to me. The ideas and values of man are fleeting and nonsensical, weak and tiny. I bring the strife and the hate and the rage. And now, whelp, I have you. You will be my bloodstained tool. You have been both blessed and cursed this day."

As it finished the last word, I felt as though I fell forward in myself and regained control of my limbs. I could feel my body again, and it was racked with pain. Every muscle twitched and burned. My legs buckled immediately. I fell face first into Joshie's corpse, feeling his shattered ribs and sternum give way to my face. The pressure of me falling on him caused blood to spurt out of his mouth and across my face. I weakly wiped the blood off my face and staggered backwards until I crashed into the thorn bush.

While I was still trying to catch breath that didn't seem to be there, the voice growled at me again.

"Put it in the hole."

"Wh-wh-what?" But I knew the answer as soon as I asked it.

"The battered shell of your friend, cram it in the hole and let's be done of this."

I crawled forward to Joshie's body and grabbed his hand. I tried to hold the bones together so it held its shape as well as possible. I couldn't restrain the sobs.

"I can't … why? Why did you kill him? Why did …"

A needle-sharp pain raged through my body as every nerve ending lit up. My strained muscles clenched, and I spat foamy drool against the mountainside. The pain only lasted a second, but it did what the being intended and seized my full attention.

"Never ask me why again, human. I savor the smell of fear and the taste of pain. I've seen your deepest darkest thoughts. You will grow to need it, to need me. The screams will become like oxygen to you. Sweet torment hangs thick in the air and will stain walls and dwellings for years. I will show you power. I will show you the pain and the desperation."

Out loud, I answered, "I don't want to see it. I don't care about any of that."

"Bullshit," it growled, using my vocal cords and throat, "If you didn't want it, you would have thrown me away. Joshie asked you to drop me." It snickered out of my throat when it mentioned Joshie. "He begged you, and you kept me gripped tight in your sweaty palms. You both knew deep down what was happening. You let me in, and I'll remind you whenever you need reminding."

While my body still obeyed my commands, like a good body should, the presence of the murderous evil was unmistakable. I could feel a tiny piece of my heart all blackened and dead. There was a hitch in my breathing, and I could feel it in my lungs, thick and toxic like fumes from a plastics factory. I could feel someone looking out through my eyes but seeing things differently. When I looked upon Joshie's body, I felt deep, agonizing pangs of guilt and shame. Yet I also felt a feeling of satisfaction and power from behind my eyes, a feeling of triumph that threatened to suffocate my conscience. I shook my head and tried to let the tears flow to release the emotional pain that was building every second I sat staring at my little buddy, now broken, now gone.

"Enough of that. If your feelings will get in the way, I'll end them for now. I wouldn't want to deprive you of them entirely, so I'll save them for you."

He spoke as though he were doing me an incredible favor.

"Your guilt and shame are delicious, and I'll feast on them again, but I think it best if you put the shell in the hole."

I felt something like a finger poke softly inside my brain. When it moved a second time, I realized it was more like a tentacle. On its third movement, I went numb. Not physically, but emotionally. I looked at Joshie, all shattered and small before me, and felt nothing. I tried to bring up old memories, but they were blurry and altered, so I decided not to press. I was emotionally frozen, and I rejoiced in the frost of indifference. I knew my hands had taken Joshie's life, but it just didn't matter anymore. When he was here, we were friends and that was neat. Now he was a shell of broken bones and ruptured organs. And I had to move the fucking thing.

"Better." He spoke with my vocal cords again.

"Yeah," I answered with the same vocal cords but in a weak, tiny, faraway voice. My throat ached and scratched when I chose the words it spoke.

My mouth curled into a twitchy smile, and I grabbed Joshie by his wrist. The bones were crushed so badly his skin hung loose and folded over my fingers when I tightened my grip. I tugged him toward me, and both his feet flopped outward in a way they never could have before that day. I stepped toward the hole, and Joshie's body followed in a half-moon movement, pulling pinecones and small rocks with it. I didn't question how I knew it was intended to go in headfirst. The body bent in half, sideways, at such an awkward angle that I was certain the spinal cord was no longer attached to anything. I stopped for a second and stared at Joshie's shell. I was sure the thing had kept its word and broken every bone. Yet, out of the hundreds of fractures, none had split the pale dead flesh. Instead of the feeling of shame I should have experienced, all I could muster was simple amazement at the brutal precision of the thing inside me. It knew my thoughts as soon as they came into being.

"You are impressed?" it scoffed at me aloud. "Years of practice. Wait 'til we rip a limb off of something."

I said nothing and tugged the body forward until the head dangled into the hole. I stepped around the mouth of the hole, twisting Joshie's arm in an impossible arch, but my weak knees buckled, and I tripped. I landed beside the hole with the arm still in my hand. When I hit the ground, a shard of bone sliced through just enough for its white gleam to stand out next to the purple and green blanket of bruises that Joshie's skin had become.

The voice growled furiously at me.

"Drop it!" it commanded.

I flinched and dropped the wrist. It swayed and lowered slowly like a fat, broken snake. I gave the corpse a good push. It held fast, and my hands sank into the gelatinous flesh deep enough to get me growled at again. It may have come with more words, but they weren't any I understood. The anger in the voice, however, was unmistakable. I shoved again, and the body still refused to budge. I lifted my foot, thinking of stomping the body into the hole, but as soon as I raised my leg, fiery pain shot up my exhausted limbs from my toes to my hips. I collapsed in the dirt next to the body-clogged hole.

"You are going to try my patience," the voice growled in my head, "and that doesn't bode well for you. I can keep you running forever. No cancer. No asthma. No sickness at all. I can heal your cuts and bruises, but I exist to destroy. I can give your body immortality and spend all that time poking holes in your mind until you spend your days covered in drool and shitting yourself."

"I'm sorry! My legs ache, and I can hardly fucking move! I'm sorry!"

A gruff chuckle answered my bubbling frustration. I opened my mouth to tell the thing inside that I really didn't want to drool and shit for eternity, but then Joshie's body lurched itself forward in the hole, and that shut me the hell up. I sat up so fast I rolled back onto my ass. I watched with a strange mix of amazement and accomplishment as the body heaved forward twice more. Joshie's feet flopped and rolled in two big, impossible circles before they kicked their way into the darkness. The feet sent up a small cloud of dust as they disappeared, and by the time the dust settled, the hole had closed in on itself.

"Whoa," I said, sounding a lot like Keanu Reeves as I stared at the empty clearing that had held the corpse of my little buddy only seconds before. As I stepped back, the thorns recoiled from us and granted us a clear path to the creek. Once we were out of the thorns and across the creek, I turned back. The landscape looked the way it always had, with thick nasty thorns crowded close up to the face of the rock wall. The clearing had vanished as if it had never existed. It felt like destiny when I looked up to the rock wall and saw one small, bloody handprint, smeared slightly, standing out in bright crimson defiance of the stark white mountainside.

It is truly amazing how the human mind handles shock and stress. Some people spend hours every day working for an ungrateful public, deprived of self-respect and treated like minimum-wage slaves. They can smile at those who treat them so, because release is only a slap away once they get home. Or a kick. Or a concussion. Some people lose those shit jobs and drive off of bridges with no intent on swimming. Some take one too many pokes in the chest and stabs in the wallet from an uncaring and greedy system and release their fury upon themselves with pills, razors, and nooses. Some turn to an addiction, inevitably a self-destructive one, to numb the redundancies of the day. The frustration of the day. The tragedy of the day. Some people get teased and picked on so much that when they find power or acceptance of any sort, they develop a soul-sustaining need for it. They look down on us all from atop podiums and behind badges. Some give away parts of themselves to fill that ever-empty void left in the wake of whatever left them. Whatever failed them. Whatever used them.

Not me. I knew as we walked away from the clearing that I was damned. The horrid thing inside me was so hideously unholy as to cause me to be damned for serving as its vessel. My mind didn't even panic. It never had time to see the full scope of my foolishness before tentacles started shutting down feelings in my brain like fuses in a fuse box. Once my fears were muffled and my raw emotions tucked deep down somewhere, I understood. My mind wrapped itself around my new reality, and that was that. I was to carry the evil and do its bidding. I was the hand of the slayer of the damned and one of the damned myself. I could sense the depravity within me and, already, the line as to which soul it radiated from was becoming blurred.

I stumbled on my weak, rubbery legs through the forest and back to the Aries. The thing inside me saw the older couple hiking toward me before I did. My eyes jerked to them, and I could feel panic drain the color from my face. My hair was clumped together with blood, sweat, and dirt. My white shirt was torn to ribbons from all the trips in and out of the thorn bush. Beneath each tear in the fabric, the bright red of fresh scratches crisscrossed my skin. My nose was swollen and bent, my eye still bloodshot and blurry.

"Oh my God, kid, are you okay?" The man rushed toward me. The thing inside me primed itself to leap forward, but I threw myself backwards before it had time to retake control of my body. The woman gasped and grabbed the man by his shoulders, halting him, which in turn relaxed the coiled madness around my brainstem.

"Get some help, Jake, the last thing the kid needs is you lumbering up on him. You probably scared the shit out of him." She finished the last with a half-joking tone, but when she looked me in my open and frightened eye, her humor washed away.

"What happened, sweetheart?" She used the word "sweetheart" like some waitresses do, as if that's how they end a third of their sentences anyway.

97

Inside my head, the harsh voice commanded, "Tell them you were hiking with your friend and you got separated. You fell down the mountainside and still can't find him. Here is your chance to whine pathetically."

I felt the tears the thing allowed. I blinked and let them wet my dry eye. They rolled down my cheek, and I wailed, "My friend Joshie and me were hiking (wheeze) … went out to hike (stuttering breath) … somewhere we got separated. I slipped and fell down the sheer side, back there … (deep breath) … and (sniff, sniff) … have been looking … (wheeze) … for him since (full on bawl)."

A group of three college kids were hiking past, but they turned their eyes away when I bawled out loud. Jake's wife slapped him on the shoulder and pointed at the kids. He nodded at her and charged at them like he had come at me moments before.

"Hey, we need help over here," he shouted, and they all stepped back, half thinking they were about to be tackled. They smiled nervously and met him in the path a good twenty feet away. Jake's wife rubbed my back softly, careful of the blood now sticking and drying. Jake talked with the kids for a minute while being careful to shield me from their conversation. Jake's wife led me to a fallen log and assured me that everything was "gonna be okay" before she jogged over to join in the hushed conversation. As she turned away, the voice growled in my head.

"Do you see how weak and foolish? We could kill these five, here and now. We could rape away the afternoon and fall asleep to tortured screams of slow dying."

I felt it move my eye to each of the five.

Jake. Then his wife, who had a fabulous ass. Two college-age guys in jeans and hoodies emblazoned with the local college emblem. The young blonde with them was wearing a gray beanie and sweatpants that said "Princess" across her ass. My swollen eye opened. I looked them over again, and my heart started to race. I felt a throbbing building at the thought of raping the two women. A strange desire to kill the men and then rape the women in their blood rose so fast that my ears got hot. I could feel the inhuman push behind the thoughts as everything became brighter and more focused. I clenched my fists and smiled.

"But," the voice stirred me from my murder-rape dream, "if they help your pathetic carcass out of here and then send your entire town of ants out here to look for Joshie and never find him, at least you will avoid trouble. And you don't want trouble, Worm. They will call you 'poor boy' and weep for your friend."

As if to prove its point, every nerve in my body came alive with the sensation of fire. I yelped and resumed my pained cries. My eye swelled shut again as if Joshie had hit me once more from beyond the grave. Jake and the other two guys came over and helped me to my feet and out of the forest.

Everything worked out how *it* said it would. The entire town did form search parties and scour the woods and mountain for Joshie. After two and a half weeks of rotating shifts of men and dogs, with helicopter support from above, they finally gave up. That day, I became the slayer of the damned and one of the damned myself. Even now, the irony makes me want to scream. Or maybe I just need to hear a scream.

Dream: Meat Hooks and the Damned

I open my eyes to fog. It drifts lazily around me, and I recognize this place. I look at myself and am not the least bit surprised when I see my plain shirt and pants, faded gray and streaked with blood. I curl my bare toes into the ashes and powdered bones beneath me. I reach up and trace the ragged edges of the fresh inverted cross carved into my forehead. The wound screams, but the pain makes me focus. I'm standing alone, but I sense other people near, the way a deer senses the hunter as it takes its final sip of water. I spin in a slow circle, and the fog spins with me.

I hear sounds, muffled sounds. I hear clapping that sounds like it is coming from every direction all at once. The fog distorts the sound, but I've been here. I hear laughter, and the hair on the back of my neck stands up. I focus and stare deep into the fog until I see a dark blur. I walk toward the blur, and it takes a more definite form with each step. The edges solidify into a black rectangle. The black becomes brown. The shape widens into a shack. The brown becomes weathered wood the color of old bone. The door to the shack slams as if blown by an unseen wind. I stand before the door, and I hear the laughter and the clapping emanating from within. The building is squat, barely taller than the door, and it only looks to be a few square feet big. Still, it weeps malevolence. The ever-swirling fog dances around it, moved by the force of the noise within.

Instinct forces my hand, and I push open the creaky door. Without taking a step, I'm standing inside the building It is massive on the inside, like a creepy wooden version of Dr. Who's TARDIS, lit by torches fixed to the walls. It towers over me, bleached wooden planks reaching twenty feet to a simple wooden ceiling where long, braided strands of hair hang down. Hollowed-out bones are braided into the hair, and they clank together, swaying in an unseen breeze. A small wooden ledge lines the wall behind me, and people sit shoulder to shoulder on it, staring past me. I feel like I should recognize the people sitting here, but my mind is blank. I walk slowly in front of them, looking into their milky dead eyes, but none acknowledges me. Each sits up stiff and straight, hands folded. Some hands are missing fingers, some faces missing strips of flesh. Some stare ahead with one eye, a gaping oozing crater where the other eye should be. Others are missing ears or wearing slit-throat necklaces. As I stare at them, they raise their hands in clumsy unison and clap in an off-kilter rhythm. Laughter erupts behind me like grenades in a barrel, and I turn around as the sitting people make screaming faces and howl with joyous laughter.

More people hang, suspended by a complex network of barbed wire and meat hooks, above a large hole in the simple wooden floor. Tears of blood stream down their faces as the wires pull taut and the hooks yank them up, down, in every direction, so that their limbs flail frantically. They cringe in agony, but they all laugh out loud as they jerk and twitch to the tug of the wires. I step forward to the man swinging nearest me and notice his eyes are alive with confusion and pain, though he screams hearty laughter in my face with enough force to speckle my skin with his warm blood. I look him over from head to toe. He has deep cuts in the flesh of his cheeks, deep enough that when he chuckles, I can see flashes of bone under the pulpy ribbons of his face. A hook pokes through his right shoulder, and another through his left thigh. An even thicker one splits his sternum open, and shards of bone stab out alongside the purple metal of the hook.

I wager a glance below his kicking feet and into the hole in the floor. Huge, savage gears made of flesh, purple metal, and pink crustaceous shell grind against each other as blood rains down on them from the twitching people above. The gears rumble, and the people dance and laugh. The people seated along the wall clap and laugh along. I stare back and forth a few times before I notice the figure standing at the far wall, his face cloaked in torchlight shadow. Everyone laughs and claps at the gory spectacle while the man at the end of the aisle works his arms, tugging at the wires that control the ghastly puppet show.

I take a step toward the puppet master, and his arms go limp at his side. In the same instant, the wires go slack, and the puppet people slide off their hooks and into the mutant gears below them. The seated people stand in the same almost-unison as their clapping, which intensifies as the bodies rend and burst in the flesh-metal-shell gears. The standing people all stare straight ahead of them, their yellow and white eyes blind to the sight of bodies grinding to pulpy smears in front of them.

I take another step, and the puppet master breathes smoke that billows out of the shadows cloaking his face and through the space between the planks in the walls. The standing people walk forward until they are at the edge of the floor, dangerously close to the churning gears. One by one, they turn around so their heels hang just over the end of the ancient wood. The figure raises his arms, and the strands of barbed wire growing from his skin shimmer in torchlight as the hooks swing down and impale the people. The people scream once as their eyes uncloud, but when the wires snap backwards, violently tugging their bodies, their screams turn to laughter. They swing back together to dangle above the gears. The puppet master exhales more smoke.

I contemplate the empty seats just as a hand, bloody and deformed, reaches out of the gears near the door. An arm follows it, and a man pulls his crushed, pulpy body from the horrible gears. Behind him, a woman follows suit, pulling her shattered body from the gears. The man stands on impossibly crushed legs and stares through me with milky dead eyes. As the woman behind him stands, the dead man takes a step closer to me. Another corpse pulls itself from the gears, forcing the dead man and woman another step closer. The puppets flail and laugh as the wires jerk up and down and back and forth in a metallic flurry. I am staring at them when the first dead man to crawl from the mutant gears slams into me as he takes a step forward to allow room for the ever-growing number of people resurrecting themselves from the flesh-metal-shell. I stumble back and notice that the dead man's face has healed—not completely, but his wounds have shrunk and closed slightly. His legs still boast compound fractures, but they are no longer crumpled to the point of being unrecognizable as limbs. He steps into me again, and I back up a few steps.

I turn around and find myself staring at the shadow that cloaks the puppet master's face. His arms work back and forth, flexing and relaxing, up and down, while dozens of strands of barbed wire reach up behind the human puppets. His body is slender but muscular, and crisscrossed with purple welts and bright crimson scars. From the mask of shadows, he blows smoke into my face. My eyes water, and red and blue spots dance behind my eyelids when I blink the burn away. When I open my eyes, I see the smoke he exhaled drift through the cracks in the wall like dust in sunshine. The dead man bumps me again, and I step toward the puppets to give him room to get past. Instead of pushing farther, he and the rest of the people who'd climbed out of the gears all sit down on the wooden ledge. They stare straight ahead with their dead eyes. The puppet master works his arms and wires back and forth, up and down, forcing the human puppets to yank and jerk against the purple hooks.

The human puppets flail and laugh, and the seated people applaud politely. The longer they clap, the brighter the torches above glow. The brighter they glow, the more the shadow concealing the puppet master's face fades. He works his arms more and more furiously until the puppets are spinning in circles, flinging fans of blood at the blind audience. I stand in front of his madly waving arms, avoiding the slicing wires as they cut the stale, blood-tinged air. He moves so fast I see tracers from the whipping wires. The dead clap, and the human puppets laugh. The torches burn daylight-bright, and the shadow hiding the puppet master fully dissipates.

I'm staring at myself. I see the thick strands of wire growing from my arms. I see where the muscles turn to wire under the stretched skin of my forearms. I can see the three tentacles connecting from the puppet master's head to the walls of the shack behind him. They are a mix of flesh and shell, like the gears below, but I see no metal as they pulse and tug at the base of the puppet master's neck. The tentacles sway, and the puppet master's arms mimic the motion, forcing the human puppets to scream with laughter as the hooks pull them in different directions. My eyes are open wide when the puppet master me exhales dark orange smoke into my face. I blink the burn away again.

I open my eyes and see the cords of wire stretching from under the skin in my arms. I feel each wire where it melds to my muscles and bones. I feel the weight of the tentacles extending from the base of my skull. I feel each throb and swing. I see time and space and beyond. I want to destroy it all. I hear drums in my head, and my arms wave to the off-kilter beat. The wires tug and tighten, forcing the human puppets to dance and sway. I look to the puppets, and each one is me. I feel the smile as I force myself to twist and jerk at the demand of purple steel. The seated people clap, and my eyes dart back and forth. Everyone sitting is me as well. Each me stares with dead white eyes at another me, twisting and twirling to the insane demands of monster me.

I see myself from everywhere. Hooked and dancing. Blind and clapping. Swinging my wires and arms.

I blow smoke and watch it drift between the planks and fade away.

My throat aches from laughing. My eyes hurt from massive, diamond-hard cataracts. My arms burn from commanding the macabre puppet show and from the wires attached to them. Each sitting me stands and claps. Again, I see time and space and beyond. I let my arms fall limp at my sides. The wires whip, and everything bleeds. I slide off my hooks and fall into gears made of flesh, metal, and shell.

My Sick Story: The Grieving Process

That day in the forest, I traded my best friend for a set of wicked homicidal tendencies. I reduced the thing inside me to its most basic quality and gave it a name, something for me to curse. I christened it Heinous, Heinous the demon. It had many names before and had little use for one, so it didn't care what I called it. I mean, would I give half a shit what my Aries called me? Heinous reminded me often, "You are my vessel; you are my tool." To me, everything about his name fits. It is even an exception to the old "i before e, except after c" rule you learn in school. And I see this entire situation as an exception to the rules of life. I'm possessed by a homicidal fucking demon. I called it Heinous that first night, and he has spent every day since proving that he deserves it.

The first few weeks after Joshie's death, Heinous would keep me awake all night, flashing visions of slaughter guided by his tentacles. I would see the visions as clearly as if I were performing whatever atrocity flashed before me, be it murder, rape, or torture. I would kill a hundred people a night as many poor fools had before me. There was nothing I could do to push the visions away. Worse still, I felt the conflict of the demon's hunger, triumph, and utter perverse satisfaction against the former host's guilt, regret, and sheer unchecked terror. I withdrew from my loving parents, knowing if I showed them any affection, we would carve them up and feed them to stray dogs. Or something worse. I started losing weight and gaining dark half-circles under my eyes. I went from fit and handsome to having the gaunt look of a heroin addict in just a few weeks.

Mom and Dad assumed I was in some sort of delayed shock and depression over Joshie's strange "disappearance."

I let them think whatever they needed to. I did think of Joshie a lot but felt nothing more than loss; that tear of separation that feels like it rips at the fabric of your soul. No remorse for doing what I did to him, no pity for his devastated and confused parents. The guilt that should have eaten my stomach alive never so much as stirred a bubble. I tell myself now that they could sense the truth. They had to. They

105

knew me too well, our happy little family, to not see the evil stirring within me. I think they may have seen flashes of the wickedness in my bloodshot eyes or seen the hateful thing move just under my skin.

Heinous and I joined symbiotically, and it hurt like a motherfucker. It burned and pulled. It twisted and cut. It stretched what felt like every nerve cluster in my body and coated them with evil. All of my joints became slightly tighter when I moved them, and a strange pressure pushed on the back of my skull. When I was allowed control, my limbs felt heavier and sluggish. I weighed myself on the bathroom scale, and I'd gained four pounds. Even as I wasted away from not being able to eat in the face of the endless morbid visions that consumed my every sleep-starved moment, I put on four pounds of ancient evil. I could feel it moving just under my ski—thin tentacles feeling their way over bones and through muscles. I could feel its hate in my veins like a thick, slow poison.

I don't know what my parents told themselves, but I'm sure they picked up on the fact that I was dealing with something much worse than a case of the dead buddy blues. I avoided them as much as possible to put an imaginary safe distance between Heinous and them. I would go days at a time without speaking a word to either of them. Sometimes while I was lost in Heinous' horrendous memories, I would hear the door to my room creak open behind me. They hardly ever spoke, and when they did, it was muffled under the screams and moans of the dead and dying; they just checked on me like loving parents do.

I spent all my time in my room when they were home, and when they left for work, I'd slink out to the forest. I'd wander aimlessly, always away from the worn paths, until we were standing in front of the thorn bush. We'd stand there, Heinous curling my lips into a smile and me thrashing within myself to leave, until a soft voice would rise from the thick of the thorns.

"Gavvvv … Gavvvvv," it would call, "are you there? I'm in here, Gavin. I'm dead, and I can't fucking scream. I laugh all the time. I can't move, Gavin." The smile on my face would stretch as the phantom voice continued. "All my bones are broken. Every single bone. But I don't really need them, because I hang like I do, Gavin. I hang all day every day and laugh the whole fucking time." As we turned away, the voice would shout, "I'll be seeing you, Gavin. You'll be here and we'll hang out again and laugh. Oh how we'll LAUGH!"

I would end up back at home without the memory of the drive every time. I swayed back and forth, confused and disoriented, for hours in my living room. When I tried to force my memory back to the drive, I'd hear the sound of fragile bones snapping. My parents would come home from work to find me staring into space. They'd rub my back and say my name softly and calmly.

"Gavin, are you okay, sweetie/"

I must have heard it a million times that first year. The amazing thing is I answered "yes" every time someone asked. I wanted to tell people I had Joshie's blood on my hands and they were stupid for not seeing it. I wanted to tell everyone about the ancient fireborn demon wrapped around my brainstem. I wanted to tell anyone who would listen that he was getting hungry again, that he would always be hungry. Feasting only whetted his appetite like some cruel cosmic joke. I wanted to slap people for worrying about hip new trends or who won on Monday Night Football. I had a demon inside me for Christ's sake! I wanted to warn everyone about him … about me. But still I answered only "yes." What could I really say? Who would have believed me?

My mind was constantly exhausted from the nonstop visions and the foulness infesting it. Heinous knew every thought I'd ever processed, and he would make me relive awkward and embarrassing moments at his demented whim. My discomfort was endlessly amusing to him, and he would flash my worst personal moments randomly, forcing me to lose concentration. As the weeks wore on, I could gradually see reality beyond the flashing visions, allowing me a slight reprieve and the ability to be a little less lethargic.

My body was in a state of sustained shock as we got used to each other. I felt him slither all over inside me. He would hit random nerves at odd times. One minute I could be laughing out loud from a rush of endorphins, and the next I'd be screaming as it felt like my nerves were exploding. Everything ached. Everything burned.

School was impossible the first month, and I was excused. The doctors gave me some kind of pill they deemed magic enough to dull me into not killing myself. I still had to do the work assigned so I didn't fall too far behind, but it was impossible to concentrate long enough to open a book. Somehow, all my work got done, and that fact gave everyone close to me a false hope that I was going to get better. By staying at home, I was spared the looks of my classmates that I knew would range from pity to fear to hate. I knew because Heinous told me.

I've heard the devil referred to as the Father of Lies. Well, Heinous never lies. The truth as he tells it is always horrid, and man does he like to tell it. He lusts for that look of stunned shock that glazes the eyes of someone who has just been told of their forthcoming doom at the hands of a loved one. He would hold onto the moment the victims realized their loved one was going to kill them and suckle the horror from it like a vampire on a jugular. He told me people would feel sorry for me, and they did. So when he told me that people would sense the change in me and react in unpredictable ways, I never questioned him. I might have been missing out on the looks, but I was still a star in the gossip and I knew it. What had happened to Joshie had stumped the local law enforcement and even the Feds who were called in after the local fuzz couldn't find even a trace of my missing little friend. So naturally, every kid in high school was working out the mystery through vigilant gossip and vicious rumor. I was the last person to see Joshie, and my going off the radar so hard and so fast raised a lot of suspicion. I was a note on a scandal no one could prove but everyone could feel.

Joshie's parents never talked to me again. They were devastated and left town after steadfastly refusing to hold a funeral for a child they would not believe had died. My mom talked to them a few times after they moved away, and she told me that they were still having a hell of a time. The stress had formed a wedge between them, and even though they were suffering over the same thing, it pushed them apart into solitary torment. Heinous laughed his harsh gravelly laugh long and loud while she told me. He laughed so loud I had to read her lips when she told me that Joshie's disappearance had been hard on everyone, not just me. I walked away, and he laughed for the rest of the night while I stared out my window and watched a hundred strangers die.

After a few weeks, my parents, principal, and school counselors held a meeting and decided that I couldn't avoid school forever and should be getting back. They assumed I would get better. My throat constricted to the point of speechlessness when I tried to tell my parents that I would never be better, that going back to school wouldn't work out happily for anyone. They took my silence as acceptance, and I went to school the next morning.

When you spend all your time watching vicious murder and rape all day and all night, you lose track of your calendar date. I walked into the school that morning without Joshie for the first time in my life only three short weeks after these hands killed him and stuffed him into a disappearing hole. I looked like twice-hammered shit and didn't care at all. Dark circles gave the illusion of my bloodshot eyes sinking into my skull. My unkempt hair hung greasy in my face, and I avoided eye contact with everyon—to no avail. Every damn kid in that school had to see me with their own eyes. They whispered and snickered as they walked away from me after telling me how sorry they were. Heinous heard every word and echoed it back in my head, the words crackling like unidentifiable uni-sex robot voices over pirate radio waves.

"I think he's using heroin to deal."

"Oh, he so fucking killed him!"

"He's crazy. You can see it in his eyes."

"Why didn't they lock him up?"

"Or at least put his murdering ass in a pycho ward?"

I heard every slam and dig the traitorous bastards whispered to each other. Heinous laughed at my blossoming rage at the hypocrites, but he went silent as their queen slithered toward us. Miss Sarah Jackson—apparently over the degrading boob ravaging scandal from the year before—walked right up to me and wrapped her arms around my neck. The reek of cheap vanilla perfume irritated my eyes even more, and I scowled as her spray-stiff hair clawed at my face while she held me tight. The urge to cause her pain rose thick and fast; stifling it sent a sharp throbbing pain stabbing into the base of my neck. I felt my hands balling into useless fists at my side, pinned in place by Sarah's blubbering form. The pressure at the back of my neck pushed so hard I thought my eyes would burst from their sockets if I didn't release the fury warming my blood by squeezing her pretty little neck shut. My muscles went rigid, and I stared straight ahead through locks of greasy hair. She gave one last tight squeeze and released me. As her arms fell away, the rage seemed to melt off me as if I'd walked from a blizzard into a sauna.

I didn't know what to say, and I turned my head to look away from her. The fact that I could still get enraged without my demon made me so happy that a grin split my emotionless face in half. I was just about to walk away without saying anything, content to leave her standing in the middle of the crowded school hallway looking like a complete jackoff, when she asked me in a whimper, "You can't even hug me back, Gavin?"

My smile cracked, and I let my jaw fall open in stunned wonder. After I grabbed her titty, every girl in the school knew about it. You would think in a high school the size of ours, at least one trampy girl would have wanted to be with a boob fondler. Nope. Not a single girl our age would talk to me for the rest of the year and half of the summer. My two fingers covering an inch and a half of fleshy mound and giving just the slightest, sweetest squeeze was enough to seriously tarnish our reputations. In her version, Joshie was my perverted little sidekick hiding in the bushes, watching and playing pocket-pool, as I pawed away her innocence like the obvious budding young sex fiend I was.

And this bitch had the gall to hug me over Joshie. Now she wanted both my long deviant arms around her, holding her close enough to feel the beat of my poisoned heart, over someone she had once referred to as "that little panty sniffer."

"Let me hug her, Worm," Heinous growled in my head, using his favorite name for me.

"I thought you hated me?" My voice held surprise even through my grin. "You hated Joshie. You told everyone he hid in the bushes and jerked off to you. But you feel bad now that he's gone, daddy, gone? Bullshit." My smile distorted into a sour pucker.

"Louder," Heinous commanded, and my voice obeyed, growing in volume and pitch. His urging washed away my restraint.

"You fake bitch! You're a liar and a hypocrite. You never gave half a glittery fuck about Joshie, but I guess it is the nice thing to do. Right?"

Sarah's lips moved, but shock stole her voice. She looked around her to see if anyone else was seeing what was happening.

"Well," I continued, "you've never been nice. Not to me or to Joshie or any one less popular than you. And, of course, nothing makes you more popular in high school than blowing the football team. Right, Sarah?"

My own sweet rage was building when I felt Heinous like an internal oil slick pulsing with malice and enhancing my fury. I couldn't clearly see the crowd around us. I could hear them like a growing buzz as more students approached the swelling circle. She was the only thing I could focus on. Even with the crowd it was just she and we, and she was weak and scared. I was breathing faster, trying in vain to catch the scent of her fear. Everything grew brighter, so I assumed my eyes were as wide and wild as my smile. Her eyes were feral, darting back and forth from me to the kids surrounding us. They were a blurry shape to me, crackling like static and tinted red.

I could feel their eyes on me. Paranoid and scared, they all plastered themselves close to the scene, speechless, while I gave little Miss Jackson a piece of my weary mind. They had all heard the worst of the rumors and gossip, maybe even adding a gory detail or two themselves before passing them on. They were starting to believe their own bullshit. I had more important things to deal with than my reputation, namely the hateful demon throbbing inside my skull, turning my vision blurry red with rage.

"Everyone knows how fake you are," I told her as I took a step forward. She took two quick steps back to keep space between us.

111

"Your whore-bag friends know the real you, so full of petty bullshit and drama. Do you really think they don't tell everyone? You think you are that fucking special?" I took another step, and she retreated as I did.

"The teachers call you a kiss-ass. They joke in the teachers' lounge about how your dad blew Mr. Sloan to get you on the cheerleading squad. Family tradition, they call it. I've seen your mom's lips; I can only imagine." She turned red at my words, her anger and embarrassment making her eyes tear and her bladder twitch.

I took a step forward and she another step back.

"Every kid in school hates you."

I heard a buzz cut through the crowd as I continued, "Everyone hates you, Sarah. We can all smell your bullshit before you enter a room. Do you understand, Sarah?"

We performed another step in our deliciously uncomfortable dance, me forward and her back. I noticed the wall behind her, and she didn't. She whimpered and looked pleadingly at the blurred shapes around us instead of answering.

"Everyone hates you!" I shouted as I took another step and she slammed herself hard into the unforgiving wall behind her. Another buzz swept through the crowd, and I felt the tension in the hall increase with every nerve in my body. I took one last step so I was close enough to kiss her. From that distance, I could not only smell her fear but taste it. It was thick and warm like hot tar on a summer highway. I wanted to grab her by the hair and stick my tongue down her throat, knowing her fear would kiss me back as it oozed down my throat.

She whined, screeched for help, and felt along the wall for a switch to flip the wall around like a secret entrance to a superhero's lair. When I spoke again, it wasn't in my voice, or even Heinous's, but in Joshie's.

"It should have been you, Sarah."

Her eyes and bladder lost their respective battles, and she broke into tears as she pissed down both legs. I smelled the piss, warm and oddly sexual, and looked to the spreading darkness on her pink plaid skirt.

"Ha!" I shouted as she pushed past me. "People will talk, Sarah! You'll never live this down! You bitch!"

I turned to follow, but our brick shithouse of a gym teacher, Mr. Apekin, and our vice principal, Mr. Pratt, blocked my path. I guess one of the throng had found the guts to ignore the spectacle of public humiliation long enough to fetch poor little Sarah some help. Motherfuckers saved her life that day.

"Mr. Wagner, come with us," Mr. Pratt ordered. I remember how weak it sounded compared to Heinous—who remained silent as the crowd began to spin around me. I felt Mr. Apekin grab my arm, but I was already swaying. I looked at the crowd, unable to focus on any one face. Instead they were all blurry shapes buzzing and spinning around me. My adrenaline crashed, and I felt a cold sweat dot my forehead. I think I managed two full steps before I passed out.

I woke up in the nurse's office surrounded by a very angry Mr. Pratt, my very worried parents, and a very unimpressed school nurse. I had no excuses. No words of apology or regret. I was suspended for "threatening a student" because "making the most popular girl in school fear-pee herself in the main hallway" didn't fit on the suspension form. My parents juggled embarrassment and worry as I stared at the lime green tile floor. The scowling nurse and the livid vice-principal insisted that I needed to seek professional help.

I was silent on the ride home, content to let Heinous replay the image of Sarah backing hard into the wall. The memory left me as unsatisfied as it did him, yet still it flashed. My parents talked quietly back and forth while stealing glances at me in the rearview mirror. My mom finally turned around and asked me if I thought a counselor would help me. I stared out the window, paying grateful attention to the visions of Heinous' past atrocities instead of the lush evergreens surrounding us. She kept talking, but the sound of people howling their death cries overpowered her soft sweet voice. I heard my mom start to sob.

"Gavin, we love you, son," my dad told me in his big booming voice, uncharacteristic for a man of his short, pudgy stature. "We'll do anything we can to help you, because we love you."

"Love." Heinous repeated inside my head. Once again his tone reminded me of the way some people say "Nazi"—like they almost choke on it and still taste it once they spit it out.

The ride home was silent. I stared out the window watching murder after murder until we pulled into the driveway. When my dad turned off the car, the visions stopped in eerie unison. The sudden silence echoed inside the vehicle, and I waited for my mom to let me out of the back of the bug. I waited for them to say something, but their loss of words was obvious to me even in my murder haze. The creaking squeal of metal on metal cut through the silence as the door swung open. I climbed out after my mom before leading our sullen family procession into the house. I walked through the darkened living room and up the stairs without turning on any lights. My parents followed behind me, turning on the lights and wanting to say something, anything.

"Are the pills helping?" my dad fumbled.

"Is there anything we can do?" my mom recovered.

My silence prevented any further plays.

I walked into my room, ignored the light switch, and sat at my desk, facing out the window. I could hear them in the hallway before they knocked softly on my door. I didn't answer, and they knocked again.

"Yeah," I croaked and the visions began.

My eyes were closed, but I was looking through a sniper's scope. I heard them shuffle into the room and approach me. The crosshairs bounced over a thick growth of trees. At first I thought I was scouring the jungle for enemies of freedom. Then crosshairs passed over four teenage boys and two girls playing volleyball, and I realized with a stuttered breath that I was looking at a park.

My dad's heavy hand reached down and rubbed my shoulder. Heinous jerked inside of me to escape the comforting touch, and it made my whole body twitch. My dad pulled his hand back and stammered, "I'm so … sorry, Gavin. I … we … Your mom and I … we just want to help you. We just don't know how, buddy."

My dad hadn't called me buddy since I used to tumble and scuff my knees. Once I was old enough to tie my own shoes and wipe my own ass, I was Gavin, Gav if he was feeling casual. He was a stiff and serious little man. He taught calculus or some math theory with a long name, some bullshit like that. I never saw him teach, but I imagined it was much like hanging out with him on the weekend: pretty fucking boring. I could see him drooling on and on about polynomials and shit, dropping sly little jokes that left only the nerdiest birdies laughing and everyone else mad-dogging the clock or pondering the quickest means of suicide in your average college lecture hall. As far as I can remember, I never saw my dad with hair or without his black-rimmed glasses. He was round and jovial looking, but his cherubic features belied his serious nature. He was not a jolly person, though he could have jolly spells. However, he was totally different around my mom.

My mom was his exact opposite in a number of ways. She was a beautiful woman full of spirit and spontaneity. My dad had the shiny, smooth dome, and she had long, beautiful blond hair into which she dyed streaks of black that matched *her* black-rimmed glasses. Her high cheekbones and bright blue eyes were fabulous genetic gifts that she passed on to me. Her smile could light up a room and could make my dad's eyes twinkle like a Christmas tree. I never ever heard them fight and only heard them raise their voices a handful of times. They really loved each other. And I knew they loved me. Part of me wanted to shake off the vision playing out behind my eyelids and crumble into their loving arms. But the other part, the part that could feel every evil pulse and twitch from Heinous, knew the slightest sign of adoration would be a death sentence for them. So I kept my eyes clenched tightly shut and stared through the sniper's scope.

The crosshairs bounced and swung so fast I could only identify people as brightly colored blurs. They finally slowed as a family sitting at a bright red wooden picnic table came into view. The scope shook more as the crosshairs lined up on a teenage boy. The muffled whimpered apology of the previous host and the ghost of Heinous' growled response echoed inside my head.

My dad opened his mouth to say something else, but the rifle cracked in the overpowering vision. drowning out his words. The sharp reverberation echoed off the walls of my skull, and I jumped involuntarily. The scope leveled back out, and a red cloud hung lightly in the air where the teenager sat seconds before. The scope swung to the left, to a middle-aged woman with flecks of blood across her shocked pale face. She looked like she'd almost caught the magic trick that was the boy sitting next to her disappearing. Another kick of the rifle and her lower jaw vanished in a smear of red and white. The jawless woman swayed back into the arms of an elderly man wearing a godawful Bermuda print shirt. His forehead caught the next bullet, which lifted the back of his skull and splattered it onto the two men behind them. The two bodies slumped forward, and I heard the muffled memory of the other people in the park screaming. I also heard my parents get up and walk out of my room, offering meager *we love yous* as they slipped into the hallway. The door closed, and I opened my eyes.

Rather than fading, once freed from the screen of my eyelids, the vision intensified and solidified. One of the two men leapt forward to the felled older man and woman. He caught them, but the dead weight was more than he could handle, and they fell backwards on top of him like they were protecting him from the same bullet-riddled fate. The other man turned to run, but a bullet to his upper spine wrecked his escape plans. The scope swung back over the picnic table, surveying a blood-splattered feast of fried chicken laid out on bright plastic plates but finding no more victims. I shuddered to myself as crosshairs swung wildly, randomly, to the scattering people below. They followed a man in khaki shorts and a Cheap Trick t-shirt to his makeshift hiding place behind a giant terracotta planter. The rifle kicked twice. The first shot kicked a rooster tail of pottery and dirt into the air. The second birthed another victorious red blur that thickened the already fading dirt cloud to an ominous black.

My mind sagged against the onslaughts, starving for the blackness of dreamless sleep. Heinous flashed the same sniper memory over and over again. He mixed up the order of the kills after the first ten times I relived it. After the memory looped another dozen times, the people getting shot were people I knew. The boy at the picnic table was Joshie. He was laughing in his high chirpy laugh the split second before the headshot that began the massacre. The middle-aged woman was his skinny mom, her flat brown hair framing her awestruck blood-speckled face. The old man morphed into Joshie's tall, skinny father seconds before the bullet sheared off the top of his head. The man who turned and ran only to catch a hot one in the back was my dad. I felt beads of sweat as he turned and waddled furiously away from the carnage only to have the crosshairs dance across his swaying back. After him, the scope swung down and caught sight of the guy in the kakis and Cheap Trick t-shirt, who now had my face on. I could see the fear in my eyes as the man ducked behind the planter as I had seen so many times before. My throat went dry as Heinous began a growling peal of demonic laughter. As the bullet shattered terracotta, my parents knocked firmly and walked in behind me.

The vision vanished instantly. The morning sun was shining through my windows, and it blinded me, completing my total disorientation. I blinked against the harsh light and rubbed my fingers over my eyelids as if I could scrub the vision away. I didn't face my parents, but I caught sight of them out of the corner of my eye. They were dressed and ready for the new day, and I had sat at my desk all night, the clothes I wore the day before plastered to my body with sweat. I heard my mom sit gently at the foot of my bed. My dad took a few timid steps and reached out a hand for my shoulder. My mom whispered his name in a voice feeble from crying. She shook her head, and he pulled his hand back, choosing instead to rub his palms on his gray slacks. His cheeks went red, and he walked a slow half-circle around me, mentally preparing the words he was about to speak.

"Gavin, we've been on the phone all morning with your school. With your principal, the school counselor, and Dr. Tock." He paused to see if I would turn and look at him. When he saw I wasn't in a *turn and look* mood, he continued, "We all think you could use a little more time before going back. Principal Miehue told us you can keep getting the weekly assignments. He also told us your grades haven't slipped at all and you haven't missed a single assignment."

"Dennis." My mom's voice was a weak whisper. I opened my eyes and looked at them through the reflection on my window. Her voice sounded so sad, so strained. I knew she had cried all night, even in her sleep. My mom hadn't sounded that sad since Grandma Rose and Grandpa Max died in a car crash near Spokane. Aside from her eyes—which glistened with tears constantly—her soft, sweet, pained voice was all that betrayed her inner sadness. A ray of morning sunlight lit a tear on her cheek, and it sparkled like a bloody diamond before slipping off her face and onto the hardwood floor. A deep pang of guilt tugged at my empty stomach for being the cause of her sadness, and Heinous let me feel all of it.

I felt the warm humming sensation of Heinous getting all worked up behind my eyes. Guilt wracked my body the way a craving tortures a junkie smelling a crack rock being smoked in the hotel room next to his. The temporary longing for my dead grandparents managed to push him that much further.

"Son, the fact that you have somehow kept focus on your schoolwork with all that has happened is amazing to us. You," he pointed at my slouching figure, "are amazing.. We are here for you, Gavin, we understand ..."

I came alive at the lie. I stood with a jolt that spooked them both. The fury pushing behind my forehead wasn't mine alone.

"Understand?" I spat. "No one understands. Not that cocksucker Miehue. Not the twat of a school counselor Miss Evens. Not that wrinkled old fuckbag Dr. Tock. And sure the shit not you!"

My dad stumbled away, a look of shock draining the color from his face. He looked from me to my mom, who had jumped off my bed when I shouted. I could see anger mixing with my dad's sadness and confusion. A hot chill tickled up my spine. My mom put her hand on his forearm, and he relented. She kept her composure better, and she tried to look me in the eyes when she spoke to me.

"Sweetheart, we may not be able to *fathom* what you are feeling for Joshie, but we do understand. We've lost people too." I felt her eyes on me, twinkling with fresh tears.

"I can give them loss, Worm," Heinous offered like a buddy grabbing you a beer when he grabs one for himself.

Panic gripped me, and I shouted, "No!"

I pressed my knuckles against my forehead, and Heinous' rage pushed back. His anticipation warmed my blood like poison. Sweat dripped down my forehead, and it felt like my shirt collar had shrunk. My vision blurred and tinted red. I backed up until I walked into my desk chair. I crumbled into it and spun back around to my desk. I clamped my hands to my face, covering my eyes.

"Gavin?" they asked in frightened unison.

"Get out!" I bellowed back. They instead each took a step toward me, and the rage behind my eyes flared bright and ominous. Before the colors could fade or my parents could take another step, I slammed my face hard onto the cluttered surface of my desk in hopes of thwarting the murderous intent rising there. I felt my nose break with a snap, and a deep pain shot from the back of my head down my jaw line and into my chest.

"Get out!" I yelled again as blood filled my mouth.

"Oh God, Gavin," I heard my mom say as my dad pulled her out of my room.

I swallowed a mouthful of my own rust-flavored blood and shouted, "Out!" so loud and hard that gobs of it splattered all over my window. I heard them close the door, but they didn't walk away. I still felt relief that they were out of my room, away from me and that much safer.

"Someone has to die soon, Worm," Heinous whispered inside my head. "Your pain is sweet, but I want to taste their blood and see for myself which is sweeter."

Big painful sobs made my chest heave and tears form in my eyes at the hopelessness I felt at his words. I wheezed through my broken nose, and my breath whistled on every third breaths

"Pleabs," I begged my reflection, "stob." My next breath was answered by a hoarse laugh.

"Ahhh, a whistling worm!" He cackled. His laughter felt acidic, like it was making my brain bleed.

"Pleabs … nob mo," I pleaded between quaky wheezes.

Heinous answered, "Get used to it, Worm. It never ends. Take comfort in the fact that I'll eventually grow tired of you and let this weak body die. Of course, death ends nothing for you."

He was laughing hard and steady as the blood flowing out of my busted nose increased. I cupped my hands in a feeble attempt to catch the seeping blood.

"A wheezing, bleeding, whistling worm!"

"Shit," I uttered as the blood overflowed my hands and splashed all over my pant legs and the hardwood floor.

"It's just a little blood," Heinous snarled at me.

I looked at my reflection, and my attention was drawn to the single bloody tear crawling down my check. Twin rivers of dark crimson flowed from my ears down my face and chest. My brown X-Men t-shirt was already dark with sweat stains, but the overabundance of my blood was turning it a sickly green color. Blood dripped through my cupped fingers to my swollen crotch. The instant I noticed my erection, the iron smell of my blood changed to a sexual musk that made me dizzy. I was in pain and aroused at my own suffering. I hadn't eaten for days, and the sight of my blood vacating my body through a shattered nose made a different kind of dizzy feeling swim inside my head.

My eyes were glued to my gory reflection as blood spurted from my ears and mouth with every pulse of my racing heart. I blinked, and more bloody tears leaked from the corners of my eyes, smearing down my cheeks.

"I can make it stop, Worm. I won't, but I can," Heinous taunted me.

I winked at my reflection, arched back and headbutted my desk with everything I had, cutting through the fog of dizziness. I hit dead center and heard a crack the same way I heard Heinous sometimes:

inside my head and with my ears. As blackness rose up to meet me, I tasted chlorine and counted drowning as a blessing.

I walked through terrors unimaginable during the time I sat unconscious over my desk. I bumbled through nightmarish landscapes that tore at the fragile fabric of my soul. I lost a good fifteen hours to the coma sleep hell that resulted from smashing my head against my desk. The first thing I realized upon waking was the delicious smell of cooked bacon permeating the house. It was sweet nectar of the gods, sending drool slipping out the corner of my mouth and deep growls up from my starved stomach. It struck me that Heinous had healed my broken nose. I inhaled deeply, as if I could eat the meat of the fabulous odor. Before my teeth could sink into the smell, a pain so intense that everything went neon orange coursed through my head. I muffled a scream of agony with my forearm, and that only amplified the pain. I clenched my teeth and eyes against the pain, and it soaked into every inch of my head like a warm wet hell.

"Good morning, Worm." Heinous chirped at me in Joshie's high-pitched voice.

"God," I groaned through gritted teeth.

"Not even close, pal," he responded in my dad's baritone voice.

"I'm hungry," I moaned, ending my unspoken hunger strike. "I can't move with this headache." Every syllable sent fresh ripples of pain through my swimming head.

"This is what it feels like when your skull cracks from forehead to base," he told me in his own vicious gravelly voice. "I healed the fracture, but I wanted you to feel the pain you left me with when your weak ass passed out. Never again, Worm."

The headache faded quickly, leaving an uncomfortable tingling sensation in its wake. I blinked away the wetness that blurred my eyes. All the blood that had flowed from my ears, nose, and eyes and splattered everywhere was gone. There were a few patches of dried brown blood from the initial breaking of my nose, but otherwise the area was clean.

"It was never there, Worm," Heinous told me as I gazed at my hands, which I last remembered catching rivers of my blood. The realization that Heinous had made the blood appear and disappear was sinking in when I heard the front door slam. I leaned forward on my desk to watch my parents leave. My dad opened the passenger door to the Volkswagen for my mom and then walked around to the driver's side. He tossed his backpack in the miniscule back seat and unceremoniously plopped into his seat. I watched the baby blue Bug until it rounded the corner before standing and stretching my cramped muscles. The smell of bacon coaxed me toward my door the way a snake charmer makes his snakes dance. My stomach ached and growled as I lumbered down the stairs to the tempting breakfast flesh waiting for me.

My parents had been making me an extra plate of breakfast every day even though I never ate it. I could imagine them exchanging sorrowful looks as they dumped full plates of breakfast into the trash when they arrived home after work. I stumbled stiffly into the kitchen and saw that they had left me a cinnamon raison bagel, two eggs, and three pieces of the applewood smoked bacon that was singularly responsible for ruining my feeble plan of starving myself to death. I reached into the cupboard for the syrup with one hand and tore the bagel open with the other. I put the cold bacon on top of the even colder eggs and put it all on the bottom of the bagel. I covered the entire thing with maple syrup and squished the top down on it so that syrup ran out the sides and pooled on the plate. My stomach kicked forcefully for the food it knew was coming.

"I'm so hungry," I moaned out loud as I gripped my sandwich.

"Me too," Heinous told me with impatience.

As he spoke, a new vision flashed clear as reality before my eyes. I was strangling someone from behind and slamming her head into the floor at the same time. I held the sandwich inches from my open mouth as the victim in the vision slouched lifelessly to the floor. The owner of the eyes through which I stared reached down and tore off a worn leather belt before ripping the dress from his lifeless victim.

"I can't eat while you do that," I told Heinous in a voice weak with hunger. "I can't do anything while you do that."

"Give me new memories then, Worm. I want new visions of rape and misery and pain."

"Fine," I told him. I would have told him anything to make it stop long enough for me to eat the pile of food in my shaky hands. I felt his need like I felt my body's need for nourishment. The vision faded slowly, like waking begrudgingly from a dream, until the only thing I could see was the stack of tasty breakfast inches from my maw. Once it had my full attention, I scarfed that bad boy in four big greedy bites.

I followed the sandwich with two heaping bowls of Fruity Pebbles in an attempt to calm my hunger-scarred stomach. I drank milk straight from the gallon jug, and it ran down my chin and neck like blood had the night before. The thought made me even hungrier, and I ransacked the cupboards for grub. I settled on a box of Saltines and a package of generic cookies. I stacked them and walked out of the kitchen only to turn right back around and grab the half-empty gallon of milk as well. I stopped at the stairs, set the milk and munchies on the bottom step, and slid open the sliding glass door to our back yard.

I'd spotted my old aluminum bat lying under a half-rolled hose next to the house. I reached down, grabbing the bat and tossing the hose mess aside in one quick movement. I scanned the trees in our back yard, a few thick pines and old cedars, and felt a rush of adrenaline I knew was Heinous. He didn't know what I was doing, but he was getting excited just the same. I spotted what I was looking for on the wide trunk of a pine right in front of the old wooden fence that separated our yard from the one behind us. I took off at it in a dead run. My bare feet kicked up small dirt clouds as I trampled over earth and pine needles toward my target. I was so focused that I didn't notice the half-gallon of milk sloshing in my stomach or the pine needles digging into my feet as I ran. An intense tingle racked my body when Heinous realized what I was up to. I raised the bat over my head and opened my eyes so wide they watered. I felt muscles flex and swell as my legs moved me faster to the tree and the squirrel clinging to it in a patch of sunlight.

I ran past the tree, swinging the bat with all my weight. My arms flexed and moved with the added power of Heinous. The squirrel was smashed between metal and tree before it knew what had happened. Fur, blood, and bark exploded in different directions, and the bat—which bent in an awkward angle from the force—shot backwards like a big metal boomerang. I felt a rising roar of laughter and stifled it, taking slow, deliberate steps around to the front of the tree.

Tufts of bloody fur floated lazily to the ground in the still morning air. A few scraps of destroyed squirrel littered the base of the pine. One still twitched for a second, but even after grabbing it and giving it a squeeze, I couldn't tell what part it was. To be honest, I don't think his squirrel mother could. I breathed deep and surveyed the carnage. A rush of endorphins tickled the back of my neck and set me swaying on my feet. I stumbled to the garage and found a black garbage bag. Heinous was replaying the squirrel death over and over as I picked up scraps from the ground and peeled others from the tree bark. I filled the bag with gore and wrapped it closed before burying it in our garbage cans.

"What are you doing?" Heinous asked me.

"Throwing it away."

"Why, Worm?" His confusion was obvious and genuine.

"So my parents don't find it. You've wrecked shop on my happy little world. If Mom and Dad start finding bloody scraps of things all over their yard, they'll put me away. Just me and you and a rubber room."

His silence signaled his understanding, but instead of a response, the vision of aluminum on squirrel began flashing again. Another wave of pleasure washed over me, and I felt like I was floating as I walked back up the stairs with my arms filled with eats and drink. Every nerve in my body was alive with pleasure. Rolling waves of euphoria emanated from the back of my neck and washed me in satisfaction. Sliding my foot into my slipper was a deep tissue massage. My t-shirt rubbing on my back and chest was a dozen silken mouths kissing and licking my chest, neck, and back. I crumpled into bed and slept the sleep of the exhausted damned until evening, when my parents arrived home.

I was sitting at my desk doing homework when I saw the Bug pull into the driveway. I watched them through the window as they waked hand in hand to the door. Once they were out of sight, I could hear them echo throughout the house. When they reached the kitchen and found my breakfast eaten and the milk supply diminished, I heard their muffled tones become more excited. I heard them chatter to each other up the stairs. They had gotten used to me ignoring their knocks, so they were already opening the door as they gave their token raps on it.

I pretended not to notice and, in a halfway cheery voice, said, "Come in."

They were already peeking in at me with slight looks of embarrassment when I spun around in my chair. I smiled weakly, but it was mask enough.

"Hi, guys. Breakfast was delicious."

My mom giggled suddenly and covered her mouth but not her smile. I saw tears of joy sparkle in the corner of her eyes.

"Are you hungry for dinner?" my dad asked excitedly.

My mom giggled again and slapped his shoulder softly. They smiled sheepishly at each other, and he nodded his understanding.

"How are you feeling, Gavin?" my mom asked, rubbing my dad's shoulder to keep from hugging me.

"Better," I answered honestly. Since I wasn't watching the murder marathon that was Heinous, I could actually do more than lie around, despondent to reality. I smiled at them and motioned to the desktop cluttered with schoolwork. "I've been working at this all day, and it's wiped me out. I'll pass on dinner, but I'll be downstairs for breakfast in the morning."

I allowed each a small hug before they left. I listened to them walking away until they were just optimistic mumbles moving through the house. I lay down on the bed and watched the exploding squirrel vision until I was completely numb to it.

Dream: Fear of the Light

Everything is black. I stand in total nothingness, free from sensation.

Then something shifts. At first I can't tell if it is something nearby in the black or if it is me. The darkness is thick and heavy. I don't physically feel a wall behind me, but I know somehow that there is one. I reach out my hand and baby step forward. I move slowly; the darkness is denser than air.

I hear sounds around me: odd shifting, shuffling, and slithering noises.

After only a few steps, my fingers find a wall. I feel warped wooden boards crammed so tightly together that no light passes through. I hear muffled laughter beyond the wall.

The darkness presses against me, coating my skin with a greasy film.

I sense movement and feel something rub against me. I move to get away, but I don't feel my legs. I feel something else behind me. My movements are wiggles and shudders. Every movement bumps me into something else. Strange skin rubs against every inch of me.

All at once, the darkness is alive and slithering against me.

Prismatic neon suddenly shines down weakly from above. I look toward the source of the lights and see a multitude of tentacles swinging hypnotically back at me. Each is lined with tiny horns, and each horn radiates a different color. A tentacle dances directly above, teasing, moving as if to cast its malevolent glow upon me. Instead it wraps around a lump of wiggling darkness next to me. It pulls its catch close to me before the neon horns shimmer brightly enough for me to see what it claims. A thick three-foot-long worm wriggles, its flesh pale against the constricting glowing tentacle.

The creature has two faces, both human and identical in features. However, one is living and one is dead. Strands of wire stitch the mouth of the living face closed. It stares at me with eyes that are terribly aware. The face next to it has the same wire stitching, this time on the sunken eyelids. The eyeballs from the eternally closed eyes are stuffed into the dead face's mouth. As the tentacle carries the two-faced worm away, the thick blackness returns.

I feel it move against me.

Another tentacle, thicker and brighter than the last, reaches toward me. The glow from the rainbow of neons stretches horrible shadows up the weathered wood walls. All around me, the darkness slithers.

I try to move, but I only twist and roll. My skin feels rough, and the darkness rubs against me. The colorful tips glow bright enough for me to see other two-faced worms all around me. They squirm weakly, as if the lights on the tentacles disturb their hellish existence. The tip of the tentacle reaches for me, the lights dancing across the shack full of worms like disco acid flashbacks.

It touches me. It tickles over my lips, plucking over the wires stitched through my mouth. It caresses my cheek. It reaches around me and constricts. In the terrible light it shines down on me, I see the truth.

My Sick Story: Broken Branches on the Family Tree

Heinous still flashed his memories but not as often. I was able to concentrate and did my best to act normal. I knew Heinous wouldn't be satisfied with a simple squirrel. He would make me kill my parents. A voice deep inside told me they knew it too. Maybe they didn't know I was to be under the executioner's hood, but I'm sure they sensed the change in me. They knew me too well, loved me too much, not to see the evil just under my skin. I think Heinous showed them glimpses of his true self hiding within me. They still smiled at me, but more with anxiety than with the excitement they showed when I started eating and talking again. I think they could feel it. I knew it, and I knew I couldn't stop him. I couldn't surprise him and blurt anything out. He'd fill my throat with thorns. I knew I couldn't stop him, but he didn't seem to be in a rush. He loved the trickle of constant anxiety I fed him when my parents were around me.

I finished the semester at home, and it was decided I'd take another shot at school when the new semester began. Everything was so crazy the first few days after Joshie's death that I forgot about the Aries. It stayed parked at the forest until the sheriff called my mom and dad to tell them someone had shattered every window and slashed every tire. I hadn't had the motivation to fix it, so it sat untouched in our garage, and my mom gave me a ride the day I went back to school. I had one last visit with my shrink, just to get my final clearance to go back to school. My mom drove me to the shrink's office and then to school after that. We were sitting in the waiting room until quarter to eleven, and by eleven thirty I was staring at the front doors of the school, gripping a bag full of generic burgers. I opened the door, but froze before climbing out. A single bloody handprint was smeared across the big glass window in the front doors.

My mom smiled at me and asked if I was sure I was up to it.

"Of course," I reassured her. "I'm feeling much better, Mom. Besides, my life can't stop anytime something bad happens, right?"

An ultra-fast montage of Heinous' visions flashed at the words. I watched a hundred snuff films in under a minute. They were over as suddenly as they began, but they left the rusty taste of blood behind.

My mom's soft, sweet voice brought me back to reality. "Gav, I know you're doing better. I believe that ... I see that," she said with a smile spread wide across her beautiful face. "But look how bad your hand is shaking, baby boy."

I followed her gaze to my hand still holding the door handle with my index and middle finger locked in a steel-tight kung fu grip on the black molded plastic. I was shaking like a meth head in court. I let go of the handle and held my shaky hand level in front of me, low enough that no one walking by would happen a glance. My hand trembled like it was in need of a fix. Watching it shake made my eyeballs feel like they were trembling too. I closed my eyes and squeezed my hand tight into a fist.

Heinous laughed a sudden harsh chuckle that made me jump inside myself. My violent twitch scared my mom, and she jumped back as well. Her door wasn't open, so she bounced her ponytail off the window softly.

"Jesus, Gav," she said with a light little laugh. "Are you sure?"

I rubbed my shaky fist with my other hand, attempting to massage the jumps right out of it. I dug deep in my sudden confusion and found the reassuring smile I had been looking for. The one that said, "I'm cool, Mom. Now go home and chill the hell out." I flashed it at her and said, "Okay, woman, if you have to hear it, then fine." I winked to back up the award-winning smile. "I'm a little nervous ... okay, nervous as hell. But I'm cooler than a polar bear's toenails."

It worked, and a kiss on the cheek later I was watching the Bug pull away. I walked in the front door and decided to get a soda out of the machine just inside. The vice principal was standing at the machine, grabbing a drink for himself.

"Mr. Wagner, how are we doing today?" he asked, sounding a little surprised to see the smile on my face.

"We," I told him with a sincere grin, "are feeling good enough to run for mayor. First step is us helping out the chess club," I told him as I slid a crisp dollar bill in the machine under the small plastic plaque that read, "All Proceeds Go to the Chess Club." Some one had scrawled "Dorks" in big letters across the whole thing.

He smiled and tipped his unopened soda at me. "I'd vote for ya," he told me as he turned back toward the air conditioning of his office.

"Lying prick," I mumbled, and Heinous growled as my Pepsi slammed into view at the mouth of the machine.

I took my soda and my hamburgers and sat on one of the hard stone benches in front of the entrance. Before I even took my first bite, the bell sounded, signaling lunch for the students. I couldn't see the back door, the one leading to the student parking lot, but I could imagine the rush of hungry bellies cramming their way through it in a hurry to grab a fast-food lunch and get back before the next bell rang. A few kids walked out the front doors without noticing me as they snuck away toward the gym.

I took big, slow bites and long, deep drinks. I watched kids mill around the quad, some reading books, others playing a rowdy round of hacky sack. I blinked and everyone was covered in mortal wounds. They didn't seem to notice their slit throats gushing blood over their No Fear t-shirts as much as I did. I took another drink, and they were back to normal when I lowered my soda.

I was just crumpling the wrapper into a tight little ball when the bell rang. In another five minutes, it would ring again and students not in their seats would be marked tardy. I tossed my garbage in a trashcan and walked through the doors and into the flood of teenagers on the other side.

Apparently, some things had changed since I had last been at school—the most shocking of which being how the tragedy of a lost Joshie could bring together Bull and Miss Sarah Jackson. They had been romantically linked since his disappearance, unbeknownst to me, of course. I saw Sarah and Bull walking toward me but didn't think anything about it.

I guess Bull still had hard feelings over me calling her a slut and such. I saw his hulking form for only half a second before his oversized fist hit me hard on my left cheek. I stumbled forward into people who were suddenly upset over their front-row seats as trickles of blood splashed at them from an ugly gash Bull's fist had opened in my face. Heinous laughed the sudden harsh laugh again as a second massive fist hit me, this time in the back of my head. I felt my anger rise faster than the pain, a fury I fully intended to unleash on Bull.

I ducked his next swing, a wild haymaker aimed at my head, and stepped closer to him. I rolled back on my ankles, ready to throw a fist hard into his tubby tummy, but my hand was impossible to lift. I felt like it was made of solid stone. My body still rolled backwards, and I twisted both ankles when my arms couldn't follow my body's momentum. Bull saw me stumble backwards, and he followed me with frenzied shots to my face.

One swelled my right eye closed, and another shattered my nose, causing a familiar flush of blood down my chin and t-shirt.

"You need this, Worm," Heinous laughed. "You are weak. Savor your pain, Worm, and the taste of humiliation. You need this."

I hit the ground and rolled onto my hands and knees. Heinous' laugh was no longer just sharp, sudden bursts; it was a constant noise in my head. The crowd was a blur as it had been when Sarah had hugged me and then pissed herself. It had become the same faceless blur that buzzed with sound but not really voices. Only Sarah wasn't blurred, standing clear as day right behind Bull with her hands curled into fists and her eyes wide with excitement at both the size of the crowd and the brutality of my beating.

Her shrill voice crackled louder than the static of the crowd as she commanded him, "Kick his ass, baby!" over and over, louder and louder. I heard each blow as it landed, echoing inside my skull. But loudest of all, I heard Heinous laughing at me. He was laughing in his own harsh bark of a laugh and with Joshie's happy chirp.

My vision went red with rage as I tried to stand. My legs shook and refused to support my weight. My clenched fists were still lead weights at the ends of my flexed and straining arms. Bull grabbed me by my collar and pulled me off the ground so he could look me in the eye without bending over. I could only see him out of one eye, and Heinous winked it at him when we locked stares.

"Motherfucker!" he growled at me.

The crowd's buzz was rising to a roar. Sarah was jumping and waving her fists in the air as she screamed even higher. Heinous roared and chirped at me. Bull tightened his fists, which in turn tightened my collar around my neck. He tugged upward and I was staring down at him at least a foot off the floor, my fists still pulling toward the ground against my will.

"Son of a bitch! Pussy!" he yelled so close to my face that he sprayed me with spittle and blasted me with oven-hot breath that smelled like hotdogs and nachos. "Fight back!"

My arms burned from my forearms deep into my shoulders, even down my back, as I strained to lift a fist to smash his big hick mouth shut. I could feel the rage pounding in my head like a drumbeat while Joshie and Heinous laughed at the trifecta of my frustration, humiliation and, of course, physical pain. As if to prove my point, Bull grunted an untranslatable curse word, lowered me to my knees, and kicked me like I was an old tractor in his dad's field. His size thirteen Nike caught me about an inch below my sternum, and it fucking hurt. He still had a death grip on my collar so tight that either my neck or his hands were bleeding. Tiny crimson droplets fell to the white tiles as my vision turned a very fuzzy, very shaky red. He had succeeded in kicking any wind I had in me out, and I gasped for air in his face, much like a fish does when he is pulled into the boat and faces the beast that caught him.

Still the laughing and the drum-like rage rolled back and forth in my head while the crowd buzzed around us.

I had been escorted out of the school just for speaking to Sarah, yet as this shit kicker was kicking the shit out of me, no one in any authoritative role was to be seen. As he let one fist unclench around my collar, I fell slightly forward and managed a few sharp gasps of air before his ham of a fist smashed into my face. Finally, after at least three more solid right hands to my face, someone pulled him off of me. I fell face first onto the blood-splattered floor, and both Bull's and

Sarah's yells were absorbed by the buzz of the crowd. As I blinked, clearing my eyes of blood and tears, I felt my hands curl under me, weak and tired from fighting against Heinous' iron control. The only sound I could hear besides the slow hushing of the crowd was the laughter echoing off the inside of my skull.

I felt a gentle touch on my shoulder and heard a soft voice that barely stood out against the buzz around us.

"Gavin … Gavin, are you okay? Jesus, what did the boy do?" The school nurse leaned closer as if trying to hear the extent of my beating. I turned my face toward her so she could see the cuts I could feel.

"Oh, sweetie," she said, and her tone made me think of my mom's soft, sweet voice.

I inched up onto my knees and elbows to get a look at her face. The woman was wearing her customary faux hospital uniform, but my mom's face was staring back at me. Her eyes were blank and dead. Her skin was so pale as to take on a soft blue tinge against the white of the nurse's outfit. Bright red wounds crisscrossed her face and forehead up under her hair. The skin of her hairline looked burnt. It looked as if someone had started to peel her face but had stopped—or been interrupted—after just getting it started. She leaned closer and the dead eyes rolled toward me. The sockets that held her eyes had the same burnt and peeling look as her forehead.

Glaring at me through hard white cataracts, she spoke. "Let me help you up and out of here. Come into my office and we'll call your parents." When she reached for me, I screamed and jumped back, falling on my ass. I hit the ground, rolled to my feet, and was backing toward the door before her pale dead hands could touch me. I stood there swaying and bleeding, looking at the now-silent crowd. The laughing and the buzz had died when I jumped back, and as I stood there, the blur died as well. I saw rows and rows of frightened faces, some alight with excitement but most just staring at me as blood plastered my shirt to my wheezing chest.

I still remember every face staring with shock as I rocked back and forth toward the door. I didn't dare turn my back, because the two teachers that had torn Bull off of me had stopped restraining him and watched me with the rest of the silent crowd. Rows of pale face stared at me, unblinking. I reached behind me for the door, missing on my first few attempts at hitting the bar that released it. As I hit it and the sound of steel separating from steel broke the silence, I could hear a buzz building at the back of the crowd. As I pivoted to leave my high school for what turned out to be the last time, I saw a few dark eyes blink as the buzz grew again to an even greater roar than before.

I spun into the sunlight and went blind until I could cover my eyes with my traitorous hands. I took long, fast strides, trying to outrun the roar that I could still hear building from inside. In a matter of minutes, I was blocks away, not really running, just walking with quick, long strides. Heinous had been strangely silent since he made the nurse look like a dead version of my mom. I felt a panic that I thought should sound like a klaxon as I ducked and hopped my way down alleys and across back yards and through more alleys. After a while, the back yards got bigger and the roads became long, lazy country roads. I was cutting through the air at great speed, but I felt no cool wind on my face. I was sweating, I remember that. A slow burning sank into my leg muscles. I had walked miles in minutes.

As I strode away from neighborhoods, over hills, and past farms, I realized I was going to the forest. I hadn't been back in at least a month, because walking around the forest by my lonesome could send the signal that I wasn't improving. I had, however, replayed that vision so many times that I knew the placement of every pinecone around us and the sound of every different bone breaking. The burning in my legs rolled higher up my legs with each step, working its way up to my hips. When the hills got closer together and steeper as I drew closer to the mountain, I eased my path onto the road. I was moving up and down the rolling hills at an amazing speed.

My body felt like it was being pushed down the hills and then pulled up them. My legs made impossibly long strides, and my bewildered body followed. We walked like the wind and as straight as the crow flies. A few more long, possessed steps and we were past the grassy hillsides and dodging around trees growing thick in the forest.

We moved so fast the scenery flew by at breakneck speed. Over fallen trees and under reaching branches we raced, Heinous still silent even as he pushed me forward.

For a few steps, we traveled along the side of the creek, and in a few more, I was standing in front of the thorns and the rock wall behind them. Without a word, Heinous relinquished control of my body and I fell forward, depleted from performing a ten- to fifteen-mile walk in a matter of minutes. I lay face down in the warm mud of the creek bed with my hands over my head, shaking as I gasped for air that didn't ever seem to satisfy my need for it. From the arches of my feet to my hips, my muscles burned and ached. I felt painful "pops" up and down my legs as tired, overworked nerves pushed to the brink finally gave and were torn in hundreds of different directions as my legs swelled with fluid wrung from exhausted tissues.

I raised my eyes to look at the high white rock wall in front of me, fully expecting to see bloody handprints covering its face. To my surprise, the rock was bare. I crawled to my knees and looked around me. The memory of that day flashed softly, and the hair on the back of my neck stood firm like a ghost was rubbing a finger over my skin.

As always with the forest, the landscape had changed in my absence. From where I knelt in the mud in front of the thorn bushes, I could see the tree where Bull had been swinging when he fell. The tree to which the rope swing had been tied had fallen. It was a thick cedar that had been used as a swing for generations of drunken tree-swingers with its wide branches and prime location halfway up the hill. Kids would jump until they snagged a fingertip on the rope, and then they could take it back up the hillside and around the trunk of the big cedar. Years of feet running and skidding down the hillside had made a natural cut in the ground that acted as both a natural runway and a ramp. A quick run and hard jump and into the air they sailed, hearts pumping, eyes wide, and smiles pure. But now that mighty cedar had fallen. It had landed downhill on another large stump that split the great cedar in two. I knelt there in the mud and thought of what the next generation of kids would do instead of swinging from that cedar. In a year or two, people would forget how much joy that one thick mother of a cedar tree brought to so many kids. How many afternoons had the excited shouts filled the forest from the rope swing? How many friendships had been forged in the shade of the massive tree? It was where Bull and Joshie had bonded over Bull's clumsy acrobatics.

I saw my memory like a ghost. I saw a skinny little Joshie help the big, dumb, embarrassed, hard-slugging son of a whore Bull to his feet next to the all-too-real cedar split in half on the hillside.

For the first time in weeks, I thought about Joshie. Not as the stomping bag that played itself over and over again in my head, but as my friend. After weeks of his vicious death replaying itself, I had started seeing him not as my lifelong friend, but as something that died fast and had to be stomped into eternity. But as I lay there, where we killed him, I couldn't help but remember him as the kind, quirky soul he was. I couldn't feel guilt for what we had done, but I felt the longing of missing your best friend. My heart ached, and I blinked, hoping for tears to wet my wind-dried eyes.

My breath hitched in my chest, and I spoke his name aloud for the first time in weeks. "Joshie ... Oh, Joshie," I moaned to the mud. I expected Heinous to scoff at my sob for my fallen friend; nothing seemed to please him more. Yet still nothing from the violent being in my head. I took a few deep breaths and looked at the thorn bushes in front of me. The stick that Joshie and I had used the morning of his death to hold back the treacherous thorn branches was holding a mass of thorny bushes now. I winced and knew I had to crawl into the mess of thorns. I stayed on my knees and crawled under the most fearsome-looking branches. My good eye looked ahead, and I noticed without surprise that the clearing had returned. I crawled into the clearing and across it to rest my still-burning legs and lie against the rock wall. I closed both eyes and let my head rest against the wall behind me.

I squinted into the sun and was startled when I heard Joshie's voice.

"Hey, Gav." I spun around frantically to see where his voice came from.

His chirpy laugh filled the still forest air, and he told me, "Down here, pal."

137

I looked down between my feet and saw the hole into which I had stuffed him. His severed head smiled at me from where it sat propped on the edge of the hole and bleeding from the neck. His eyes were held open with long thorns that could have been plucked from any one of the branches around us. I would never have recognized him looking as he did, but for the fact that we had made him look this way. His skinny nose was broken and bent so it resembled that of a boxer. His smile was unnaturally wide because of the fractures of his jaw. It was broken in three different places, including at his chin, so his whole face looked almost comically elongated. His smile had gaps where teeth had been knocked out with fist or foot. Some teeth were broken and chipped but remained covered in dark brown bloodstains. Gashes cut across both cheeks. His head was terribly misshapen. It was caved in at sharp angles on the right side, just at his forehead, from a stomp, and the entire back of his skull was concave where the rock had crushed through to his brain, killing him.

"Long time no see, Gav," he told me, and blood trickled from his wide broken smile, dripping down his chin and into the dirt. "How have you been?" he chirped at my shocked expression.

"Shitty," I told my buddy's decapitated talking head.

"Fuck you," he told me with the same happy voice and wide madman grin. "You have no idea about shitty, my friend." He didn't sound like he was even a little bit mad, but his eyes were skinning me alive. Other than his newfound use of profanity, he seemed in great spirits. He stared at me with his angry eyes, smiling, waiting for me to say something. I realized that since he was dead, he could wait in uncomfortable silence longer than I, so I asked the first thing that came to my head.

"Are you in Hell, Joshie?"

His loud, chirpy laugh rang out again, sounding excited at the thought.

"Oh no, good buddy. I'm in the place people in Hell have nightmares about."

He laughs again, and his lips split a little. His smile grows even wider, reminding me of the Cheshire cat.

"Surely you have begun to understand what has happened, right, Gav?"

"Heinous … He made me kill you," I stammer.

"Ironic. Heinous is where I am too. It's so bad, Gavin. The screams are laughter and the pain eternal." He chuckles more of his happy-sounding laugh while his eyes try to scream in agony.

"Where time doesn't even exist, how long is forever, Gav?" His head rolls a little to the side like a dog with a question. The movement rustles pinecones and spills more thickened blood into the hole.

I knew something was inside of me. I knew that the thing inside of me thrived on pain and misery. But I only knew it as a something. A something named Heinous. I knew the past few months hadn't been a dream, despite hoping so on countless sleepless nights as I watched the murder visions flash nonstop. I guessed Joshie knew more than me, even in death, and it was tickling rage somewhere deep down in my belly.

"You are a vision he is making me see." I told the head at the edge of the hole. "Like the school nurse and the bloody handprints on this rock wall." I jerked my thumb over my shoulder at the wall. "He made me see the handprints even before we killed you, before he climbed inside me. So you can't be real. You're just here because he's messing with me."

"Fuck you twice, my friend!" he squealed and then roared with laughter.

He wheezed through his broken nose and coughed up more dark brown blood to trickle down his chin.

"I'm the vision? Ha! I told you to leave that stone alone and you just fucking couldn't, could ya?" His harsh words and perky voice were a stark contrast to each other.

"I'm not the only one here, Gavin. And we'll be here forever. You too eventually, you know. But not right now."

"What …" I started to ask, but he interrupted.

"I'm here and you are standing outside your parents' bathroom, seconds away from killing your mom. See you again, Gav, sooner or later."

His voice faded and I was standing in the darkened hallway outside of my parents' bathroom. I stood in the shadows and heard some dumb game show on the seventeen-inch television that Mom insisted on watching while she soaked in the tub after a long day of teaching the disenchanted youth of today. I heard water splash and my mom scoff at an answer given by the current contestant.

"Welcome back, Worm," Heinous greeted me inside my head.

Before I had time to say anything or even think anything, my hand reached up and turned the doorknob. My body lunged forward through the door, and I felt pinned inside myself again as we stepped into the room. I was looking out my own eyes like they were the eyes of a stranger again, and the tiny piece of my stomach that was still mine started to turn.

"Gavin, get out of here!" she yelled at me as she jumped backwards, covering her breasts with her arm. My right hand shot forward and pushed my mom's television set into the bathtub with her. My gaze locked on her panicked face as the set hit the water. I felt Heinous' sick thrill rising with my mom's loud panicked breaths. As the television sank, the lights blew out in a spark. With a loud electrical hiss and a sick sizzling pop, we were left standing in the dark in total silence. I could smell the thick odor of burnt flesh, but my vision remained black. My mom's deep breaths had died as instantaneously as the lights before she even managed a single scream of pain, depriving Heinous of the possibility of a sound he could relish over and over again in my head. He knew as well as I that my mom was dead, flash fried by the television set she insisted on keeping perched precariously while she bathed.

Like a selfish lover, she had reached her climax first, leaving Heinous unsatisfied and confused, standing inside me in the bathroom as the smell of burnt flesh and burnt wires filled the air. He had expected to see her flail in the water, lights flashing, panic and pain drenching her screams, terror and agony radiating from her eyes. As it was, he had no vision to replay over and over. A small sense of triumph rose inside me at his failure, even as my mom lay slaughtered and cooked in the bathtub beside us.

Joshie had died too fast as well, but Heinous had the time to make me break every bone to give him something to cherish. As the smoke from the bathtub and sockets burned my eyes, the sound of sirens cut brashly into the silence.

He didn't have time to do anything else, no postmortem atrocities for my mommy. I couldn't cry for the woman who had clothed me, fed me, comforted me and above all else, loved me. The pain of her loss was like death to me. I felt so much hope drift away on wisps of smoke from the bathtub. I felt helpless already without her, and she was only ten seconds into Hell, but no tears would come. At least I thought to myself that there was nothing more we could do to her. *Team Wagner wins the battle, but not the war,* I thought madly to myself.

My sense of triumph grew even more at the greatest gift I could possibly give my mom under the insane circumstances: the gift of a quick death.

A fury rose hard and fast at my happiness. The eyes through which I was looking were overtaken by invisible thorns that twisted into me. Every nerve in my body was set aflame at once. My body felt like the old iron maiden torture devices from an even older England, trapping my soul to endure incomprehensible pain. My mind unraveled, and my entire being seemed to scream in pain and beg for mercy at once. I was torn apart with jagged blades over and over again, all while my body turned and strode out of the bathroom. I suffered a thousand deaths thrashing inside my prisonlike body as it walked down the stairs to the front door.

As my body started down the stairs, the sound of someone pounding on the front door broke into my pain and gave me something to focus on. I heard the knock again, louder and clearer, and the pain stopped as suddenly as it had started. My body fell limp and I vomited over the railing before I tripped the last few stairs to land hard on my elbows and my tender face. The force of my landing reopened the gashes on my checks and eye that Bull had inflicted, and blood stuck like a web between my face and the floor. I let loose a scream of pain and frustration, and whoever was knocking heard me and opened our door, blinding me with flashlights.

I screamed again, partly because the unexpected brightness had scared me and partly because my entire being still throbbed at my punishment. I flinched at the beams of light cutting through the smoke-filled house to blind me and let my scream taper into a bloody spit. I was going to tell them that I had killed her, that he had made me, that we would never stop, that I had to die, but when I started to speak, thorns rose in my throat and Heinous screamed out words in my voice. "Oh my God! She's gone! Mommy!" he wailed out loud for the rescuers to hear, laughing inside my head all the while.

"Why?" Blood trickled out of my mouth as he wailed on. "God, why? She's gone! My mommy is dead! Someone, please help me!"

A blanket was thrown over my sprawled form and someone's arms helped me to my feet. As we were being led out the front door amidst billows of rancid-smelling smoke, we saw a fireman wave his hand in front of his face, gag a few times and vomit next to mine.

Heinous chuckled and told me, "It never ends, Worm. Never."

I was starting to believe him.

I was taken to the hospital for smoke inhalation, but of course, I was physically fine. I would be fine as long as Heinous wanted me that way. I sat at the hospital until my poor distraught dad came to pick me up. His eyes were swollen and red from constant crying. He grabbed me firmly in a big, sad dad bear hug. He was shorter than I, just a pudgy little man who had lost the best thing he had ever known, and his head rested on my shoulder. Within seconds, he was blubbering on me, soaking my t-shirt in fresh salty tears. I held one arm around his back and rubbed his bald head with the other.

Sadness was one of the only emotions Heinous hadn't taken from me, and I felt it in spades now. My heart sank for my dad. He had lost his parents in high school ("Just like you, Worm."), and my mother was his world. He got an insane settlement from his parents' death. Goofy as he was, he could have had any piece of eye candy swinging on his elbow and spending his money, but he met my mom at school and fell in love. He was a nerdy kid and lived like a broke college student, tracking his money meticulously, spending only for tuition and basic human needs like shelter and food. She didn't even know he was filthy, stinking rich until after their wedding night. She loved him and respected him. He bought her a nice house, and she gave him a son. A son who would toss a television set into the bathtub with her one fine afternoon, but a son nonetheless. They both made fairly good money teaching, and they both loved doing it.

They really were the two most compatible people I have ever seen, before or since. Opposites only in the physical sense, they had the same taste in movies (cheesy, feel-good family crap and brainless buddy comedies), music (easy listening and longwinded hippie blues jam band), and the outdoors. I had been going with Joshie to the forest for a long time, but I had been going with my parents since before I could walk. They loved the trees and the mountain air, and they instilled that love in me, but I enjoy heavy metal and horror movies instead of their pallid fare.

It hit me one day when I was fifteen. We sat down to watch the Lion King, and I hated it. I hated everything I had sat through and smiled at a thousand times. I made a point of playing my headphones as loud as mechanically possible anytime I had to be in the car with them for any extended amount of time.

I played my music loud and covered my walls with posters of the walking dead and skeletons. I stole their pot and smoked it with my friends and had no qualms about going through a wallet or a purse for cash. I guess something inside me had always been slightly heinous on its own. Maybe that was why I wanted the stone and Joshie didn't. It doesn't matter now anyway. What's done is done.

My dad cried on my shoulder for a good half-hour before he even tried to talk. Heinous sucked in the sadness and cherished it. He was still insanely angry at how Mom's death had ended, up but my dad's pure heartbreak was like wine to the fiend inside me. For some reason, he could only hold onto emotions if he had the vision and soundtrack to go with it, so he drank his fill of sadness as he could get it. My dad was currently a supercharged battery of sorrow for Heinous to feed on. He had been leeching off of my sadness over her loss from the instant the TV sank, but I had no guilt or shame, only sadness. My dad blamed himself, as is common when a loved one passes, and Heinous relished it. My dad cried into my chest that we were going to be okay. He told me he didn't know how, but we would.

"We still have each other," he reminded me through tear-filled eyes. "God, I loved her more than anything, Gav." He inhaled deeply and sobbed big wet sobs as he exhaled. He patted me on the back and hitched up his pants. He blinked his swollen red eyes at the rows of fluorescent bulbs overhead before he started crying again.

"I don't want to go home, Gav," he confessed. "I don't think I can, at least not for a few days. It'll take a few days to get the smell ou-" He broke into huge sobs again, and I helped him to a chair in the long, empty hallway.

"There's a hotel just two blocks down, Dad," I told him while rubbing his back. "I don't want to go home tonight either. Let's stay at the hotel, at least for tonight. We both need sleep."

"Yeah," he agreed as he stood up and began shuffling down the long hallway. "I loved her so much, Gav, so much."

"I know, Dad. Me too," I told him as we left for the first night without my mom.

We buried her three days later, on a cold Thursday morning with fog hugging the town like a sorrowful mist. For the three days leading up to the funeral, I watched my dad slip deeper and deeper into depression. He refused to go back to the house and stayed at the hotel, paying day by day, of course. Heinous made me spend all day trying to comfort my dad so he could feed off his mood.

At night, he would make me drive the Volkswagen home, where he made me sleep in the bathtub. The nonstop visions returned with his frustration. I lay sleepless, missing my mom in the bathtub where she died and watching Heinous' memories of slaughters past for three cold, insane nights.

The morning of the funeral, my dad came home early and started coffee like it was just any other day. I climbed out of the bathtub with a shiver of disgust for Heinous and for myself. I snuck out of the bathroom and tiptoed down the hall, then opened my door loudly and stumbled down the stairs with a clatter to make sure he heard me. He poked his head out of the kitchen and into the foyer at the bottom of the stairs.

"Good morning, son," He said, managing a weak smile. His eyes were still puffy and red, but it looked like he'd run out of tears at some point in the middle of the night and had made the decision to move forward with his life.

"Morning, Dad," I said and gave him a good heartfelt hug. He hugged me back, and even that didn't bring tears, though it took all my self-control not to twitch as Heinous slithered uncomfortably within me. My dad grabbed a bag off the kitchen table, brought it to the foyer, placed the bag on a small table there and pulled out three ties.

He held all three across his hands and stared at them for a minute.

Without looking away from the ties, he spoke. "Can I ask you a favor, Gav?"

"You can ask," I answered honestly.

He smiled at the ties and spun toward me.

"Can you help me pick a tie for the funeral?" His voice quivered a little at the mention of the funeral but he again worked up a little smile in place of tears.

"Sure, Dad."

He turned his hands, and I could see price tags hanging from the backs of the ties. He went and bought three new ties rather than going upstairs into the bedroom he and my mom had shared.

Heinous barked a harsh laugh at this.

"He is scared of the room they shared, Worm. He knows deep down her fate and his. He is right to be afraid. He'll die by your hand soon, Worm, after this day of sweet, delicious pain," Heinous cackled in my ear while I examined the three ties.

I picked a blue one with silver stripes and dark purple circles.

"I think Mom would like that one best."

He smiled a sad little smile and nodded. "That was the same one I was thinking. She would have picked it as well."

He turned and walked back toward the kitchen, still smiling that sad little smile. I watched him until he disappeared into the kitchen before I ran upstairs and started getting ready. When I was done, I found him standing at the foot of the stairs, looking at the family picture that hung there. I noticed again that he had no tears in his eyes.

"We've had a lot of good times, right, Gav? The three of us?"

I put my arm around him, gently leading him toward the door and away from the picture.

"Of course, Dad. I wouldn't trade my childhood for anyone else's," I told him as we walked into the cold to bury the woman who was my mother and his wife.

Rows of black, with eyes as sad as the sky, surrounded her casket at the graveside service. My Aunt Sally—my mom's sister and my only aunt—flew in from a town outside of Reno, Nevada to be with us. The three of us had the only three chairs, and we sat while people said remembrances for my mom. Sally bawled silently through the entire service. Neither I nor my dad ever broke down, but as the casket lowered, we both started leaking tears. Not crying or sobbing, just tears that slipped out without restraint. They were good honest tears, tears from our hearts, not our eyes.

We talked to the people in black for much longer than any of us wanted to. Nothing anyone had to say could make us feel any better. An hour after the last shovelful of dirt was tossed onto her grave, we finally left for home.

Sally followed us back to the house in her rental car to share a meal before flying back to Nevada. We all ate dinner of tilapia, wild rice and kale (my mom's favorite dinner) in the dinning room. Sally wasn't one for uncomfortable silences—or even comfortable ones—so as soon as we sat down, she started talking.

"Gavin, how much thought have you given to going to college at UNR?" she asked as she heaped her vegetables on top of her rice just like my mom.

I looked to my dad, who was watching her with the same sad smile I saw before the funeral.

"None," I told her as I stabbed the flaky white fish on my plate.

They both chuckled at my honesty. It seemed to do my dad good, as for the first time all day, he joined in the conversation.

"Where *do* you plan on going to college, Gav?" he asked as though he had realized only seconds ago that I was about to graduate thanks to my home studies.

"I don't know, really," I said and then took another bite. "I had always supposed I'd go to school around here. You know with you and mom, dad." That was bullshit, and I didn't know why I said it. I had very little interest in school and had truly given college no thought whatsoever. The thing in my head that was making me kill my loved ones was taking priority over all else.

We had been to visit Aunt Sally a few years ago, and I hated it. Where at home, we were surrounded by trees—big beautiful evergreen trees—all of the trees in Aunt Sally's desert town were dying and pathetic. The whole state was half dead and wretched. Nobody smiled, and everyone was shitty to each other. Here, we have rolling hills with lush grasses or crops. There, it is flat and barren, with sand everywhere. It was an ugly modern-day wasteland. I hated Nevada as much as I loved Idaho. My dad smiled meekly at my comment and told me, "Maybe you should give it a try, Gavin. Reno is close to Lake Tahoe, and you'll love it there. Also, Northern California is as beautiful as anything you've ever seen."

He poked at his rice, and after a deep breath, he told me, "I think I'd like to get away from here too."

"But Nevada?" I asked, unable to hide my disgust at the idea.

Aunt Sally laughed out loud, and after a big bite of rice and veggies, she retorted, "Nevada isn't as bad as you make it out to be, Gavin."

147

She smiled a sweet smile that matched my mom's. I looked at my dad, who still wore his own mournful smile. I couldn't feel sympathy for him—Heinous wouldn't let me—but I could see his heart breaking for the thousandth time this week.

"It's a twenty-four-hour state; everything is open all night. Are you kidding me?" she said and then scoffed. "Can you say Partyville, Gav?"

I took the last bite of my dinner, looked her square in the eyes and told her, "No, Aunt Sally, and you should never say it again either."

I winked at my dad, who returned my grin weakly and stared into space, lost to memories of Mom, no doubt. They finished their dinner, and after a short hug-filled goodbye, Aunt Sally drove off to fly home to her shitty little Nevada town.

As her rental car pulled out of the driveway, my father turned to me and said, "I'm tired as all get out, Gav. This week has worn me down. I love you, Gavin. I'm going to bed."

Without any thought at all, I asked him, "In your room?"

He stopped on the third stair and looked down at me. "Yeah, Gav. I have to." As he spoke, his eyes wandered to the family portrait hanging on the wall.

"Goodnight, Dad. I love you." I spoke before I could stop myself, and Heinous sneered at my declaration of love as acid coursed through my veins as punishment.

My dad slunk away silently after a tiny wave and disappeared over the top of the stairs. I walked into the kitchen and started picking up plates from our dinner. I figured that since I'd gone that far, I might as well clean the rest of the kitchen. I cleared the counters of junk mail and other debris, tossing them into an overflowing trash bag. I sighed out loud and pulled the bag out of the can, picked up all the scraps that had fallen, and headed out the back door. I walked barefoot to the outdoor garbage can and tossed it in. But instead of returning, I walked around back to my dad's tool shed. I opened the door and stared into the darkness. Without me telling it to, my hand reached into the darkness and reappeared with the axe my dad used to cut firewood.

148

"I feel like killing vermin, Worm."

As soon as the fiend finished his sentence, the visions started flashing, beginning with Joshie, the sound of his bones overlapping all others. The pictures were so vivid that I couldn't see through them. Sightless but sure of foot, my body turned and started back toward the house, axe in hand. Heinous piloted my legs, relishing the never-ending scenes of violence as I walked into the house. We walked through the sliding glass door, through the kitchen and into the foyer were we stopped, facing the stairs.

As my feet started a slow, blind march up the stairs, I watched the brutal rape and murder and then rape again of a woman dressed in the style of the Wild West, with bloomers and all. As the fiend from my memory climbed on top of her after stabbing her, my mom's voice echoed in my head.

"Gavin, split his head wide, sweetheart."

Then Joshie's voice joined in. "Maybe you could take it clean off if you swing hard enough, Gav!" he shouted excitedly.

"Gavin, I remember when you were a nice boy, never killing your parents," my mom's voice mocked me. "As long as you're going to kill him, you might as well make him suffer." Her tone was conversational, like she was telling me to drop off something at the post office on my way to school.

The visions faded as the voices become clearer and louder. By the top stair, I was staring down the dark hallway at my parents' bedroom door. I tried to stand still, but Heinous moved my legs for me in quiet, deliberate steps. I could feel him throbbing with anticipation. Panic clawed at the base of my neck, and Heinous let me feel it.

I knew what was coming, and I knew I couldn't stop it. My easy defeat thrilled Heinous and pushed him further.

"I think you should take your time, Gav," Joshie's high, excited voice chirped. "You only have one dad to kill. I say take your time and do it right. Maybe start by taking his eyes out with your bare fingers. You should eat them, Gav, or feed them to me!"

"I agree," My mom joined in. "Let's take our time here and really make a mess."

They sounded like they might as easily be talking about a birthday party as about the slaughter of my father. This pushed the panic until it evolved into rage. I tried to turn and run down the hallway and away from everything. Heinous reacted more quickly than I, and I felt a thousand blades inside me, holding me in place, marching me forward in my own body. I was the ultimate Trojan horse, a heartless monster that thrived on pain and suffering, hiding inside the son my dad had known and loved since birth.

"I say we cut off his hands first and nail them to opposite walls," my mom said, cackling with a wickedness that was alien to me. "Then we'll start chopping from his ankles up!"

A chorus of laughter rang out in my head. At first I heard only Heinous, my mom, and Joshie, but soon there were hundreds of laughs that were oddly familiar. Sharp blades stabbed me forward until I was standing at my dad's bedroom door, axe in hand, breathing hard.

"We don't need to do this," I pleaded in a weak whisper.

"Yes we do, Worm. We both need this. He needs this," Heinous told me in his gravelly voice.

"Besides, you've already killed us, Gav. If you kill me and not him, you're playing favorites, and that hurts people's feelings," my mom's voice mocked me.

"He'll be depressed for a long time. You can feed off that. That's what you do, right? Like a leech?" I asked in a high, whiny whisper.

"A leech?" he asked.

"You really are a sack of shit, Gavin, you want to follow your dad around and feed off his misery for the rest of his pathetic life?" Joshie's voice was almost as sharp as the blades holding me outside the door.

My left hand gripped the axe while I watched my right hand reach for the doorknob. I felt Heinous' excitement rise as the knob turned. It popped quietly as the door opened into the room just a few inches. A light shone out of his room into the dim of the hallway where I stood. My heart raced, and I could hear not only the echo of my hard breathing in my ear but that of my mom and Joshie breathing hard and excited as well.

"Please," I begged quietly as my hand pushed the door open more.

"Enough, Worm," Heinous scolded me.

My legs moved me into the room and stopped. I felt a smile start to form on my face in the ruin of Heinous' shock. My dad's bare feet were dangling right at my eye level. The sadness was too much for him, and he had hung himself from the ceiling fan above their bed.

We stared up at him as he slowly spun through the air. As his face came around, I saw his eyes bulging intensely out of their sockets, his tongue hanging long and limp out of the corner of his mouth. I saw with a hint of happiness that he was still wearing the tie I had picked out that morning. My laugh rose before I could even try to stop it. It rose so quickly and happily out of me that Heinous didn't have a chance to stop it. Tears filled my eyes, and I dropped the axe. I stood laughing like a maniac while my dad swung slowly by his neck from the fan above us. There was nothing more we could do.

I grabbed my dad's foot as it dangled in front of me.

"Good for you, Dad. I'm going to go ahead and score that for Team Wagner."

I gave his foot a little shake and let it go. It made his body swing as it turned. A loud creak from the chandelier cut my laughter into a giggle. My dad was a portly little man, and that port was pulling hard against the brackets holding the chandelier in place. I reached for him after another creak ended with the harsh scraping of metal on metal.

"You get to keep your hands, Dad," I told him as I centered him under the chandelier. I knew I would have to sleep on his bed with him spinning slightly above me all night. We would call in the morning to report it, but tonight my suffering and longing would sustain Heinous until he thought of a new game to play. The three people about whom I cared most were all dead and gone, yet none had satisfied the fiend inside. I found the irony hilarious and laughed even harder.

I started pulling back their sheets and climbing into their bed even before he told me to, laughing out loud the entire time. I stared up at my dear old dad, heartbroken and dead, swinging a foot above and away from the foot of the bed. Tears came as freely as my laughter, and they felt every bit as good.

Within just a minute or two, my pillow was wet alongside my head and down my neck from my falling tears. My true vision blurred, and the inner visions started. Joshie screamed at me as my dad swung behind him, like a double-exposed picture.

Still I laughed. I laughed at the demon's growing frustration. I laughed at my family's sad little victory. I laughed at madness and with it. The sounds of Joshie's bones echoed over a vision of someone stabbing a cousin while drowning her in a kitchen sink. Behind that, my dad swung. Still I laughed. I laughed and wheezed and coughed. I laughed and cried and laughed and cried.

Heinous ended my laughter with six short words.

"Worm, we are going to Nevada."

Dream: The Ash of Trees and Dreams

I'm standing in a forest. Lush, damp, and full of life, it surrounds me. A creek babbles a cold wet song as it rushes under fallen logs and a makeshift bridge to my left. Sunlight shines through the evergreen branches crisscrossing the pinecone-littered ground with spiky shadows.

Suddenly the air is alive with laughter. It raises the hair on the back of my neck and sends shards of ice through my veins. I raise my head slowly to look for the source of the laughter, which seems to rain down on me from above.

Tied to each and every trunk with spools and spools of barbed wire is everyone I have ever known. I see my mom and dad held tight to opposite sides of the same wide tree, their outstretched hands failing to touch each other by mere inches. I see Joshie and his family. I see Bull and his bitch-ass girlfriend, Sara, wrapped to a tree with football players and cheerleaders hanging from the branches by barbed wire. Behind them are teachers, gas station attendants, and other people I recognize from around town. All screaming tortured laughter as the wires dig into their flesh.

I open my mouth and scream. An honest sound of fury, shock, and pain leaps from my open mouth, and it turns to flames once exposed to the moist forest air. I spew my pent-up feelings of frustration and my forgotten feelings of regret as a massive neon fireball. The bushes and fallen logs catch first, but the flames surround me quickly, eating their way up the ancient trunks of the forest.

The laughter swells as the fire chars bodies and wood alike. I can't scream anymore. The forest burns to nothing all around me. I kneel in the sand and laugh as black ash drifts on the air. The tears in my eyes blur the barren fog-ridden landscape and catch ash as they trickle down my cheek.

My Sick Story: Heathens in the Sun

My last days at home were a hazy blur. Heinous was furious with me and near-constant visions of astounding clarity made communication with anyone almost impossible. Everyone assumed me to be in some state of grief and shock, but truth be told, the visions were so clear it was as if I were there, doing the killing and raping with my own hands and dick. I stared blindly at people standing in front of me, as I could see only dark distant shapes behind whichever murderous vision was flashing at the time. The visions were so loud, echoing and overlapping inside my head, that I hardly heard people's words. I heard them more as muffled voices alien to visions that I was starting to recognize, even if the person talking to me was standing close enough to put a sympathetic hand on my shoulder.

Which, by the way, would conjure feelings of extreme pain, replacing any comfort anyone tried to bestow on me with agony—and when you're a kid with two parents dead a week apart, everyone wants to hug you or rub your back. Every time, instead of feeling the warmth of another human being, I felt a hundred tiny little mouths tearing through my skin and deep into my muscles. Hugs felt like acid burning my flesh and my bones. I would recoil from the slightest bit of human contact, but still people touched, and still it ate and burned my flesh and Heinous laughed. He laughed in a hundred voices, my mom's, my dad's, Joshie's, and a host of people slaughtered by the evil inside me. His harsh laugh was a constant as the others faded in and out. No matter what vision was being relived or who was mumbling at me back in my crumbling reality, I heard him.

I felt him twist and squirm, growing more comfortable inside me. Every twist was the twist of a tiny razor-sharp blade cutting inside me, every squirm a shock, half electric burn and half sharp stab. I curled within myself and died a thousand times. I felt the pain until it reached an excruciating climax ending with a split second of glorious death before I was reborn into the pain again.

My sense of time was extremely skewed, and I have no idea how long it was until we buried him, or how many days it took my aunt Sally, who had come out to set up the sale of my parents' estate and a trust fund for me with the lawyers, to finish her business before flying back to Nevada to wait for me as I drove a moving van full of my life and towing the shitty little Bug my parents drove for so many years, to arrive in her little shitball town.

Heinous walked my body through the days while I tried in vain to avoid the agony about me. I was aware of my body moving, but between the pain and the visions, I was helpless, trapped and tortured in my body. He would walk me through my day, my real eyes blinded by murderous memories, and the eyes everyone saw dull and empty. He'd shuffle my feet and walk me into walls, laughing at me the entire time. Always, he laughed.

The only time he stopped the visions was at my dad's open-casket viewing. I had had no idea as to my whereabouts when the vision I was watching (the sniper fire tearing through a once-pleasant park, always a Heinous favorite) faded like smoke in front of my eyes and I was left standing on weak legs inches from my dear dead dad. As the echoes of high-power rifle fire died in my ears, I heard the ocean of mourners behind me, weeping and whispering about me. I looked into the coffin to see my dad still wearing the tie I had picked out the day of my mom's funeral, the blue one with silver stripes and purple circles. The satin on which he lay was a very light purple, and his tie seemed overly bright against it.

When I looked closer, I could see that the tie was tied far too tight, slipping into a deep red groove around his neck. As I stared, it grew tighter and tighter. I looked at my dad's face just in time to see his eyes open sluggishly. His bulging eyes were bloodshot, each pointing in a different direction but both looking at me. I felt a swoon coming and gripped the sides of his coffin with both hands. I heard the people dressed in black behind me make a worried sighing sound almost in perfect shocked unison. His bulging eyes darted madly from side to side, so swollen that blood began to drip from both of his eye sockets and down his bloated cheeks.

He tried to open his mouth, but with his tie so tight, he couldn't manage a sound, just strangled, silent gasps for air he'd never breathe again. I felt a familiar panic that I assumed by then was madness; it tickled more than burned as it climbed the back of my neck. His right hand slid slowly and silently as it off of his left and groped for my white knuckles, which gripped the side of his casket. I took a deep breath that hitched in my chest, like when you can't stop crying even after hours of it, as he reached for me. Another sound of group sympathy came from the gallery behind me, reminding me that, no matter what, I couldn't freak out. If I were to turn and scream to them what I was seeing, what I had been seeing, what I would see forever, they would lock me up in a hospital.

I would be poked and prodded. I would be dissected and studied. I don't know if those thoughts were mine or not, but they scared me enough to make me not want to find out. I saw ancient tortures and the devious devices that delivered them. Something told me then that Heinous had memories he wouldn't flash for me, memories of pain and fear inflicted upon him and his host instead of the other way around. He loathed and feared these memories, and until the thought of capture flashed through my mind, he had managed to keep them hidden from me.

As I came to this amazing realization, my dad's cold dead hand slapped soundlessly against my hand. I looked at him, and both his swollen eyeballs burst with a sick gushing sound I heard only in my head, where it echoed like a scream in a cave. His mouth, no longer gasping for air, curled into a tight little grin that pulled back just enough to look sinister and out of place on my dad's face. The swoon I felt coming before returned, and I tightened my grip on the coffin. I heard people start moving across the hushed room to comfort me, and I curled against the coffin and tried to brace for the burning and stabbing that I knew would be heralded by their sympathy. Tears started without me knowing it, and my vision blurred as I watched the blood continue to flow out of his ruined eyeballs and down his face.

As the hands fell on my back and the teeth started chewing, I heard Joshie's voice in my head telling me, "We should have eaten those eyes, Gav. What a waste."

As he continued to *tsk tsk* at me, my eyes rolled back and I crumpled into a heap on the funeral home floor, where what felt like a million hands touched me and tried to help me up. Every kind touch burned and bit. I felt like I was being fed to hellhounds there on the foul yellow-and-red flower-patterned carpet, but I couldn't scream out, and my throat closed tight to prove it.

On the ride home in my Aunt Sally's rental car, the visions returned, as clear and dominant as before, and so returned my staring blindly into space with falsely vacant eyes. My aunt tried to talk to me, but compared to the sound of Joshie's bones breaking and bouncing off the inside of my head, she sounded not just distant, but almost as if she were talking from somewhere else entirely. She sounded like a scream three blocks away on a dark night, haunting and vague compared to the horrors I heard as the visions flashed.

Heinous, who still hadn't spoken to me since silencing my laughing fit, let enough of my aunt's words float through the soundtrack of his memories to let me know what was going on and how helpless I was to stop it.

First, I was moving to motherfucking Nevada.

I still had a few months before I turned eighteen, and Aunt Sally was my guardian according to my parents' wills. I was going to live with her until I could finish my high school work through the mail and could start college in Reno, whenever that would be. She lived an hour away from Reno, and even though her sister and brother-in-law were both in the ground, I could tell even in my stupor of pain and confusion that my lonely old aunt was happy to have me—much happier to have me than I was to go.

She could not bear children herself but had always loved them, born with a natural mothering instinct as strong as my mom's but without anything to heap it on. It was a hole in her soul that she filled by heaping upon me, her lone nephew, love and gifts and support, all in near-suffocating levels. But I loved her and didn't want her to die. I did, however, feel that Heinous had let his cards show a little more than he meant to. Her dying would lead to suspicion, which would lead to capture, which of course would lead to torture. He would let her live

157

as long as he possibly could resist killing her, and he would do it out of fear. Thinking him in any way weak was a blasphemy and resulted in feeling of tiny, jagged knives stabbing inside my skull until I passed out. He knew my every thought, conscious and subconscious, and any attempt to relive the memories of torture that I'd glimpsed ever so briefly was punished immediately and with such ferocity that I made considerable effort to wipe them from my own memory.

Second, even though I was acting as dazed and crazed as a shithouse rat, I was the heir to the Wagner family bank account. Of course, I had to pass a battery of psychological tests before I could touch it, but it was there on the horizon. I had no reason to worry about college, as I had money now, enough to attend any school in the country, and Reno's instate tuition was moderately priced. I had enough money to never work, much less go to college, but I knew I would. Heinous had plans for me, and they didn't include a lifelong vacation. He hadn't told me, because he didn't have to. He knew that hearing it from a million random voices discussing my future while my body sat slumped over with vacant eyes would be enough to fill me in while also keeping me confused.

Maybe "confused" is not a strong enough word. I had lost any sense of time after lying in my dad's bed. Different visions flashed at different speeds, so nothing ever felt right, though a maddening order to the hundreds of visions made me realize what atrocity I would be seeing next. I was hardly in control of my physical body for those lost days or weeks. I felt huddled inside myself, trying in vain to escape the incredible pains that apparently fed on my very soul, since my body still walked in slow stagger steps like a slow-learning infant and mumbled nonsense words through spittle on my lips, just as Heinous directed it to.

And when the time came for me to make the improvements needed to be deemed sane enough to inherit my parents' monies and move with my sweet, unsuspecting aunt to Nevada, Heinous pushed me down deeper inside of myself, and damned if he didn't pull a full recovery better than any con man ever could. He fooled everyone. No one ever suspected that the sad yet handsome boy answering them with tears always looming like fall thunderclouds wasn't really me, but the terrible thing inside of me. My aunt Sally gave me long heartfelt hugs that Heinous wouldn't let me shy away from, hugs that burned like battery acid on a fresh third-degree burn. I felt it all inside myself like my body was dripping acid onto my soul and then combusting over and over and over.

I was slowly becoming more aware, still not in control, but I could look out of the eyes that weren't mine and watch the demon walk me through my day. The hugs gave way to sad looks and pats on the hand, and the feeling of burning and being eaten alive relented as well. He still wouldn't let me control anything, and the visions never once stopped or even waned after my dad's viewing, but sometimes I could see through them to what was going on outside me.

He didn't speak to me in the gravelly harsh voice again until right before he returned full control to me, which, of course, wasn't until we were already in Nevada. The sound of his voice was so terrifying and familiar that, had I been in control of my eyes, I would have wept.

"Wake up, Worm. Crawl out of your belly; we have a lot to talk about."

It was like hearing the voice of God. A cruel and hateful god, but the only god I had truly known. On his command, I relaxed. I waited to see if it was a trick, something to torture me even more as I waited for sweet freedom that was never destined to come. I stretched out inside my body, where I found no pain and no burning. I pulled myself up until I was staring out of my eyes at the blank Nevada landscape.

He had driven the moving van from our little Idaho town, and after making it a hundred miles through the Nevada desert nothingness, he stopped at a rest area. Heinous parked the moving van and walked me inside the little stone shitter that counted as a rest stop. Once inside, he locked the door behind us and, without a word, relinquished control of my body back to me. I experienced the feeling of falling forward within myself.

I blinked my eyes to find I was looking with my own eyes, not just looking through them as I had minutes before. No visions obstructed my view of reality, even though my current view was that of a brown stone wall covered in graffiti done in black marker. My body felt warm and comfortable. Oh how I had missed it. I fanned my fingers and giggled out loud as they wiggled back at me. I told my toes to do the same, and when I felt them obey, wiggling against the inside of my shoe, I smiled even bigger. I took a deep breath and felt the dry desert air fill my lungs. I felt like I had made it through a horrible accident, one that had left me in a state of fear, pain, and coma. Wiggling my digits and breathing hot desert air, I felt alive again.

My body felt relaxed and well rested, though my soul felt the opposite. I felt myself climbing fully into my skin suit, inch by inch, organ by organ, feeling like me again. I sat on the cold steel toilet, a smoothed tube of metal sticking up from a twenty-foot-deep stone room full of shit and piss, and looked at my hands like I was a baby seeing them for the first time. Everything felt strangely new, every limb taut and strong as if I had gained muscle mass in the past few weeks. My blond hair fell across my eyes, and I excitedly pushed my right hand up and through my errant locks.

I stood on firm, strong legs and walked the three steps to the restroom mirror. I wiped the layer of fine dust off the mirror and smiled at my reflection. I looked healthier than I ever had. And—dare I say it?—I looked happier than I ever had. I was still gazing at myself when I saw a tiny flash in the reflection of my eyeball. As if for one second a dark light had gleamed at me from within myself. The color was like none I had ever seen. It was as if a light had blinked on a beacon far away, through the stars, on a strange alien planet, and through some tear in the cosmos, a slip in reality, it had reflected in my eye. I blinked my eyes slowly and opened them so I was looking dead into them in the mirror. Again the dark light shone from my eyes, brief like a whispered farewell, but unmistakable.

Then I felt Heinous move. He had physically grown so great that I felt my skin ripple as he squirmed beneath it. As I felt his mass curl and settle, I gripped the sink in front of me with both hands, fully expecting great pain and the sickening roll of my stomach that always accompanied it when he slithered around inside me. Instead, he settled quickly and painlessly, and he winked my eye at me in the mirror.

A nervous chuckle escaped me, and I glanced away from my reflection so I didn't have to look at my eyes anymore. I looked down at the sink as I reached to turn on the cold water, and I noticed a large knife, at least a foot long and fuck-off nasty, lying behind the knobs against the wall. I stared at it with my head cocked to the side, trying to take it all in as I twisted the cold water to life. I let my fingertips dance under the flow as the simple feelings of cool and of liquid, feelings of which I was deprived while in my shell, flowed over me, causing exaggerated pleasure to tingle from my hands to my feet and to the back of my neck, where Heinous twitched slightly as it passed. I never took my eyes off of the huge gleaming blade.

I knew without him telling me that he had brought it in with him and set it here seconds before he released me back into myself. I knew this, but nothing more. I cupped my hands together under the water and let them fill, then overfill so that the cool water ran in erratic streams down the muscles of my forearms to my elbows, where it fell to the floor in large drops, making small puddles on either side of me. I splashed two palms' worth of water on my face, and the feeling of pleasure tingled across my face and down my neck to all of my lower body in turn. Still looking at the blade, I wiped my face with my hands and waited for Heinous to speak.

When his harsh voice came, it was so gravelly that it almost felt abrasive inside my head, yet it was so eerily familiar and oddly comforting that I devoted my full attention to it.

"Only a handful of times in my eons of life have things not gone for me the way I have guided them." As he rasped the last word at me, a rush of memories I had never seen flashed. Even in their brevity, the terror they radiated was incredibly intense. I felt the thing inside tighten in what I assumed was an involuntary movement at reliving the tortures and horrors when they were inflicted upon him and his poor unlucky hosts.

The visions flashed fast and left a sinking feeling in my gut. I could differentiate only three different times, all centuries away from each other, the most recent in an age in which men wore ties and drilled into the side of people's heads, trying in vain to cure mental illness. The oldest seemed to come not just from a different time, but from a far different place entirely, where ugly human-like things released swollen worms covered in slime and teeth into people's ears to eat the evil that hid there.

My stomach rolled at the feelings of terror and pain, and I puked into the sink. I splashed more water across my face to wash the vomit away, and the pleasurable feelings rushed over me again, calming both me and Heinous.

"I am old now, Worm, and I have learned much in my time. I was brash once and acted on my every impulse as it occurred to me. I would force my host to perform whatever act of murder or depravity I craved. I am an agent of chaos, Worm, a vast and wild cosmic chaos far beyond your comprehension. Bloodlust drives me; I feed upon misery and pain, murder and rape."

I looked back at my eyes in the mirror. As he talked, the dark light shone from time to time, as if an alien fire were burning inside me.

"I have had hosts even more worthless than you." Disdain dripped from his voice, and I averted my eyes from my reflection in shame.

"Three times before, my hosts have been captured for their crimes, my crimes. Three times before have I had to outlive my host as men poked and prodded clumsily and violently at the human brain, which happens to be where I take up my residence. I have been seen by more than just my hosts; men of science and medicine have gazed upon my dark skin and seen me coiled and living, feasting on my hosts' brains."

With the last revelation, I froze and felt myself go sickly pale. I felt lightheaded and grabbed the sink in much the same way I had grabbed my father's casket. His barking laugh shook some of the nausea away as he continued.

"Relax, Worm. I'm not eating your brain. I won't end you as I've ended countless others. I tried to take everything you love, and as pathetic as they were, I got no satisfaction from their demises. Far too quickly they all perished. So now, Worm, we will do it how I did it when I was young. You will kill whatever, whomever, whenever I say."

Without meaning to, I looked at the humongous knife, blade alight in the dim glow of the stone bathroom.

"The price for your weak and unsatisfying family is that now we will spread our chaos and pain farther than I had planned, and you, Worm, will kill and torture and rape until I'm finished. I've taken everything you've ever loved, your parents and your best friend. I've taken you from your peacefulness in the trees. We won't kill Sally right away, but we will kill her too. Anyone that you ever felt anything for, we will destroy."

Even as he spoke, the words sounded harsher than his tone. He had shown me what he was capable of doing, and I had no choice but to submit, to kneel before my reflection and grimace at my fate.

"It starts now, Worm."

With that he stood me to my feet with sharp shots of pain that ran the length of my legs, and he reached my arm up to flick the lock back to open. I looked at my reflection, and he was smiling at me. When he talked next, he used my mouth but his voice, so I could see my lips move as he told me, "Grab the knife."

I hesitated only a split second before what felt like a million spikes started twisting inside me. I reached for the knife, and the pain stopped as soon as my fingers wrapped themselves around the hard wooden handle.

"Now we wait. When that door opens, YOU will kill whatever unlucky soul opens it. This is your last chance, Worm. No matter what blood will be spilt here today. The decision you need to make is if you or I spill it. I can promise you now that if you let me down again, I will stab you so far down inside yourself that you will know only pain for all time."

He had proven the truth of his words to me, and I knew he meant it. My shaking hand brought the blade before me. I twirled it in the air in front of me, silently amazed by its sheer girth. I was staring at it when I heard a car door slam in the rest area parking lot. I looked at my reflection to see a wicked grin and the strange light glowing in my eyes.

I heard footsteps fast approaching the door, and I moved so I was positioned far enough behind the door that I wouldn't be hit when it flew open. As the footsteps reached the door, I turned and looked in the mirror that was now next to me. The instant before the door swung open, my reflection winked at me. The door swung wide, and a big fat man in a dirty tan shirt with sweat stains in the armpits stood shocked before me.

He looked at me with surprise on his face, and for a split second, I thought he would excuse himself and leave me standing there spinning my big blade in the air. He didn't. He farted and growled at me, "What the fu-," but before he finished his sentence, I dove toward him, swinging the massive blade at his ample gut. He jerked backwards, and I reached for him in a fury with my slashing blade. Instead of opening the door and running away, he swung the door closed and shuffled his fat ass around me so I was standing by the door and he was left looking scared in the corner from which I had just sprung. He hadn't seen the blade at first, but his eyes went wide with fear after I slashed it at him. He was panting and stuttering words, but I swung at him again while noises rose from within me like those of some strange animal.

He managed to dodge the first wild swipe of my blade, but I reversed direction in midair and dragged the heavy blade across his arm and belly with a howl of excitement. I felt all my senses come alive. My skin tingled with pleasure, and in the mirror next to him, I saw the wide wicked grin across my face as I swung the blade again and again, back and forth. He had backed himself fully into the corner and was whimpering as his blood gushed to the concrete floor. I leaned at him and slashed across his right leg, and he fell first to a knee and then flat back on his ass. He leaned against the stone wall and moaned something into his hands. He looked at me through his fingers, and I could see the skin around his frightened eyes going pale with blood loss.

"Finish him, Worm. Cut him into pieces, for his salvation and yours!"

I looked at the blood pooling on the floor, and it was the most beautiful color I had ever seen. A bright, rich crimson swirled with a black darker than night that made me think of eternity. It sparkled and glittered before me on the dirty concrete floor. The room was full of the smell of blood, which was overwhelmingly sweet, and the warm musk of his fear. I rolled my eyes back as the sensations of smell, sight, and feeling washed over me like a silken river of ecstasy.

I heard a skidding noise on the floor and opened my eyes to see him crawling through his own blood toward the door. I stood alongside his crawling form and kicked it with all my might. He rolled into the wall with a half-sob, half-grunt, and I fell on him, stabbing and slashing until his screams stopped. Heinous was laughing his harsh, barking laugh, and as I slashed and the fat man's blood flew about the room propelled by my blade, I realized I was laughing as well. I backed away, breathing hard and dizzy with excitement. I put the massive blade, now covered in blood and gore, back where I'd found it. I looked at myself in the mirror, and I smiled my own smile at my blood-splattered visage. I turned the knob on the sink and again let the cool water flow over my hands before splashing it on my face. My body still trembled with excitement and fury.

"Very good, Worm," Heinous told me.

"And now our adventure really begins."

I grabbed the knife from the sink, but I didn't bother to turn the water back off. I walked from the dimness of the stone bathroom into the hot, bright Nevada sun, never casting a backward glance.

With the slaying of the fat man in the sweat-stained shirt, I had crossed some kind of line. I knew it; I could feel it as I shifted the van into drive and started down the long, flat highway. I had lost everything, and now I simply quit caring about other humans. It was them or me now.

"And it will never be me," I spoke out loud with a glance at my reflection in the rearview mirror.

He knew my thoughts, so he understood I had given myself to him. I had given up. He had to take control of my body in order to kill Joshie himself. He again had to force my hand in shoving the television set into the bathtub with my mom. He would have forced me to kill my dad if he weren't already swinging from his neck when we came in, axe in hand. The animals I had slaughtered before to buy me time weren't the same as the fat man I had diced up like dog food in the bathroom. This was different blood. It was a different kind of power. It was the better sacrifice.

The fat man died by my hand, not that of the murderous thing inside me. It left him swollen and appeased, and I watched the road through the memory of him dying so violently over and over and over again.

By the time we pulled into my Aunt Sally's driveway, I was shaking with excitement to kill. Heinous' bloodlust had joined with me with the slaying of the fat man. My stomach grew tight, and I couldn't focus my thoughts. I closed my eyes, and the vision of my first murder flashed again, so vivid this time it was as if I weren't remembering it so much as reliving it. The feelings of euphoria returned, though with less intensity now that the act itself was over.

"And they never will," Heinous growled at me.

I opened my eyes and winced at the bright Nevada sun. I surveyed everything around me and sighed in tired submission. The block on which Aunt Sally lived was long, flat, and more sand than concrete.

The houses were all old and either a dusty white or a dingy tan. From where we parked, I could see to the corner on my right; I could see the four houses, two on each side of the street, three whites and one tan. To my left, I could see halfway down the dirt street and at least the next dozen houses, six on each side of the street. Aunt Sally's house was the tan color that to me looked like something the desert had puked up. The entire block, in fact, looked like the sand had spit it out from a colorless void under the rolling hills of the desert to rot under the sun. The block held at least twenty houses, and only a handful of trees dotted the landscape. They were all tall old elms, and they were all dead or dying. I found out later from Aunt Sally that there was an infestation of elm beetles that the city had ignored to the point of negligence. Of the houses I could see, at least five were empty. Only two looked as if they had been recently inhabited; the other three looked as if they should have been condemned decades before. A lot of the houses on the block had had new foundations put in, as the sand underground still shifted slowly, and foundations cracked and crumbled more quickly than in the solid of the big city with all its concrete and rock. The empty houses stuck out like sore thumbs amongst the inhabited houses and gave the street an air of neglect and decay. After talking with Aunt Sally, I learned that almost every block had at least one empty or deserted house, most of which were owned by rich, prominent men in the town. They cut every corner possible, employed laborers who traded work for meth, and used ancient heaters and water heaters just waiting to explode and take unsuspecting families to the fog beyond, but because they were on the city council, they all got away with murder.

As she explained how the rich old men had been bleeding the little desert town dry, Heinous curled and settled, appeased by his choice to move us here. The little town was as corrupt as cities ten times its size, and Heinous reveled in it. The decay and corruption the little town exuded thrilled him to no end. His harsh chuckle built slowly in my head while Aunt Sally talked on and on. She was an obnoxiously optimistic person, and not even she could put a positive spin on the rotting little town. She told me she couldn't give up her job. She made too much money to leave the little town, whether it was dying around her or not. As she showed me to my room, she told me she understood that I would want to move to Reno for school soon, but she assured me that I could take my time.

"Gavin, I know that you've been through things no one should ever have to go through," she started before tears filled her eyes without warning. "But I want you to know I'm here for whatever you need."

She reached to rub my back, and I recoiled instinctively, causing Heinous to bark his harsh laugh inside my head.

"Sorry," I told her, looking sheepish and feeling foolish.

Tears slipped out of her eyes and dripped down her soft, smooth cheeks.

"No, I'm sorry, baby. I've been gabbing this whole time, and I'm betting you are ready to just take a minute, right?"

"Yeah, Aunt Sally," I told her with a wink. "A lot of shit to take in."

"I love you, Gav," she said as she put something on the windowsill in front of me. "Have a good night, and make yourself at home, sweetheart."

"I love you too," I told her as she disappeared to her room for the night. I turned and examined what she had dropped in front of me; it was a joint. As soon as I realized what it was, I snatched it and ducked out onto her back porch. The sun was dipping behind the roofs of the houses across the street, and the light was a sickly yellow orange that seemed to make the dust in the air glow unnaturally. I lit the joint and inhaled deeply, letting the high wash over me. I held in the hit and greedily pulled another three or four more before a coughing fit made me drop it. I put it out to smoke as a roach later. I blinked my eyes, and the ever-blowing sand stuck to the moisture, blinding me temporarily. I blinked and rubbed until the sun had fully set and droves of mosquitoes infested the night sky. I scooted back inside, away from the bugs and sand, blinking and slapping until I was in my new bedroom, where I walked to the long skinny mirror and looked at my reflection. My eyes were red and irritated, and a mosquito bite swelled slightly on my cheek.

My mind raced over the things Aunt Sally had told us about the corruption of the doomed little town. The decay and rot must have spilled over from the houses and buildings into the townspeople, making them so greedy as to let their home strangle itself. Heinous started flashing the visions as he grew more and more excited about our new playground. My face was smiling, and my lips moved when Heinous growled, "Home."

Dream: Wall of Dead Flesh

I'm kneeling in the gray sand as the fog dances close around me, welcoming me back. I look down at myself and notice I'm covered in blood. My shirt and pants stick to me like a slippery second skin. I look at my hands and see blood, dried and brown, flaking and drifting to the ground when I move my fingers.

I realize I'm kneeling in front of a morbid wall that reaches high above me into the fog. The wall looks to be formed completely of severed limbs, torsos, and heads. Arms overlap legs so that fingers and toes point lifeless accusations at the sky and ground. Long hair from the decapitated heads hangs down and blows slightly from a wind I don't feel against my skin. The sand nearest the gate is clumpy and wet from the blood drizzling down the wall of gore. I can see faces on the blood-soaked ground, all silently screaming their agonies at me.

I hear a mumbling voice and stand up to find its source. To my left, I see myself standing on a stepstool fighting with a female's limbless, headless torso halfway up the wall. I approach him slowly, admiring the violent architecture and dragging my feet through the harsh sand. He doesn't face me, but I see beads of sweat form on his bald head as he tugs at the torso. The other me grunts and tugs the torso with so much force that he falls backwards into the sand with it clutched to his chest.

He lies in the sand, breathing deep, with his arms around the naked chunk of human meat in an exhausted lover's embrace. As I approach, I hear him whistling a quiet lullaby to it.

I stand directly above him. After a few minutes, he opens his sparking blue eyes and notices me above him. I offer him a hand to help him back to his feet. He scoffs at my offered hand and tosses the torso off of himself before he stands back up. I don't know how to respond to his unexpected attitude, so I stand silent and watch him. He stares at me with eyes damp and jittery with emotion but says nothing as he climbs back up on the stepstool.

He resumes his macabre task of tugging at body parts. I take a step even closer and notice he isn't tugging; he is untying strands of barbed wire that hold the gory trophies in place. The other me twists two tightly wound strands of rusted metal apart, causing the arm they hold pinned to slip a few inches. He nudges a disembodied leg out of his was way while searching for the other wires holding the arm in place. He finds the next knot and begins working on it.

I'm watching his fingers when he drives the pad of his thumb onto a barb with an accidental squish. The other me howls in pain and yanks his hand away, leaving a thin strand of blood hanging between his punctured digit and the rusted barb. I watch the barbed knot he was working on tighten itself back down so that the wire digs into the rotting flesh of the arm until the knot is buried in the decomposing limb.

The other me doesn't see the disappearing trick. Instead, he squeezes his wounded thumb, which has quickly swollen to a grotesque degree. From the wound, intermittent drops of red and green ooze and fall to wet the sand. He squeezes until the swelling relents and drains what looks like a half-gallon of blood and slime onto the sand below. Once the swelling goes down, I see several tiny black webs of necrotic tissue dotting his fingers and arms. Swollen red and green lines connect each dead wound buried just under the pale pallor of his skin like internal lightning.

He looks at me, the whites of his eyes sickly yellow, and spits a gob of blood at my feet. He turns back to his task, sighing loudly when he notices the wire dug deep into the dead arm. The silence between us whistles in my ears and makes me more uncomfortable than the barbed wire and flesh wall.

He won't even look at me, so I go back to looking at the wall. Long blond hair hangs upside down from a head I should recognize but don't. I wrap my hand in her hair and tug the head toward me for a better look at the semi-familiar face. As the head comes free, barbed wires pulled taut snap loose, cutting the air by my face and nearly slashing the other me as he jumps away. A large section of the wall collapses, revealing a gate made out of thick steel bars hidden under the corpse wall. The limbs, torsos, and heads form a sickening pile of half-decayed human parts that separates me and the other me, now standing next to his stepstool.

I smile at the progress I made with one curious tug, and he scowls back at me. I don't understand his scowl until I look back to the gate. It is once again covered with severed body parts, this time twice as thick, even though the ones between us remain.

"I was just trying to help," I blurt out in confusion.

"Help?" he says in my own pained voice as everything around me begins to drift and fade. "You fucking did this!"

My Sick Story: Decades that Bled

Rather then enroll in school in a new town for the last month of the school year, I finished working toward my diploma through the mail. I received an envelope at the beginning of each week with that week's assignments, and an envelope around Thursday that contained my graded assignments from the previous week (always one hundred percent correct). We did the folder full of school work the day it arrived, but I wouldn't mail it out until I received the folder with my graded work. Heinous gave me answers to everything, and it was he who insisted that everything be perfect and that college was to come after and was to be done perfectly as well. I never missed a question or a deadline.

Aunt Sally worked five days a week at the Department of Mosquito Abatement five miles out of town. She did something or other in the busy office. Whatever it was, the county paid her damn fine to do it. She assumed I spent my days working through the pile of papers that she eyed incredulously every time she walked past it and playing video games. She urged me to get out of the house and try to meet people. She thought hanging out with kids my age would make me feel better.

I knew it wouldn't. What could I possibly have in common with normal kids getting ready to graduate? They were getting drunk and banging each other's brains out in pickup truck beds surround by miles of salt flats and tumbleweeds. And all I wanted to do was cruise local hotels for victims.

I would skulk in dark alleyways and let Heinous pick travelers at his own random whim. We would snatch them right outside their cars in the pitch-black parking lots, or we would follow them down empty hotel hallways and spring as they opened the doors to their rooms. We carried men and women into the rooms they had rented, beating them, raping them, hurting them, killing them.

Rape wasn't nearly as sexual an act to Heinous as murder was. It was just another way to pull sweet pain from a human. I had no homosexual feelings, but the persistent evil inside me would rape a man—or rather make me rape a man—if the urge struck him. Raping the women victims was more common but still hardly sexual. Catching the last breath from a dying person was a euphoric feeling that left me weak from physical and mental ecstasy. I'd use my victims' cars to drive their bodies out into the desert that surrounded and isolated the shitty little town. I'd take any cash I could find and then I'd dig a hole and add a name to an ever-growing Missing Persons list.

And so passed the next few weeks: a blur of quick, efficient homework and picking up hapless travelers from local motels. Never once did Aunt Sally suspect anything. I received a load of recruitment letters from schools across the country due to my astonishing 4.0 grade point average and equally impressive test scores, and still Heinous insisted we only move the hour to Reno. My high marks had earned me scholarships I didn't need because of my trust fund, but would use anyway. I visited the Reno campus and enrolled so I would begin in the spring and still have a few more months to relax before I had to move.

I killed my first hooker after leaving the campus that day. We picked her up off a barren street corner where she stood, slightly pigeon toed, with makeup applied by shaky hands. She climbed in and offered a chipped-tooth grin and gracious little conversation before she undid my pants and pulled out my cock. She asked me for a twenty, and as soon as it was tucked into her sports bra, she took my flaccid manhood into her mouth. I drove while she did what she did. I drove to the tallest point I could see, and she never came up. I turned up the volume on the radio so I didn't have to hear her pathetically fake mumbles and moans of pleasure. I parked at the edge of a road with a high rocky cliff that gave way to a spectacular view of the lights of the town—so many that a cloud of light floated above the city like a low-hanging moon. She still worked up and down in my lap, and I still hadn't finished. I knew I wouldn't; I had to take to be turned on. Besides, her excessively slobbery suck job wouldn't have turned me on even if I didn't have a demon inside, silently begging to see her flayed open and gutted.

I glanced from the wide view of the city lights overtaking the darkness above to the tousled hair of the hooker's head in my lap. With a half-grunt, half-sigh, I grabbed the door handle with my left hand and a handful of greasy hooker hair with my right. In one smooth move, I opened the door and stepped out, pulling the whore by her hair. She stumbled as I lifted my hand higher in the air and walked her quickly toward the edge of the cliff. She bawled a scream that sent a quiver through my loins and finally made me hard. She sobbed out loud and yelled a strange string of curse words the last few feet before I led her, head first, off the cliff to break upon the rocks below.

I stood and stared at the panoramic view above the city as the dirt disturbed by her headlong tumble clouded the brightness of the lights as it shifted and resettled to the dirty cliff side. I walked to the edge and saw her body stuck on a pile of sharp rocks only a dozen yards from the house closest to the high cliff. I saw, with a wide grin, her arms and both her legs bent in unnatural directions across the jagged rocks. Blood ran from every orifice on her head, and high crimson splashes of it colored the surrounding boulders. I came without touching myself. Heinous erupted in hollow, sharp laughter. The euphoria overtook me, and I swayed at the edge of the cliff while the lights blurred and blinked before me.

"You just walked her right off the cliff, Worm!" Heinous laughed as I climbed back in the car with a satisfied look on my face. As soon as I pulled away, Heinous flashed the vision from the time we picked her up to the last long glance down at her broken and bent remains. It repeated over and over again, so vividly that the road on which I drove became a dream that floated over the Reno skyline. The dizziness returned, and I gripped the wheel tighter. I pulled off at a rest stop fifteen miles out of the city to let the visions come, strong and vivid, without worry of crashing the little Volkswagen. As the most recent kill gave way to older ones, I smiled and laughed out loud.

In the few weeks I had been in Nevada, I had more than made up for the disappointment of my family's weak death in terms of vivid memories for him to relish. When the memories flashed, more often than not they were of a piece of prey that Heinous and I had killed, rather than any other of his hosts, even in their vast numbers.

I was his favorite. I enjoyed the killing and the raping. I enjoyed the torture and the pain. Because of this, he allowed me to feel the dizzying euphoria more than any other host. He had bonded physically more with me than with any other host, as strands of his strange body were in almost every part of my body, bound to bone and muscle. With every person I slaughtered, I felt it more and more. I was less I than us, and he was becoming us as well.

We flexed *our* muscles. *We* killed *our* prey. *We* enjoyed the visions of *our* killings.

The last two months before we moved were the cold winter months, and we were so anxious and full of bloodlust that it was impossible to stay home. Aunt Sally took extended holiday trips to Las Vegas to stay with a long-distance flame. Heinous and I never killed anyone in her house, though he wanted to every damn day. Instead, we drove to neighboring towns and stole people back to the desert between our town and those of our victims. We took our time and sometimes spent entire cold winter days slowly torturing poor damned souls to death in the barren and unforgiving bleakness of the desert. We stole cars and cruised to Reno, where the number of people nobody would miss was greater.

The weekend before we moved, we found a father and son camping in the high desert. We sat in the shadows and listened to them talk. Real intense father and son stuff. Dad talked little Jimmy through the perils of crack addiction and the innumerable pluses of prophylactics. He explained to his son that even though his parents were no longer living together, it didn't mean they didn't love him. They hugged and shared a good manly cry. By the time we stood and stretched in the shadows, Heinous was quivering within me so hard that my extremities went numb. We didn't make any effort to silence our approach, and the hatchet in my hand proved our murderous intent.

The father dove at me, protecting his son, and got my hatchet to his gut for his effort. I tossed him aside, crumpling their two-man tent. Little Jimmy pointed all his adolescent rage at us, but I swung the

175

handle of the hatchet at his forehead hard enough to knock him into their campfire. We stuck the dad to the ground with the tent stakes and dragged a screaming Jimmy out of the fire pit. We spent the next few moonlit hours giving them the grisliest father/son bonding anyone could ask for as we slowly hacked them to bits.

Once Heinous was sated, I stood, covered in pulp and gore, surveying the carnage of the secluded campsite. The mess was overwhelming; the tent was shredded and blood soaked, all of their supplies were scattered and destroyed, and a twenty-foot circle of blood had dyed the sand a gritty black. Heinous spoke words in a harsh garbled language I didn't understand. At once, the ground swallowed the entire terrible scene. The ruined tent and savage chunks of father and son sank into the sand with amazing speed. Once the last scrap of evidence had sunk, clean sand bubbled out and erased any sign of our atrocious evening.

The next decade and a half blurred together. Heinous did the schoolwork with the same quick perfection as he had during high school, and college flew by in four short slaughter-filled years. We cruised the streets, collecting whomever we wished. By the time I graduated, we had doubled the number of visions in Heinous' vast and vivid memory.

I never made friends, but I was damned friendly to everyone—unless, of course, we were killing them. I was charming and good looking enough that people just assumed I had friends and a very active social life. In reality, I didn't even have a steady weed dealer anymore and would buy some whenever I got the chance off some random person. I didn't want anyone to mistake my friendliness for my actually being a friend. My trust fund allowed me to live without roommates, without the need to sacrifice my privacy in a dorm. We wore a damn charming mask to hide our ugliness and our depravity. Everyone knew me or at least knew of me. I was the kid from Idaho with an unthinkable past and a smile that couldn't help but make you smile too. I was he of the flawless academics. I had an endless string of excuses for avoiding large public gatherings or any social interaction beyond that which was absolutely required by school.

I feared silently the entire four years that someone might talk to us for too long, might see through the disguise that felt so paper thin at times. In a sense, it kept us cautious and taught us both some restraint. We were both enjoying our situation enough that a careless kill was not worth it. We avoided the school when looking for something to torture and kill. We never hunted down students, as we were students, and we needed no eyes prying into our lives outside of school. Those four years, we killed only from the waves of the downtrodden and forgotten that littered Reno's streets, slept in her parks, and camped under her bridges. Four years of killing only whores, junkies, and poor unlucky homeless people. By the end of the four years, these victims started to feel more like the squirrel I had sacrificed in trying to buy my doomed parents more time than like actual people.

It was harder to draw the fear and pain necessary to achieve the utmost euphoria at the killing time. Most of our prey had already given up on life, whether they knew it or not, and some even welcomed my hideous gore-stained blade.

One crack-addled whore my senior year even thanked us when we sank our blade deep into her stomach. Being in the role of dealer of a merciful death didn't sit well with me, and it certainly did not sit well with Heinous. A feeling of deep sickening revolt rolled in our stomach, and we backed away like a vampire from a cross as she slid off the blade. Her eyes filled with tears, and she pleaded with us to finish her. We turned and left her to bleed out in the third story of the abandoned warehouse to which we'd taken her in anticipation of having our kind of fun. We heard her screams fade as her blood ran dry as we left hurriedly and disappeared down the dirt alleyways that surrounded the warehouse district. It was an uncomfortable and unsatisfying death that reminded me, in its own sick way, of my parents' deaths. Sitting there angry and frustrated, even I felt that my parents' deaths were unsatisfying. We needed pain for the feelings of ecstasy. We needed fear to tint the metallic taste of blood with satisfaction.

We spent our spare time killing, remembering killing, or planning to kill. That was all my life was. For years, I lived for the kill.

I lived for the elation the evil inside allowed me to feel when blood was spilt for him. We would do whatever we had to in order to keep people thinking us the most perfect guy ever.

After graduation, I secured a high-paying job in Reno at a company called Killkin Brothers Enterprises. They were a high-powered financial conglomerate that acted as a payroll company to a few studios over the hill in California. They also collected and distributed cash and cash-equivalent prizes (gift certificates, prize vouchers, and coupons) for large companies that had franchises across the Untied States. It was a well-to-do company that hired me fresh out of school at a salary that should have made me blush.

The Killkin brothers were Ted and Gary, and they were as different as night and day. Ted was very tall and very thin, whereas Gary was short and quite overweight. But their differences didn't end at their physical attributes. Ted spent very little time in the office and was always flying here or there for this or that. He was the long, skinny arm of the business, reaching out and making new friends, new connections, and new clients.

Gary was the fat, comfortable rear end of the company. He was in the office day in and day out, working alongside their employees in their day-to-day endeavors. Where Ted was brisk and professional, Gary was attentive and jovial. Ted knew how to charm clients and prospective clients, but had a hard time socializing with the employees that worked in their office every day. Gary knew the name of every employee and the names of everyone in each employee's family. He was the best boss most people in the office had ever had. He was friendly and outgoing, even to the kids who fetched coffee and delivered the mail. He was fair and honest to his employees, and they respected and adored him, whereas most of the office workers viewed Ted with a quiet and uneasy fear because of the cold, nearly emotionless way in which he dealt with them.

Gary took me under his flabby wing, and I rose quickly through the ranks of their well-built and thriving company. His jolly girth and easy grin reminded me in some ways of my own deceased dad, and he filled some sort of vacant father role for me. Eight years

178

into working for them, I had earned myself a top spot in the company as the unofficial number three from the top.

We spent our days watching visions of our atrocities while my body and mind worked nonstop, controlled on some subconscious level by Heinous. I sat through meetings, talking, sharing ideas, and making presentations, all without ever knowing what was really going on around us. I hid in my shell and watched while we walked through our day, excelling at any task given to us, all without stopping the visions of murder and pain that drove us and sustained us.

Days blurred together into weeks, weeks into months, and months into bloodstained years. Until the day Elisha walked into the office with a flyer depicting her missing older sister Tina. Dark brown eyes that seemed covered with a sheen of sorrow peered back at me from behind her black-framed glasses. Long blond hair framed her high cheekbones and brushed softly against her tanned shoulders. She was the most beautiful woman I had ever seen. I stumbled for words when she caught me staring at her lovely face, and she giggled a sound like angels weeping.

"Hi," she offered in a voice like rumpled silk. "My name is Elisha. I'm hanging up some flyers in hopes that somebody recognizes my sister, Tina."

She handed me a flyer, and with great effort, I tore my gaze away from her sorrow-tainted eyes and flawless face. Tina smiled back at me from the flyer with a chip-toothed grin I saw in visions almost daily. I suppressed my own grin at my dark secret as Heinous cackled rudely.

"I'm sorry, I don't recognize her," I said in my practiced empathetic voice as I handed the flyer back. She reached for the flyer, revealing a thin purple scar running the length of her forearm. I held onto the flyer and stared into her eyes. The sorrow there was a pool in which I could feel myself drowning. I spoke my next words without thinking.

"I can take the afternoon off and help you pass these out, though."

Her smile was electric and her eyes thankful as she nodded. I left with her, and we talked as we hung pictures of the familiar chip-toothed grin all over town. Once her pile was depleted, I offered to buy her a coffee. We talked more, and a cup became six.

She told me of Tina's disappearance from their Lake Tahoe home after an ex-boyfriend got her hooked on meth. They lost their mother when they were very young, and Tina's disappearance has almost broken their father. I listened to her pouring her heart out while I stared, through the vision of her sister sucking and dying, to Elisha's sincere eyes beyond. I told her about my past: the loss of my best friend, then mother and father in quick succession. I left out the fact that their deaths had all been because of me, of course. She grabbed my hand and stared deep into my eyes, something no one had done in decades.

"We are both haunted, Gavin," she told me in her weeping angel voice.

I should have told her to stay away. I should have, but I couldn't. She reminded me of the human I once was. Being with her, staring into those haunted eyes, I forgot about killing for the first time in fifteen years. I should have told her to stay away, but instead I drove her home and made a date for the weekend.

Dream: Wagner Family Reunion

Laughter. Overwhelming, disorienting laughter. Laughter I recognize.

I don't want to open my eyes.

But then I catch the faint whiff of cherry blossom perfume. The laughter stops, and my eyes open. The orange-peel glow of flickering torches lights the solid black rock walls of the cave in which I'm standing. The ground is littered with mutilated corpses rather than bones. I see fist-sized bright white beetles, each with a single bright red fingerprint on its back, skittering over the bodies and feasting in festering clumps upon them. I watch one pull away a triangle of dead flesh from a gray face, revealing the dull white of cheekbone.

I hear the laughter again, more distant than before. The sweet cherry blossom fragrance drifts up my nostrils with it. My feet step over the bodies in my way as I chase the source of sound and scent slowly through the torch-lit cavern. Faces carved into the deep black stone walls wail and weep at me as I pass, each a face from my past. I stumble over an ever-growing stack of corpses until I see a wide archway ahead of me, casting long streaks of torchlight over the dead. The laughter echoes off the walls, pulling me hypnotically through the arch and into the massive hall beyond.

The hall is cyclopean in size and design. Stout stone columns line the wall and hold up a ceiling lost to darkness. Torches flicker and spit from the high stone walls, down across a vast, mostly empty space. Situated in the middle of the giant room is a table. I take another step into the room and I'm standing at the table, looking at my parents. Their eyes are sewn shut, but they feast with primal greed on chunks of rotten meat strewn across the table. My dad has his tie, filthy and speckled with blood, bound tight around his neck, but it doesn't slow him down as he tears a chunk from a fist full of green meat. My mother still wears her black-rimmed glasses over her eternally closed eyes. Her naked skin is crisscrossed in vibrant bright red scars, and burnt, blackened flesh peels from her hairline and neck. Her nipples are black, and blackened veins spiderweb her breasts. She grabs a fruit so covered in mold that it possesses no distinguishable features. She digs her teeth into it, spilling fetid fluid down her chin, before she turns her blind eyes toward me and asks, "Gavin? Is that you?"

My dad stops his ravenous feeding and casts his blind eyes my way as well.

My voice leaves my mouth as a whimper as I answer, "Yes."

"Well, sit down and eat, son!" my dad says and pushes a plate of stinking meat across the table to me.

My mom ravages the moldy fruit and tosses the remaining pulp over her shoulder before grabbing a long greasy strip of dead flesh from the plate in front of her. She gnaws at it, tearing with her teeth and claw-like fingers.

"No thanks, guys. I'm not hungry," I say, fighting the disgust bubbling inside me.

My mom spits the rancid meat from her mouth and gapes at me.

"But you provided the food, sweetie."

"And the company!" My dad laughs out loud and tugs at the tie digging into his neck flesh, to no avail.

"Sorry about that," I say, and the words feel weaker than they sound.

They ignore my flat apology and continue gorging on the spoiled foods before them. I turn back the way I came, and the archway has vanished, leaving only solid stone wall where it once sat. When I turn back around to the table, there is a chair made of bone beside me. I drag it back through the harsh gray sand and take a seat.

"So, Gavin, do you ever see Joshie?" my dad asks through a mouthful of gore.

"No," I answer flatly.

"Bullshit," Joshie's voice responds from somewhere near. I don't see him sitting at the table, but I feel his eyes burrowing into my soul. I scan the table frantically and find him. His decapitated head rests in the middle of the table like a morbid centerpiece. Two white candles are stuck to his forehead like horns, and the wax melts down over his bloodied face and shattered jaw.

"You can be such an asshole, Gavin," my mom tells me as she leans blindly across the table, spilling festering meat from the heaping plates that hold it as she reaches for Joshie's head.

"He was your best friend, Gavin. I mean, everyone wants to kill their parents; we can understand that. But your little buddy?"

As she fishes his head from the piles of meat, he smiles his wide broken grin at me. She pulls him close to her naked chest, and his eyes shine wickedly at me as he latches his broken maw onto her breast and begins sucking obscenely.

"What else is new, Gav?" my dad asks and I'm able to divert my gaze from Joshie and my mom's tit.

I clear my throat and answer, "I graduated college. Four-point-oh GPA, even."

"Big whoop," my mom says, cradling the suckling Joshie head. "We used to teach college. Four-ohs are for limp-dick losers with no friends."

Joshie pulls away from my mom's blackened nipple, leaving a dribble of blood connecting his mouth to her breast, and tells me, "See, fuckrag, you shouldn't have killed me."

My mom rolls his head back and forces her nipple into his mouth. She weeps and sobs, but no tears flow from her ocular stitches.

"Now you've gone and upset your mother," my dad chastises. "It wasn't enough that you killed her; now you have to hurt her feelings. Sheesh, Gav, we should have had you aborted."

My mom and dad break into pained laughter. Joshie laughs around the dead breast on which he sucks. The meat on the table starts crawling.

"I met a girl!" I shout, filled with a strange hope.

All the laughter stops. The only sounds in the hall are the squishing of meat crawling over other meat and Joshie sucking greedily on my mother. My dad gets up and walks away from the table, shaking his head sorrowfully as he does. A noose of barbed wire hangs down from the darkness, and he wraps it around his neck. His mouth curls into a grin, and he flips me the bird as the wire jerks him up into the darkness. Blood rains down on me.

I wipe the blood from my face and turn back to my mom. She holds Joshie's head to her chest and reaches her other hand up to her eyes. She tears at the stitches until blood runs down her smooth cheeks in crimson ribbons. Her eyeballs are black and cold. They stare into me as she tells me, "That poor, poor girl."

My Sick Story: Resolution Reeks of Gasoline

I drove Elisha home to the secluded Lake Tahoe cabin she shared with her grief-stricken father. Her dad regarded me coldly with tortured eyes until Elisha explained my presence. His smile was weak and insincere, but he welcomed me in for dinner. We ate deer steaks and drank dark ales while they talked about Tina. Heinous flashed Tina's death over and over the entire time I was there. He spoke no words, but I could tell he was enjoying the suffering for which we had been responsible.

After dinner, Elisha walked me out to my truck. I didn't know how to proceed, since my only experiences with females had been either humiliating of fatal, so I stood there staring into her sorrow-stained eyes. She smiled softly and kissed me. Heinous recoiled within me, but I leaned into her and returned the kiss. Our tongues met and twisted over each other. She sighed deeply and pulled away, still smiling at me. I tasted blood and smiled back.

"Can I see you again?" I asked as she backed slowly to her door.

"Do you want to?" she asked, honestly confused.

"I do," I whispered in the cool wind crawling from the high mountain lake.

"Then yes," she said before she disappeared inside the cabin.

I climbed back in my truck and thumbed the CD player, bringing the ferocity of the Black Dahlia Murder to volume. The beats and growls stirred the demon within, and I felt him uncoil inside me.

"How shall we kill her, Worm?" he asked.

"We shouldn't," I answered coldly. "Having a steady girlfriend will only make this mask more believable."

"You have a point," he grumbled. Surprisingly, he spoke no more on the subject.

Over the next few weeks, I saw more and more of Elisha. She would drive her dad's beat-up old Chevy into town and pick me up for lunch. We plastered her sister's chip-toothed grin all over town. True to his word, Heinous did nothing to spoil the budding romance except for flashing her sister's death whenever she was around.

After two months of courting and dating, she finally agreed to sleep at my place. We ate a dinner of fish and rice and found ourselves wrapped around each other on the living room couch. Her lips kissed my neck and cheeks as she tugged the shirt from my back. She licked my chest, drawing heart-shaped lines across it with her saliva. Moans, honest and longing, rose from my throat as I lifted her sundress over her head. She undid my pants and tugged them down, using her feet to fully remove them. She pulled her white panties to the side and perched herself on my throbbing dick. I grabbed handfuls of her ass and pulled myself deeper inside her.

As she bucked and moaned, I felt my world spin. Blues and reds danced around me until they blurred into a pitch black. Her soft cries of pleasure faded as I passed out.

When I came to, I was standing naked in the center of my living room, swaying on weak legs. I opened my eyes and saw the walls of my apartment coated with a slick layer of blood. I felt weight in both my hands.

In my left hand, the familiar wooden handle of my knife warmed against my palm. My fingers went numb and dropped the tool of death to the blood-soaked carpet. Wet strands wrapped around my right hand. I lifted my hand up and came face to face with Elisha, fear now frozen in the pools of sorrow. Blood dripped freely from her neck and ran down my arms in small streams.

I felt the swoon coming, and Heinous erupted into sharp laughter as the blackness swirled back around me. I dropped Elisha's head and crumbled into a weeping mess.

The next thing I remember was my truck navigating the dirt road leading to Elisha's cabin. The sun teased at rising, casting long daggers of light up from behind the mountains. Elisha's dad's pickup wasn't parked out front. Heinous reached my hand to the door and opened it. He walked me around to the back door.

"Why are we here?" I asked.

"Because I want to be, Worm," he growled at me.

He raised my fist and punched it through the window on the door. The tinkle of shattering glass echoed through the trees surrounding us. He reached in and opened the door. My legs followed his orders as we walked into the kitchen.

"We can't be here. We should be at work … they are delivering the five-hundred-dollar gift cards for the new Northeastern Automobile Association's prize packages … people will be suspicious." My excuses were as weak and tired as my soul, and Heinous disregarded them quickly.

"Nonsense, Worm. People are late for work every day. Nice try. And besides, I just want to leave the old man a gift."

We turned down the hallway and into her father's bedroom. The sound of the old Chevy pulling up didn't seem to bother the monster inside of me.

"He's back! We have to leave now!" I whisper-shouted.

Heinous ignored me still and pulled Elisha's severed head from my blood-soaked backpack. He plopped the morbid trophy on the old man's dresser. Then he reached my fingers into her dead mouth and forced her stiff lips into a grin. The front door opened with a creak.

"Gavin? Elisha? Are you two here?"

"Back here, Dad!" Heinous shouted in Elisha's voice.

"Oh, good to hear your voice, Leash. I had the most disturbing dreams last night …" He rounded the corner into his room and froze. His eyes barely regarded me and went straight to his daughter's head staring at him from his dresser. He turned to me, anger forcing his tears.

I wanted to tell him how sorry I was. How it wasn't me. I wanted to tell him I knew what he was feeling. I wanted to comfort him. Instead, what came out of my mouth was a noise no human had ever made, a deep, yowling, hissing snarl that froze the man even in his newfound state of rage. He charged me and we knocked his ailing form into his dresser. His nose hit the wood first and shattered, spitting blood all over him and the dresser. Elisha's dead eyes held his gaze as he wailed at her. Heinous reached down and grabbed a claw hammer from the nightstand, where it sat next to a half-empty box of nails and a beat-up old tape measure.

"Why?" the old man screamed.

"I couldn't help it." Heinous let me speak the words.

Her dad spun back on us, his sorrow warping into murderous rage. His eyes narrowed, and he screamed a tortured, insane scream that made Heinous sway with pleasure. We didn't even allow him a single step before Heinous swung the hammer, claw side first, and sank it into the charging man's skull. He crashed into the wall, and Heinous hissed the demon sound again as he ripped the metal hammer from the screaming man's skull and slammed it back even harder a few inches from the first gaping wound. The old man turned and tried to run, but his feet became tangled, and he landed head first, digging the hammer still deeper into his brain. His mouth filled with blood that dripped out of the corners of his lips, and he mumbled quiet words that we couldn't hear. The old man's left hand twitched wildly and knocked the leg of the table next to him, forcing several pictures to fall and shattering the glass that had protected them in their frames. A pool of dark blood had already soaked the carpeted floor around him, and the newly dropped family pictures were slowly soaking up blood, blurring in a red haze. The flow of euphoria oozed into me, and we stumbled back the way we came.

"Why? Why did we do that? We're going to get caught! What the fuck?" I yelled out loud and punched the steering wheel and dashboard in frustration.

"Because you have forgotten your place, Worm." It was his only response as the vision of the old man's death began its cursed eternal loop. To prove his point, decade-old visions danced before my eyes as he drove us back through the rising sun to Reno.

I pulled into the large parking lot of the office complex where Killkin Brothers was located. I glanced at the clock again and could barely make out the numbers telling me I was a full half-hour late through the vision of my dad swinging by his neck and laughing at me as he spun. I stumbled toward the door, dragging Heinous' weight with each step.

"Tonight we'll go visit Aunt Sally. Give her a hug and a fuck before we tear her apart. I warned you long ago, Worm," Heinous growled at me as we walked hurriedly into the office. I ignored him as best I could and rushed in to find Gary standing at the front counter, looking scared and pale.

"Damn, Mr. Killkin, I'm so sorry I'm late. It'll never happen again. Did I miss the delivery? I can work late if I have to, to make up for it. Or I can come in this weekend."

I realized suddenly that I was rambling and he was still looking pale and frightened. When I stopped talking, he spoke without looking at me. "I'm Gary. Mr. Killkin is my dad."

I turned slowly and saw the thick barrel of a revolver pointing at my face, the head behind it hidden by a ski mask. Heinous laughed, and I felt again the feeling of the oncoming kill ooze into me. I forced myself, as much as I loathed it, to think about stepping to the old man, hammer in hand. Heinous couldn't help but start flashing the vision of our most recent killings.

"This gentleman is here for the gift cards, Gavin," Gary told me, still staring at the gunman. I held my hands up and took a slow step backwards toward Gary. I kept my eyes on the massive barrel and moved slowly and deliberately around to the service side of the small counter. As I took physical steps backwards, Heinous and I stalked forward down the hallway in the ultra-vivid memory.

"Well, if they're here, I can get them," I told the gunman in the calmest voice I could muster.

I rounded the waist-high counter and stood next to Gary. I glanced down and, by pure dumb luck, saw the empty box left over from the last set of gift cards on a shelf under the counter. I nodded toward it and glanced at the man.

The gun shook, and the man under the mask told me, "Give them to me and no one has to die."

I waited for the vision to progress, and as I leaned toward the empty box of cards, Heinous swung the hammer at the old man's skull in my vision. As I stood, the pleasure from the kill washed over Heinous, and he reveled in the recent kills as well as the one he

189

assumed was coming. I felt the dizziness, but held my eyes to the tip of the gun and let Heinous enjoy the full effect of his euphoria.

I placed the empty box on the counter, and the gunman took a step toward us. As he reached for the box, Heinous swung the hammer at the father's head a second time in the vision. I felt his sickening ecstasy at his memories as he rolled back into himself on a wave of remembered pleasure so vivid it was as if he were still staring at the man's feet twitching in the hallway before we left.

At the moment the gunman realized I'd handed him an empty box, I shoved Gary as hard as I could through a closed office door slightly to the right of where we were standing with our arms in the air. With my force and his girth, he demolished the wooden door and fell to the floor with a crack and a thud. I turned to face the gunman, Heinous still swooning and confused, and I told him with a grin, "Someone always has to die."

He yelled at the empty box, crumpled it and pointed the gun at me. I heard Gary rolling around on the office floor, panicked but alive. Heinous was still swooning, and not even his demon speed could save us when the gunman fired.

I was still staring at the tip of his gun as smoke and bullets flew out of it. I counted five loud shots and felt five hot balls of metal rip into me and slam my body into the wall behind me. I felt blackness overtaking me as I slid down the wall. I heard Heinous' gravelly voice as I faded into the darkness. He told me it wasn't over, but as I slipped away, I disagreed.

Hours later, however, when I awoke racked with unbelievable pain, I realized with a sob that he was again telling the truth. We lay in a hospital bed, hooked up to machines and with an IV strung to us and dripping. With Heinous' angry voice came a wave of pain that made me curl in on myself.

"It ends my way, Worm," he told me, and for the first time ever, I sensed weakness in his voice. He answered my thought quickly.

"Your little glory show has ended you. I'm stretched too thin. I can't sustain you and maintain myself anymore."

I groaned as he made me sit up and swing my feet over the edge of the bed. At the sound of me moving, a young black nurse came running into the room.

"Whoa, hold on there, stud," she said as she reached for me. I held up a hand to keep her at bay.

"I can't believe you're alive! Hell, no one can." She stared at me, and I could see that she really was amazed to see me not only alive but sitting at the edge of my bed.

"How does it feel to be a hero?" she asked with a sheepish grin.

"Sickening," Heinous answered out of my mouth before I could speak.

"I'm sorry?" she said and leaned in closer, not believing what she'd heard.

"I feel sick," I told her feebly but quickly.

"Oh I don't doubt that. Five bullets tore through your body, but lucky you, they all passed right through."

"What about the man who shot me?" I asked weakly. "What about him?"

"Well the police say he shot himself after shooting you. Between him filling you full of lead and whatever he was after not being where he thought it would be, he just killed himself."

As she finished her last words, a vision started flashing, vivid and clear. I watched the bullets as they came at me. I felt each hot piece cut into me, and everything went black. Suddenly my eyes opened, and despite the roaring pain throughout my body, I stood. The gunman was walking in circles, cussing and yelling to himself. Heinous walked my broken body around the counter and behind the panicking gunman. With Heinous' hypersensitive hearing, I heard Gary whispering frantically into the phone in the office. My arms wrapped around the gunman, and Heinous grabbed the hand holding the gun from behind. The would-be robber fought, but the demon was too strong and forced the man's gun hand to his own temple. He tried to struggle, but Heinous squeezed so hard on the man's hand that his fingers broke as the trigger was pulled. Blood and brains splattered the wall, and Heinous dropped the body. He walked back to the blood-streaked wall where I fell. We heard Gary telling the police he'd heard anther shot. Heinous lay back in the exact spot where my body had come to rest, and everything went dark again.

"I'm in a hospital then?" I asked the nurse once the vision stopped.

"No, you are at Peaceful Grove, a private recovery center. Mr. Killkin has paid for this room for you and told us no expense was to be spared."

I knew the building when she said the name. It was a hospital for people too rich to die with the common folk who littered public hospitals. It was a diamond-shaped building in the hills just outside of town. It was somewhat like the Pentagon in construction, but with only four sides. In the middle was a large garden, visible from every patient's room and used for its healing value. Through my window, I watched a maintenance worker move two five-gallon jugs of gasoline and put the weed eater he had been using back in the storage shed just down from my room.

The sun was going down, and soon the night shift would come in. The pretty nurse told me she had to go inform a doctor that I was awake. She disappeared, and Heinous hopped us out of bed. With every step, pain flared and burned, from my chest and stomach to my thighs and shins. Still, I hobbled down the hallway and out into the large garden. I walked to the shed and grabbed the two full five-gallon cans of gasoline that I had seen the worker move.

Heinous had to strain as hard as I did to carry the full cans of gas. Once inside, we found a small cart with syringes and other medical supplies. With a grunt, we brushed everything into a heap on the floor and put the cans on the cart.

My hospital gown swung open as I started sprinkling gas along the hallway floor and splashing it on the walls. I pushed the cart with my hips as I went, swinging the can back and forth. I went into my room and poured gas on the bed and swung the can so it splattered on the walls. I found my jeans folded neatly next to my bed, and I dug into my pockets for my Zippo lighter. I started back down the hallway, continuing to spill the flammable fluid all over the floor and walls.

For some reason, an old song came into my mind, I remembered the beat but not the words, and I sang my own words to myself as I worked at soaking the hospital in gasoline.

I have no name. No genus or species. I've been called many things throughout time.

I rounded the first of four corners and saw no one down the hall, so I continued splashing and singing as I worked my way down the hallway.

Demon, Devil, Monster, He Who Follows the Shadow, Harbinger of the Damned, the Hate Within,

I felt my own torn muscles, and I could feel Heinous' thick, greasy form as he literally held me together as I walked, dumping gas as I went.

The Slouching Beast, the Fourth Eye of T'Nartha, and many more that would make no sense to you.

I sang while Heinous started to laugh his harsh laugh, weaker than before.

You will be my blood soaked tool ...

A sob hitched in my chest, and I looked back down the deserted gas-soaked hallway behind me. Still facing backwards and splashing gas, I sang on.

You have been both blessed and cursed this day.

Heinous laughed, and I turned the cart around the corner and stopped. The nurses' station was at the far end of this hallway, and the three nurses were running around in a panic. I stood and sang quietly to myself as I watched them.

We walk in nightmares and darkness. We are the uneasy feeling in the air and the stirring in the calm. We are every unnatural fear, every starving child, and the very idea of war. We walk between Life and Death, before the Beginning and after the End.

Heinous twitched as he struggled to hold me together, but I sang on.

I have made brother kill brother, parent kill child, lover kill lover, Worm kill everyone.

The three nurses and one scared-looking doctor ran back around the back corner, leaving the hall deserted. I started down the hall, splashing walls and floor and singing.

What is sacred to you is laughable to me. The ideas and values of man are fleeting and nonsensical, weak and tiny.

Halfway down the hall, I heard a weak voice trying to shout for the nurses who'd fled.

"What's going on out there?" someone asked as I peeked into the room. I couldn't see where the feeble voice was coming from, but it spoke again. "I smell gasoline," it whined. "Get the nurses."

I started singing again as I pulled the door closed.

I bring the strife and the hate and the rage. You have been both blessed and cursed this day.

I got to the nurses' station, the first can of gas ran out, and I opened a door, set it inside and went on my way with the second can. I walked back into the nurses' station and poured it over desks and left puddles in the garbage cans. I rounded the last corner and could hear more panicked talk past the steel double doors at the end of the last hallway. I walked faster and splashed more wildly, quickly forgetting what I had been singing.

The voices started to fade as I stumbled my way down the hall, leaving my fuming trail. The nurses and doctor had made it to my room and found it and the hallway wet with gasoline. My body groaned, and I fell to one knee, but weak spikes jabbed me forward. I spilled the gas more the faster I walked but still had a quarter of the can when I reached the closed double doors. I grabbed the Zippo lighter we had salvaged from my pants off the medical cart that now reeked of gasoline.

"Hurry, Worm," he gasped, and I felt him twitch fiercely as I flicked my finger and watched the flame come alive. With a cry of shocked pain, I tossed the lighter to the gas-slick floor and pushed the big steel door shut.

I heard the roar as the hallway ignited and the crackling of the blaze as it rolled down the hall after the nurses and doctor.

I felt a ripping sensation that dropped me to my knees. The tearing came a second time, and it felt like my back was being ripped off beneath my skin.

Heinous snarled and grunted, and I felt his form heave within myself, like a rabid dog throwing itself at a wall. As the monster of a blaze rounded the last corner to face me, I heard a chorus of screams erupt, and for the brief second before one last terrible ripping of separation, they all sounded like laughter.

I crumpled weakly to my stomach. Face down on the floor, feeling my body go into the shock of my symbiotic separation, and in agony from the five searing bullet wounds, I stared blindly at the fire as it licked the walls and ceiling.

Before it engulfed me, I felt the full impact of the guilt and shame my violent crimes deserved. The anguish and remorse Heinous had stifled returned a thousandfold. I was finally confronted with the human feelings for everyone I had killed. The flames danced on me, burning my hair and clothes, and my tears were for my mother and my friend, for the hundreds of unlucky strangers that had crossed our path, not my own selfish pain. Faces flashed, and my heart broke a million times as I burned.

It never went black. There was only the all-consuming glow of the roaring blaze and then the fog where I sit now, huddled in the gray sand, trying not to scream.

About Jonathan Moon

Jonathan Moon is a horrorcore writer living in the Palouse region of Idaho/Washington where there is an abundance of trees and decrepit shacks to fuel his twisted muse. He writes his own brutally beautiful brand of horror and strange dark fiction such as HEINOUS, Stories To Poke Your Eyes Out To, Hollow Mountain Dead and Worms in the Needle. He is also the co-author of The Apocalypse and Satan's Glory Hole with Timothy W. Long. Mr. MoOn was born the same day Cthulhu rises in the classic H.P. Lovecraft story 'The Call of Cthulhu'...he does not believe this is coincidence.

You can find Mr. MoOn online at his Monkey Faced Demon blog (www.mrmoonblogs.blogspot.com) where he reviews, interviews (home of the DEATHMATCH Question), and offers up stories and such. Follow him through the darkness in the hearts of men and hold tight to your slippery sanity.

www.ingramcontent.com/pod-product-compliance
Lightning Source LLC
Chambersburg PA
CBHW021147130626
46554CB00005B/1706